3396862

THE
UNLEASHED

PRAISE FOR THE JONATHAN QUINN SERIES

"Brilliant and heart pounding."—**Jeffery Deaver**, *New York Times* bestselling author

"Addictive."—**James Rollins**, *New York Times* bestselling author

"Unputdownable."—**Tess Gerritsen**, *New York Times* bestselling author

"The best elements of Lee Child, John le Carré, and Robert Ludlum."—**Sheldon Siegel**, *New York Times* bestselling author

"Quinn is one part James Bond, one part Jason Bourne."—**Nashville Book Worm**

"Welcome addition to the political thriller game."—*Publishers Weekly*

ALSO BY BRETT BATTLES

THE JONATHAN QUINN THRILLERS
THE CLEANER
THE DECEIVED
SHADOW OF BETRAYAL (U.S.)/THE UNWANTED (U.K.)
THE SILENCED
BECOMING QUINN
THE DESTROYED
THE COLLECTED
THE ENRAGED
THE DISCARDED
THE BURIED

THE REWINDER THRILLERS
REWINDER
DESTROYER

THE LOGAN HARPER THRILLERS
LITTLE GIRL GONE
EVERY PRECIOUS THING

THE PROJECT EDEN THRILLERS
SICK
EXIT NINE
PALE HORSE
ASHES
EDEN RISING
DREAM SKY
DOWN

THE ALEXANDRA POE THRILLERS
(with Robert Gregory Browne)
POE
TAKEDOWN

STANDALONES
THE PULL OF GRAVITY
NO RETURN

For Younger Readers

THE TROUBLE FAMILY CHRONICLES
HERE COMES MR. TROUBLE

THE
UNLEASHED

Brett Battles

A Jonathan Quinn Novel

To my friend Jim Hardwick
for his infectious enthusiasm and unwavering support

CHAPTER ONE

BANTEAY MEANCHEY PRISON, CAMBODIA

THE DELUGE HAMMERED against the tiled roof, drowning out all other sounds.

It had started before sunset, and continued unchecked into the night as if plotting to go on forever. The storm was the remnants of a late-season typhoon that had finally lost its lofty status after slamming into the coast of Vietnam. But while the winds may have lessened, the rain still drenched the countryside as it moved into Cambodia.

"He's late," Chayan said.

Though the lights were off in building seven, enough illumination from the exterior flood lamps drifted in through the chain-link-covered windows to paint the room in murky grays.

"You know these animals," Mee Noi replied. "Never on time. But he'll come."

Chayan glanced at him. "And if he doesn't?"

Mee Noi said nothing, sure their wait wouldn't last much longer. He had worked hard to put the plan in place. Money had been slipped into the right hands to obtain a meeting with the new prison director, a man much more malleable than those who had previously held the position. The new head of the facility hadn't blinked an eye at the cash offered to look the other way. More payments were made to Captain Keo and the men assigned to the task.

Admittedly, Chayan did have cause to be concerned. This wasn't the first time they'd tried this. Which was why Mee Noi was not relying simply on the bribes. A backup plan had been arranged. If things didn't proceed as expected, the prison director's family would go missing within twenty-four hours, at which point it would be made clear to the man that his wife and their children—and mistress and *their* children— would not be returned until his promise had been fulfilled. A similar fate would befall Captain Keo.

Mee Noi was confident it would not come to that. The director might not have been the smartest of men, but he was intelligent enough to know money does not come for free. Especially from someone like Chayan.

So far, everything had gone exactly as expected. The prison, like all Cambodian prisons, was overcrowded to the point of ridiculousness. At Banteay Meanchey the population was nearly three times its maximum capacity. That meant at night, each building was stuffed full of prisoners sleeping on whatever small section of the floor they could claim. Tonight, though, building seven only contained Chayan and Mee Noi.

Over the roar of the storm, Mee Noi could now hear a faint rumble and splashing. He rose, walked to the door, and placed his ear against it. The rumble grew louder and then disappeared in a squeal of brakes.

"They're here," he said as he returned to his boss's side.

Chayan's expression remained neutral.

A few minutes passed before a key was inserted in the lock and the door swung open.

In walked Captain Keo and two of the bought prison guards.

"Inspection!" one of the guards announced in Khmer, a language both Chayan and Mee Noi were now well acquainted with. "Remain where you are."

The flashlight beams swung side to side as the guards walked through the room. Keo, a short man with a barrel chest and matching stomach, watched from the doorway as if his mere presence guided the guards' every move. After a few moments, he appeared to tire of this and sauntered over to Chayan and Mee Noi, a broad fake smile plastered across his face.

"My apologies if we have disturbed your sleep," he said in fairly proficient Thai. "Are you aware of any contraband items your fellow prisoners might be hiding? Perhaps any forbidden activities they might be up to?"

"We are aware of nothing, Captain," Mee Noi said.

"No one with plans to attack my men? Or maybe sneak out of the prison?" The smile again, this time accompanied by a chuckle.

"No, sir," Mee Noi said, reining in his anger at the man's foolishness.

Keo focused on Chayan. "And you? Nothing?"

Chayan looked at him, his lips a flat line.

"I guess that's no," Keo said.

"Captain," one of the guards said. "Inspection completed. Everyone is…um…accounted for."

"All right, then. Let's move on." The captain nodded to the two Thai prisoners. "Have a good rest, gentlemen."

Mee Noi and Chayan watched the men exit. When the door shut, as per the plan, it was left unlocked. The two prisoners waited a moment, and then crossed over to it. As Mee Noi reached for the handle, Chayan touched his arm, stopping him.

"The captain needs to learn respect," he said.

"I will make sure the message is passed along."

Chayan removed his hand and Mee Noi opened the door.

Waterfalls of rain poured off the roof, adding to the growing lake that all but covered the ground between buildings seven and eight. Sitting in the middle of the water was the prison van that had brought the captain and his men. The trio was now in the neighboring barracks, conducting another inspection.

Mee Noi hurried over to the vehicle. As expected, the van's single back door was unlocked. He opened it and checked inside.

The box was right where it was supposed to be, masquerading as a wide bench running down the driver's side of the cabin. Opening the door had also opened a panel that covered the back end of the box, via a cord tied between them. The space inside the box would be tight, but Mee Noi was a small man and would take up much less room than his taller, well-toned boss.

He motioned to Chayan, letting him know all was ready, and then helped his boss into the box before slipping in himself. A makeshift cloth handle had been attached to the back of the panel. By pulling hard on it, Mee Noi was able to shut both the panel and the van's back door.

With their hiding place now in total darkness, Mee Noi had to feel around to find the knotted end of the cord that connected the panel to the van's door. It took him a moment, but he was able to undo the knot and push all but the very tip of the cord back through.

"They're taking too long," Chayan whispered a few seconds later.

Mee Noi said nothing. Again, it was just his boss's frustration at their inability to fully control their current situation. But building eight was packed even more than usual, and they were both aware it would take the guards extra time to finish their inspection. The plan would work best, after all, if things appeared normal.

The rain pounded relentlessly on the metal roof, echoing through the inside of the van. The wood surrounding the two men barely dulled the noise. It was so loud they didn't hear the van's doors open, and only realized the guards had returned when the vehicle rocked as the men climbed in.

A creak of the box down near their feet indicated one of the guards had sat on it. Moments later the engine started up, and the van began to move.

Four minutes passed before the van slowed to a stop. Mee Noi could hear voices, but the downpour made them impossible to understand.

When the vehicle moved again, it was soon going much too fast to still be inside the prison. If Mee Noi needed further proof they had passed beyond the gates, he received it moments later when he heard several motorbikes zip by, the rattle of their engines delivering the relief he'd long been waiting to feel.

Four years he had been in that prison. Four years since he'd purposely let himself get arrested so he could join Chayan inside. Four years he had served his boss there, passing Chayan's orders on to their organization, and working to get his boss and himself free.

This was their third escape attempt. The prison riot meant to facilitate the first one had fizzled before it began, and their second effort was thwarted by a "clean" lieutenant who had thought of himself as a Western-style anti-corruption official. The man had paid the price for his "superior" values, of course. His body was found tangled in a clump of trash floating down the Serei Sophorn River.

One would think a message such as that would make others more cooperative, but instead there was a crackdown that saw the removal of most of the prison staff Mee Noi had in his pocket, forcing him to start at the beginning again.

On the van went, curving through streets, splashing through water and bouncing from pothole to pothole. After a while, Mee Noi realized the ride was lasting longer than it should have. Of course, the rain and the atrocious Cambodian roads weren't helping, but still, they should have reached the drop-off point by now.

Nearly a half hour passed before the van pulled to a stop and the engine shut off. The vehicle rocked again as the guards exited. For several minutes there was nothing but the sound of the rain. And then the back door finally swung open.

A knock on the panel of their hiding place was accompanied by Captain Keo saying, "Please, join us."

Mee Noi did not like the man's tone.

"Open it," Chayan whispered.

Mee Noi hesitated, and then pushed on the panel.

Bright light flooded into the box, forcing Mee Noi and Chayan to squeeze their eyes shut.

"My apologies," Keo said. He barked an order to his men and the flashlight beams moved away. Another shout and a man was next to the box, grabbing Mee Noi by the shoulders.

"Can do myself," Mee Noi said in his patched-together Khmer.

The man pulled as if he hadn't heard, so Mee Noi slapped at the guard's arms.

"I said I can do!"

"Let him," Keo said.

The guard backed away. Mee Noi saw there were now three others in addition to the captain and the two camp guards. None of the new men were wearing uniforms. They were, however, similarly armed.

Mee Noi pulled himself out of the box and set his feet on the wet ground. Their release was supposed to have happened inside a storage building on the edge of town, but they were outside in a clearing surrounded by jungle, the only structure in sight a decrepit hut. A glance around revealed but a single road leading in and out of the clearing.

As Mee Noi always suspected, the captain had changed the plan.

When Mee Noi leaned down to assist Chayan, he conveyed their situation to his boss with a look. Chayan was also not surprised.

Once they were standing outside the van, Captain Keo donned his ugly smile and held his arms out wide. "The air of freedom. Smells so good, doesn't it?"

Mee Noi and Chayan said nothing.

Keo looked at them, disappointed. "At the very least, I would think I'd have your thanks."

"You received our thanks already," Mee Noi reminded him.

"I received *some* thanks."

And there it was. Some people didn't know when they already had a good thing.

"Come," Chayan said to Mee Noi.

He took a step to the left as if intending to walk away. Immediately the three non-uniformed men pointed their rifles at the two Thais.

Chayan halted, and very slowly turned back to Keo. "What is it you want?"

"What is it I want?" Keo laughed. "Only a fair price for my services."

"You've been paid a more than fair price," Mee Noi said.

"You may think so. I do not."

Mee Noi had worked for Chayan long enough to know when he should talk and when he should say nothing. This was one of those latter times.

Chayan said, "And what do you think *is* a fair price?"

"Oh, I'd say at the low end at least double what I've already received." He gestured to the others with him. "And of course some for my men."

"Of course," Chayan said. "I suppose we are to remain your guests until that happens."

"I like that term. *Guests*." Keo paused. "Naturally it would be bad business to do things any other way."

The rain continued pouring down, soaking everyone to the bone as Chayan and Keo stared at each other.

"Or," Keo said after several seconds, "we could shoot you here, and claim we tracked you after you escaped. We'd be given medals. Maybe even a reward. Admittedly not as much as we would get from you, but still something to compensate us for our time. And the attention would be...enjoyable, I think. So tell me, which would you prefer?"

"Neither," Chayan said.

"Understandable, but that's not one of your options."

Chayan glanced at Mee Noi and nodded.

As a boy, Mee Noi had worked the passenger boats on the Chao Praya River, where he learned the art of whistling to communicate with a boat's pilot as they approached a pier. He used that skill now, letting out two loud, quick shrills.

Five gunshots, grouped so close together they sounded like one, echoed across the clearing. The two prison guards and the three other men dropped to the ground, dead.

Keo jerked in surprise and fumbled with the pistol in the

holster on his hip.

"That would be a very bad idea," Chayan said.

Keo froze, undoubtedly realizing he would never get his weapon drawn before he received the same fate as his men. When he moved his hand away, Chayan gave Mee Noi another nod.

This time Mee Noi's whistle was a single long note. From out of the darkness came ten rifle-toting men, weapons pointing at the prison captain.

"You should have been happy with what you were given," Mee Noi said.

The captain's gaze flicked from the armed men to his fallen companions before returning to Chayan and Mee Noi.

"Go ahead, then. If you're going to kill me, kill me." The words might have been brave, but the tremor in the man's voice belied them.

Chayan walked over and removed the pistol from Keo's side. He checked the chamber and then shoved the barrel against the captain's temple. Keo tried to pull away but Chayan kept the gun pressed to the man's skull. The captain finally stopped struggling and began to cry.

Chayan sneered. "I want to be very clear about this. You *are* going to die." He pulled the gun away. "But not tonight."

It took a moment before Keo worked up enough courage to open his eyes again.

"Tonight you have work to do," Chayan said. He gestured to the dead men. "Clean this up. I don't care how you do it, but none of it comes back on me or my people."

Keo hesitated a moment, and then nodded.

"The longer no one comes looking for me, the longer I don't come back for you. Understood?"

Another nod.

"Good."

Chayan flipped the gun so that he was holding it by the barrel and slammed the grip into the captain's head. Keo fell into a pool of water, moaning in pain.

"That's so you don't forget."

The dead men's rifles were retrieved, and Mee Noi and

Chayan's team escorted them to the waiting vehicles.

"The border?" Mee Noi asked the team leader after they climbed in.

"Everything is set."

"What about the list?" Chayan asked.

"Prepared and waiting for you."

"Then let's go home. We have a lot of work to do."

CHAPTER
TWO

CLAIRE LOOKED AROUND, taking everything in as Quinn carried her off the plane and down the roll-up staircase to the tarmac at Samui International Airport. Right behind them came Garrett and Orlando.

"It's so hot," Garrett said.

"Oh, really?" Orlando said. "I hadn't noticed."

He looked back at her as if she were crazy, but when she smirked, he rolled his eyes in annoyance. "You're hilarious, Mom."

"So you keep telling me."

This was the end of over twenty-four hours of traveling—San Francisco to Hong Kong, Hong Kong to Bangkok, and finally Bangkok to the island of Samui—and the first time they'd been outside since they'd started the trip. Garrett had been in the tropics before when he and Orlando lived in Vietnam, but that had been eight years ago, when he was five. Since then, he'd seldom gone far beyond the considerably more temperate San Francisco Bay area.

As for six-month-old Claire, this was her very first trip out of the country, and she seemed intent on not missing a thing.

Airline employees pointed the arriving passengers to open-air trams that drove everyone toward the small, open-air terminal—the perks of island living. As she had done since the beginning of the journey, Claire made friends with anyone who looked at her, smiling at them, and sometimes hiding behind Quinn's shoulder before popping up again and laughing.

"She is *adorable*," said an Australian woman sitting in the seats behind them.

Quinn looked back. "I'm afraid she knows it, too."

"Clearly." The woman laughed.

The walk from the gate to the baggage area took only a minute. When they arrived, a familiar voice rose above the din. "*Sawadee khrap*. Welcome to Samui."

"Uncle Daeng!" Garrett yelled. He ran over to where their friend stood by the luggage conveyor. Instead of hugging, the two performed the intricate handshake they had invented long ago.

When their ritual was done, Orlando wrapped her arms around the former monk. "It's been too long," she said.

"It's good to see you, too," he replied.

Daeng looked over at Quinn and Claire, his smile growing even larger. "Oh, my God. Look at her. May I?"

Though Claire liked to flirt, she didn't easily go to someone she didn't know, and the last time she'd seen Daeng was the week she was born. As far as she was concerned, he was a stranger.

Quinn said, "You might have to give her a day or so before you—"

Claire extended her arms toward Daeng and made the "unh-unh" noise she always did when she wanted something.

"Okay, never mind," Quinn said.

Daeng took her and raised her high above his head, resulting in a laugh from her loud enough to be heard throughout the baggage area.

"Uh...good to see you?" Quinn said as he watched his daughter be entertained by his friend.

It seemed to take an effort for Daeng to pull his attention away from Claire. Shifting her into the cradle of his left arm, he extended his hand to Quinn. "*Sawadee khrap*."

When Quinn shook it, Daeng pulled him forward and gave him a side hug. Claire laughed again, delighted her father had joined her in Daeng's arms.

"There's our bags!" Garrett shouted and hurried over to the conveyor.

After they collected their luggage, they loaded it into a van Daeng had rented and piled in.

"How far do we have to go?" Garrett asked as they drove away from the airport.

"Not too far," Daeng said. "Twenty minutes or so."

"Will we drive by the beach?"

An exaggerated look of pain crossed Daeng's face. "Oh, did no one tell you?"

"Tell me what?"

"There was a big storm last week. The beaches are all closed until the end of the month."

Garrett's eyes went wide. "What?"

"He's kidding, honey," Orlando said.

A grimace and a huff. "He's almost as funny as you are, Mom."

PRAVAT LOWERED HIS binoculars.

"What's he doing?" Narong asked.

"Waiting," Pravat said.

"For what?"

"How the hell should I know?"

They had been on the job for two weeks now, following the target around Bangkok, and then almost losing him eight days ago when he went to Suvarnabhumi Airport and caught a flight to Koh Samui. If the plane had been fully booked, Pravat and Narong might still be searching the island for the man. But there had been several seats available and they'd had just enough time to grab two and get on board.

Since coming to Samui, they'd spent a lot of time waiting around while the target holed up in a private, walled-off compound on a small cove south of Chaweng Beach. One day Pravat had become so bored, he left Narong to watch the main gate and went to Chaweng Beach, where he arranged for

24

a speedboat to take him along the coast, past the compound. For an hour he sat several hundred meters off the beach and watched the house, but didn't see the target even once.

After the first two nights, it became clear the guy was content to stay where he was, meaning there was no reason to keep him under twenty-four-hour active surveillance. Pravat had arranged for some gear to be sent out the next day. When it arrived, he and Narong installed the camera across the street from the compound's entrance, and then linked it to monitoring software on a laptop. If a specified target in the camera feed moved—for example, the compound's gate opening—an alarm would sound. Though technically they could use the setup to watch the villa's entrance around the clock, they only used it at night so they could get some decent sleep.

It proved to be a sound choice. Over the next several days, the only activity occurred during daylight hours when Pravat and Narong were nearby, and even then it was just a few deliveries bringing things into the compound. The target himself remained on the other side of the gate.

Until this afternoon.

The day had started off in the same monotonous, frustrating way the others had. No alarm during the night, and a morning spent parked at their usual spot, watching the gate. But at 12:45 p.m., the gate opened and the van they'd followed to the villa their very first day there pulled onto the road, the target behind the wheel.

They had followed the van north all the way back to the airport. Concerned that the target was going to catch a flight out, Pravat left Narong in the car and followed the man into the terminal. But instead of checking into a flight, the target had proceeded to the baggage claim area.

Confused and curious, Pravat had retreated to a point where he could see the area but wouldn't be noticed, and texted Narong to join him.

"Is he meeting someone?" Narong asked.

Pravat looked at his colleague, wondering, not for the first time, at what age Narong dropped out of school. "It's an airport. So yeah, he's probably meeting someone."

"Who?"

Pravat lifted the binoculars and looked at the target, not even pretending to consider answering the question.

A few minutes later, a jet landed with a screech of rubber and taxied out of sight on the other side of the terminal. Ten minutes passed before passengers started arriving via the airport trams and trickling into the luggage area.

At first, the target stoically eyed the growing crowd, but then he smiled and appeared to say something. A second later a boy ran up to him, a young teen by his height.

His son? Pravat wondered. He and Narong had no information about any family.

A woman approached next. *Wife? Girlfriend?*

No, he realized a few moments later. There was a man with her, a Caucasian, holding a baby. Though the target did take the girl for a bit, she was clearly more familiar with the other man, and in the end wanted to be back in his arms.

As the group made its way to the van the target had arrived in, Pravat and Narong returned to their own vehicle, where Pravat made a phone call. "He has visitors," he told his boss, Virote.

"Do you recognize them?" the man asked.

"No. There's a man, a woman, and two children. A baby and a boy who's maybe fourteen or fifteen. I'm not sure."

"Send me pictures."

"Of course."

"And keep me updated."

"Yes, sir."

Pravat hung up.

"So what do we do now?" Narong asked.

"The same thing we've been doing. Watch and wait."

THE BEACH RETREAT hid behind a solid metal gate that slid open and closed via remote control. The road on the other side weaved through the lush jungle and down a slope toward the cove, ending in a circular parking area. The villa itself was all but hidden from the driveway by an expertly landscaped menagerie of orchids and ferns and palms and the like. The only thing visible was a covered wooden walkway to the house.

The building came into view halfway down the walk, its teak façade a mix of traditional Thai and the modern world. Though it had only one floor, it was spread wide.

"Whoa!" Garrett said as they entered. He dropped his bag and ran straight to the sliding glass panels that made up the wall on the ocean side of the room. "No way!" He looked back at the others. "Mom, we're right on the beach." Again he turned to the window. "And there's a pool!"

"Hey," Orlando said as he started to pull one of the sliders open. "Let's get settled first and then we can go out."

"Ah, come on!"

"It'll only take a few minutes."

"This is your living space," Daeng said, gesturing at the room. "Kitchen, dining area, living room." He pointed off to either side. "Two wings, four bedrooms each. Your choice. Right or left."

"You guys take right. I'll take left," Garrett said, already running back to grab his suitcase.

"Not so fast, smart guy," Orlando said. "We'll be staying in the same wing."

"Why?" Garrett asked. "It's not like I'll be in a different house."

She carried her bag toward the wing to the right. "Come on, or I'll pick out your bedroom for you, too."

Resigned but clearly wanting to control some of his destiny, Garrett hurried after her. He picked the room closest to the common area, undoubtedly because it was the farthest from the gigantic master suite Quinn, Orlando, and Claire would be using.

Quinn and Orlando hadn't even opened their suitcases yet when the boy rushed into their room wearing a swimsuit and nothing else.

"Now?" he asked.

"All right," Orlando said. "But swimming pool only until one of us joins you." As he started to run out, she added,

"Sunscreen!"

"Yeah, yeah."

"Garrett, I'm serious!"

"I'll do it, I'll do it," he yelled, his voice trailing off as he ran down the hall.

"You know he's already forgotten, right?" Quinn said when she turned from the door.

"Naturally."

Quinn situated their luggage while Orlando laid Claire on the bed and checked her diaper. "Ugh, change time."

"My turn," Quinn said, heading over.

She didn't even hesitate to step away. "Be my guest. I'm going to take a shower."

Quinn put a new diaper on their daughter and carried her to the living area. Three of the glass partitions were open and Daeng stood just inside, keeping an eye on Garrett at the pool.

"Just yell out if he starts to drown," Quinn said.

Daeng looked back and smiled. "He's quite a swimmer so I doubt that's going to happen."

Quinn joined him and took his first good look at the view. As Daeng had promised when he told them about this place, it was gorgeous. The oversized infinity pool paralleled the back of the house. Just beyond it was a sandy beach and a quiet cove shared by only a handful of other equally impressive homes.

"May I hold you again?" Daeng said to Claire.

This time she turned her face away and leaned against Quinn.

"Long trip," Quinn said.

"I'm surprised she's doing this well."

"We had a little rough patch as we took off from San Francisco, but after that she's been pretty good."

"You're blessed.

Quinn looked back outside. "I am."

At the opening of the cove, he could see a motorboat drifting by. Tourists, it looked like, trying their hand at fishing.

"So you're staying in the other half of the house?" Quinn

asked.

Daeng shook his head and pointed out the window to the right. "I'm in the guest house. The path's over there if you need to find me. Up the hill a bit. I promised you privacy, remember?"

He had indeed. When Quinn and Orlando decided to take a vacation, their first thought had been Bali. Around that time, Daeng had called to check in, and Orlando mentioned the plan. He told her he knew just the place for them to go, a beautiful home on a tropical beach with all the privacy they could ever want. The place belonged to a friend of his and would come free of charge. It wasn't that Quinn and Orlando were hurting in the money department, but a beautiful house and the chance of spending some relaxing time with Daeng was more than enough to change their destination.

"I might have to return to Bangkok for a day or two, but I'll be around most of the time if you need anything," Daeng said.

"Whenever you're here, we expect you to hang out with us," Quinn said.

Daeng scowled. "If I must."

"You must." Quinn glanced at Claire. Her eyes were shut and her face slack with sleep. "I'm going to go put her down and then maybe you and I should join Garrett."

WHEN IT BECAME apparent the van was heading back to the house behind the gate, Pravat had Narong drop him off near the beach where he'd hired the boat a few days earlier. The same vessel was there, and the captain was more than happy to repeat their previous journey.

Instead of stopping at the cove on this trip, Pravat had the man slowly cross the end of the small bay while he pretended to fish off the side.

Holding the pole in one hand, he scanned the compound through his binoculars. The boy played in the swimming pool, jumping in and making big splashes then hopping out and doing it all over again. At first, the target and the other man stood just inside the house, and then the other man disappeared for a few minutes. When he returned, he had changed his clothes. While he went to join the boy at the pool, the target moved around the south side of the house and disappeared. When he came back, he too was wearing a swimsuit and jumped in the water with the others.

Pravat saw no sign of the woman by the time the boat reached the far end of the cove. He was tempted to tell the captain to do a repeat performance in the other direction, but if the target noticed him, the man might become suspicious. Given the luggage the target's friends had brought and the way they seemed to be settling in, Pravat felt sure they were planning on staying for a while.

"Take us back," he said.

On the return trip to Chaweng Beach, he called Virote and gave him an update.

"Where are those pictures?"

"Haven't been able to get close enough yet."

"Make it happen. You know Mee Noi and Chayan will want to know who they are right away."

CHAPTER
THREE

HASAM KAZI WALKED into his two-level, sixteenth-floor apartment with his mobile phone pressed to his ear.

"I don't care what they are saying," he yelled. "We have a deal, one that *we* have honored over and over again. You tell them to pull their heads out of their asses and send their pickup team with the money within the next thirty minutes or we will find someone else who wants our product."

Hasam hung up and tossed the phone onto the couch on his way to the bedroom. A moment later, Mee Noi and Chayan could hear the distant sound of the master bathroom shower.

Finding the traitor had taken longer than it should have. This was due to the condition in which Chayan and Mee Noi found Chayan's organization after they escaped the prison. Chayan's brother Kwanchai had been put nominally in charge. He was to handle only the most trivial decisions, while everything else was supposed to have been run by Chayan and Mee Noi. Many things had not reached the two men's ears. Still, if Kwanchai had been even half the leader his brother was, perhaps the status quo could have been maintained. But he was not.

In the years Chayan was in prison, whole sections of his illicit business broke free from the organization's control, former employees setting themselves up as new crime lords.

If not for the blood of their mother flowing through Kwanchai's veins, Chayan's brother would already be dead. As it was, Chayan had banished him to a do-nothing post with one of his smuggling operations in southern Thailand. If karma existed, Kwanchai would do him the favor of making a wrong turn into oncoming traffic.

It had been two months now since they had left Cambodia, and most of that time had been spent sewing the organization back together and repairing damaged customer relationships.

Chayan's normally calm exterior was often overtaken by anger and frustration at having to deal with things he shouldn't have had to worry about. Mee Noi was equally irritated. Their plan had always been to take care of those responsible for Chayan's imprisonment within the first few weeks of their newfound freedom. But Kwanchai's failures had put all that on hold. The best they could do for now was keep an eye on those connected to the incarceration.

Business, after all, came first. Hence the reason they'd come south to Indonesia.

Hasam had once been one of Chayan's trusted lieutenants. Mee Noi had helped groom the man after finding him scamming tourists in Bali. Eventually they'd put him in charge of the very lucrative methamphetamine operation near the Myanmar border. After the drugs crossed into Thailand, it had been Hasam's job to make sure they made their way safely to Bangkok, where couriers would ferry them to the West.

When Chayan was put behind bars, Hasam had seen the opportunity to take over the operation and strike out on his own. With the drug money now all his, he'd set himself up in a luxury apartment in his parents' home city of Jakarta. Kwanchai had made a feeble attempt to bring him back into the fold, but Hasam had beefed up his own security force, and that had been enough to scare off Chayan's brother. Another thing Chayan and Mee Noi were not told about.

Hasam had escaped retribution because of the long list of more pressing things that needed handling. But his time had finally come.

And he, like the others, had no idea.

When Chayan and Mee Noi discovered the chaos the business was in, Mee Noi had suggested they keep their prison escape a secret, revealing it only when necessary. Their ghost-like status had proved to be a powerful tool. When those they confronted realized the truth, their shock and fear had been palpable, with several literally soiling themselves.

Chayan and Mee Noi heard the shower shut off.

Chayan reached for another *salak* from the dish on the dining room table, peeled off its scaly brown skin, and bit into the flesh. He gestured to Mee Noi to take one, but Mee Noi shook his head. The fruit was not one of his favorites.

While his boss had chosen to sit at the table, Mee Noi was standing to his side, next to one of the windows. He glanced out at the Indonesian capital in disgust. He hated the city. To him, it was a sprawling mess almost impossible to navigate. He knew some said the same about Bangkok, but that was home.

A noise from the bedroom, a drawer opening and closing.

Mee Noi turned from the uninspiring view and moved into position behind his boss. Hasam reentered the living room a few moments later, wearing only a pair of boxers and a towel draped over his shoulder.

His multimillion-dollar apartment was a big place so it wasn't surprising that he didn't notice his old employer right away. He picked his phone up off the couch and focused on the screen as he walked into the kitchen. From the wine cabinet he removed a bottle, uncorked it, and poured a healthy amount into a glass.

He was in the middle of a drink when he turned toward the dining room and saw his guests.

"What the fuck? Who the hell—" It was as far as he got before he recognized the two men.

"Hello, Hasam," Chayan said.

Mee Noi dipped his head a fraction of an inch. "Hasam."

Hasam stared, mouth agape.

"Wh-ho…g-g-g…"

"I'm afraid I don't understand." Chayan glanced over his shoulder. "Mee Noi, did you catch that?"

"I believe he's asking how you are."

"Oh, isn't that nice. I'm fine, thank you. Well, I have to admit I *am* a bit confused."

Hasam stammered again, still rooted to the kitchen floor.

"Come," Chayan said, gesturing to the chair across the table from him. "Sit."

Looking like he wanted to do anything but, Hasam glanced toward the kitchen cabinet next to the refrigerator.

Mee Noi said, "Go ahead. Push it if you want."

There were several alarm buttons throughout the apartment that would signal Hasam's security detail, located in a much smaller apartment on the other side of the same floor.

"I insist," Chayan said.

Hasam hesitated, and then raced over to the cabinet, pulled out one of the drawers, and reached under it.

"That make you feel better?" Chayan asked after the man had pressed the button on the bottom of the drawer. "I hope so. Now, please sit. We can pretend to wait for the people you think are coming."

Hasam looked toward the main door. When no one came rushing in, his fear turned into panic.

"I said, sit," Chayan said.

Hasam forced himself to do so.

"I could use a glass of wine," Chayan told Mee Noi.

"Of course," Mee Noi replied. He headed for the kitchen.

"Pour one for yourself, if you'd like."

"Thank you. I will."

Chayan said nothing more until Mee Noi returned with his glass. He took a sip and looked at the wine appreciatively. "Oh, that is good. Where is it from?"

Mee Noi went back and picked up the bottle. "Argentina."

"Take a picture of the label and order a case when we get back home."

34

Mee Noi did as ordered.

The sweat on Hasam's forehead began dripping down his face.

Chayan took another sip before setting down the glass. "So, my friend, how's business?"

Over the next hour, Chayan and Mee Noi extracted all the information they needed in order to reacquire the wayward meth operation. Hasam was very forthcoming; just the threat of violence was enough to get his tongue moving. When they were through with the questioning, he may have been mentally drained but physically unharmed.

Chayan stood. "All right, time for us to go. Get up."

Hasam looked at him. "But-but...I've told you everything. I've cooperated."

Chayan's eyebrow rose. "You've cooperated? You mean by stealing my drugs and my money for the last several years? Is that the kind of cooperation you're talking about?

"You-you can have it all back."

"Everything?"

"Everything."

"Every *baht*?"

Hasam realized the trap he'd fallen into. "Everything I still have. I'll give you my accounts. And...and you can have this apartment."

"That's very kind, but we've already taken over your accounts and this apartment," Chayan said, looking around. "I don't think we'll keep this place, though. I doubt I'll come to Jakarta enough to use it." He paused. "I said get up!"

Hasam jumped to his feet.

The poetic solution would have been to throw him out the window of his precious home and let him think about his life choices as he plummeted to the ground. But even if the window had been easy to break, doing so would lower the value of the property and prevent them from getting every cent they could out of the place.

They chose the less spectacular method of strangling him in the backseat of their rented SUV on their return trip to the airport. They then dumped him in a waterway that should shepherd his corpse into Jakarta Bay.

"Who's next?" Chayan asked as he and Mee Noi waited in the first-class lounge for their flight home.

"We have only a few offenders left. There's the matter of Aawut in Issan that still needs attention." A provider of girls, both of age and not, who had taken to skimming far more than his share of the profits.

"What else?"

Mee Noi hesitated before saying, "Well, there's always your brother."

Chayan shook his head, obviously not ready to cross that bridge yet. "That's it?"

"As far as business-related matters are concerned, yes." Another pause. "We could, of course, move on to the other list." That was the list of the three people most responsible for Chayan's imprisonment. "We have everyone under surveillance already."

The hint of a smile graced Chayan's face. "Something different *would* be enjoyable."

"Would you like to start with the monk?"

Chayan thought for a moment. "No. We'll save him for last."

"Mr. Kim and Mr. Maddox, then. They are both in Bangkok. I believe we could easily deal with both tomorrow. Do you have a preference for who's first?"

"Let's start with Mr. Kim."

CHAPTER
FOUR

BARCELONA, SPAIN

THE CROWD ROARED as music played over the stadium speakers and the starting teams for FC Barcelona and visiting Granada walked onto the Camp Nou pitch, each player holding the hand of a kid wearing a team uniform.

It was week nineteen of the La Liga schedule. Barcelona was top of the table, while its opponent was flirting with the relegation zone at the bottom. Nate had explained all of this to Liz on their way to the stadium, but her eyes had glazed over not long after he began.

Having lived in Europe for a few years now while attending grad school in Paris, she couldn't help but be familiar with many of the continent's biggest football stars from the sheer number of commercials and advertisements that featured them. Beyond that, though, all she knew about the game was that players kicked the ball back and forth, hoping to get it into one of the nets. She didn't hate sports. She was just much more passionate about art.

Nate had been visiting her since five days before Christmas. Once the holiday had passed, they headed off to Spain. But their time together was drawing to an end, and in another few days they would be returning to the French capital so Liz could get back to work on her dissertation and he could return to California.

Their relationship was a patchwork of vacations taken

when Liz needed a break from her studies and Nate had some time off from his work with her brother, Quinn. While it had been serving them well enough, she'd begun to wonder how long they could keep it up. They had shared some incredibly intense times, but had never lived in the same place at the same time and therefore hadn't tested the bounds of what it really meant to be a couple. Given Nate's exciting covert life, she was more than a little worried he'd become bored with her.

She glanced over at him. He was staring down at the pitch, his smile as wide as she'd ever seen it. After a moment, he noticed her attention.

"What?" he asked.

She grinned. "Nothing. Just looks like you're having fun."

"How can I not?" He motioned to the field with both hands. "This is Barcelona. They're like the best team in the world."

"Didn't you once tell me Bayern Munich was the best team?"

"Okay, *one* of the best in the world."

She snickered. "So are we totally blowing off your job or what?"

A bit of the glimmer faded from his smile. "Right," he said. He lifted his binoculars and looked down at a row of seats far below them.

The game had not been part of their vacation plans. In fact, if they had stuck to their original schedule, they would be in Madrid right now. But three nights ago, Nate had received a call from Helen Cho, one of his and Quinn's clients. She had a mission for him right there in Barcelona, one she had said shouldn't occupy him for more than a handful of hours over the next couple of days. He'd been less than enthusiastic but Helen had kept pushing, and he'd taken thirty minutes to think it over and discuss it with Liz.

"There's no guarantee it'll stay within her forty-eight-hour window," he'd told Liz. "You know how these things go."

"Do you want to do it?" she asked.

"Of course not. I want to spend this time with you."

She knew he was telling the truth, while also holding something back. His sense of duty to his job was fighting with his desire to be with her. But she understood what he did for a living, knew how different it was from what others did, knew it was important though few would ever know it.

Nate and Quinn were cleaners. They made the dead disappear. Liz probably shouldn't have known that, but she'd seen them at work, and—much to her brother's dismay—been pulled into a couple of operations herself, where she had proved surprisingly useful. The organizations they worked for tended to be associated with US intelligence, so that made her boyfriend and her brother spies of a sort.

Helen Cho was in charge of one such organization. The mission she had given Nate, though, had nothing to do with body removal. Per Nate, it was to be a simple observation job that required him to be at certain places at certain times. How Helen had known he was in Barcelona he didn't say, nor did Liz ask. She'd seen enough of his world to know that if someone with means was looking for you, they'd find you.

"I'm telling her no," he finally said. "She'll have to figure out how to get someone else here to take care of it."

She stopped him as he reached for his phone. "She wouldn't have called if there was someone else. It's just a few days, and if she's right, there will be plenty of time in between for us."

"You're sure?" he asked, surprised.

"I'm sure."

And now here they were, as he predicted, on day three of his two-day assignment, with no end in sight. At least she'd been able to tag along, which was more than either of them had expected.

The subject of Nate's observation was also attending the football match. The man's seat was considerably better than theirs, only eleven rows up from the pitch, near the center of the field. They had seen him twice the day before—at a restaurant for lunch and at a theater in the evening—and twice more on the day before that, arriving on a boat at the marina near the Hotel Arts and that night at the beachfront club Opium. So it was easy enough for her to pick out his bald head and large frame even without Nate's binoculars.

Who he was and why her boyfriend was observing him, neither she nor Nate had any idea.

Another roar from the crowd signaled the start of the game. For a while Nate forgot about his task and enjoyed the action on the field. Even Liz couldn't help feeling some excitement, especially when one of the Barcelona players scored only eight minutes into the game.

After that, Nate went back and forth between watching the game and checking on his target.

The match was nearing the thirty-minute mark of the first half when he looked toward the lower seats and said, "Oh, crap."

Liz glanced at him, and then down where the bald man was sitting. Or, rather, had been sitting. Several people were standing in the area, looking at the ground.

"What happened?" she asked.

"He's on the floor between the rows."

"Did...did someone—" She stopped herself before she asked if someone had shot him. This being Europe, chances were most of the people around them spoke some English. She leaned against Nate and whispered, "Is he dead?"

"Can't tell. Too many people blocking the view."

Here and there, spectators in the rows near the man began standing and looking over, visually spreading the news that something had happened. Movement drew Liz's attention to the top of the stairs that led down to the man's seating area.

"EMTs," she whispered. Four of them were hurrying down the steps, carrying a stretcher.

Nate cursed under his breath.

"Is this what you were waiting for?"

He tore his eyes away from the binoculars long enough to glance at her. "What?"

"You were waiting for something to happen to him, weren't you? Is this it?"

"No. I was just supposed to note who he met with. That's all."

"Do you think your client lied to you?"

A shrug. "Wouldn't be the first time."

The EMTs disappeared behind the standing crowd when they knelt next to their patient.

When they lifted the man onto the stretcher, Nate grabbed Liz's hand. "Come on."

They hurried down the steps and into the tunnel under the stands. Once inside, Nate turned right and rushed over to the stairs that would take them down to the section where the bald man was.

They came out on the lower level very close to the man's aisle. Several people were standing at the top, staring down the steps. Nate and Liz joined them. The EMTs were working their way up the stairs, carrying the man on the stretcher. Behind them came two other men. Liz recognized them as having always been with the bald man whenever she and Nate had seen him.

The crowd at the top parted as the EMTs neared. Nate maneuvered himself into a front position and Liz tucked in beside him. As the stretcher went by, Liz realized the only reason the sheet covering the man's body hadn't been pulled over his face was to keep the crowd from panicking. But thanks to her brother and Nate, she'd seen enough dead bodies to know the man was gone.

Nate put a hand on her back and gave her a tug, indicating they should meld with the onlookers and head out. But before they could disappear, the gaze of one of the men following the paramedics fell on Nate.

"Hey," he said. "I know you."

"Keep moving," Nate whispered.

Curious eyes in the crowd turned toward Nate and Liz.

"Stop there," the man said as he started after them.

"Run!" Nate yelled.

The man tried to grab him, but his hand caught only air as Nate and Liz sprinted away.

The concourse was filling with people trying to get in a

bathroom break or buy some snacks before halftime. As Nate led Liz through the mess, she could hear the chasing guy's shoes hitting the concrete only steps behind them.

Nate pulled her around a man and a boy, twisting sideways so he wouldn't hit the child but losing momentum in the process.

A hand snatched at the back of Liz's shirt, almost grabbing hold.

"He's right behind me!" she said.

Nate glanced over his shoulder and then tapped her hand twice, telling her to be ready. Ten feet farther on, he squeezed her hand and lunged to the right toward a set of stairs under a sign indicating a stadium exit.

When they reached the landing, though, instead of going down, Nate jerked to the side and pulled Liz behind him. The man's shoes skidded on the floor as he reacted to their sudden halt. Before he could stop, Nate shoved him toward the stairs, sending him stumbling down. Nate grabbed Liz's hand again and took off back onto the concourse. Once they reached the middle of the crowd, he slowed.

"Do you see him?" he asked.

Liz scanned ahead. "No."

But they weren't out of trouble yet. Security officers were heading in their general direction, though it appeared they hadn't spotted Nate and Liz. Nate hunched down to avoid being one of the taller ones in the crowd and led Liz to the side. As soon as the officers passed by, Nate guided her to another set of stairs, as if he'd been in the stadium a hundred times before. This, she knew, was due to the prep time he'd put in that morning, memorizing Camp Nou's layout and that of the surrounding area.

After they reached the bottom, they headed for the nearest exit, but as it came into view, Nate muttered under his breath, "This just isn't our day."

A half dozen guards stood near the exit, scanning the faces of the people as they left.

"We could go through separately," Liz suggested. "They're probably looking for two people together."

Nate thought for a moment, and shook his head. "I don't want to take that chance."

He looked around. Suddenly he grabbed her and moved her against the wall. Turning his back to the crowd, he leaned close like he was going to kiss her. Instead, his eyes moved side to side, checking his peripheral vision.

"What is it?" she asked.

"More security."

She pressed her face into his shoulder and peeked over it at the busy walkway. Four more guards were hurrying through the crowd. One of them glanced in Nate and Liz's direction, but dismissed them.

"They're gone," she whispered a few moments later.

"No more coming?" he asked.

She checked the walkway in both directions. No more guards, but she did spot something that might help them get away.

"Wait here," she said, moving around him.

"Where are you going?"

"Trust me."

Though her Spanish wasn't nearly as good as her French, it was improving, and she had no problems making a deal with the woman who caught her eye. When she returned, she motioned for Nate to follow her to a quieter spot off the main passageway.

"I'll do you first and then you do me," she said.

"Do what?"

She held up the two sticks of colored makeup she'd bought off the woman with the blue and red stripes on her face.

"Nice," he said, impressed.

"Should one of us do red and the other blue?" she asked.

"Obviously you're not a Barcelona fan. Do half and half."

Liz quickly painted his face, and then he did the same with hers.

"Is it going to work?" she asked as he looked her over.

"Here's hoping."

"You were supposed to say yes."

"Right. Then yes, it'll work."

They waited until a particularly large group of people were walking by, and then moved through them toward the exit. Since it was halftime, only a handful of people were leaving.

"Act like you have a stomachache or something," Nate said.

"Uh, sure," Liz replied. Putting a hand on her abdomen, she scrunched her face into a look of extreme discomfort. "How's this?"

"Perfect."

They approached the exit, Nate's arm around her as if he were half guiding, half holding her up. The officers closest to the gate looked them over and quickly waved them through.

A couple blocks away, Nate said, "It's okay now. You can stop."

Straightening up, she asked, "What happened back there?"

"That is an excellent question."

THE FIRST THING Nate did when they returned to their hotel room was to wash the makeup off. While Liz did the same, he called Helen.

"Mr. Roberts is dead," he told her, using the name she'd given him for the man he'd been watching.

"Dead?" Helen said. Her surprise seemed genuine, but in this business it was hard to be sure. "What the hell happened?"

He described what he had seen.

"Cause?"

"No idea. At one point he's fine, and the next time I check he's lying on the concrete, probably already dead."

"You didn't have eyes on him the whole time?"

The question was considerably more accusatory than he would have liked, so he answered in an equally clipped voice. "That would have raised a lot of questions, given my surroundings."

She was silent for a moment. "I suppose. Dammit. I can*not* believe this."

"I take it he wasn't supposed to die."

"Of course he wasn't supposed to die. Dammit. This really puts a wrench in things." A pause. "Hang tight. I might need you—"

"Whoa, hold on there. I've already been on this job a day longer than I was supposed to be, and in case you've forgotten, I'm on vacation."

"I realize that."

"You can get someone else to find out what happened to him."

"I wasn't suggesting you find out what happened. What I *was* going to say is, I might need you to fill in for him."

"Wait. He was working for you?"

"In a manner of speaking."

"What the hell does that mean?"

Another pause. "He was not necessarily aware he was doing something for me."

"How could he—" Nate stopped himself. "You know what? It doesn't matter. My girlfriend is waiting for me so I'm off the clock now. I'll bill you for my time when I get back home."

"Do I need to call Quinn and have him tell you to help me?"

Nate had to work very hard not to squeeze the phone into pieces. "Excuse me? Quinn is *not* my boss. He hasn't been for a while. He's my partner. He doesn't tell me what to do."

If Quinn had been having this conversation with Helen, he would have hung up by now. But while Nate was indeed a partner, he hadn't reached a point in his career where he had the clout to piss off their best client without ramifications. Yet he also couldn't set a precedent of allowing her to say anything she wanted to him.

"I apologize," she said after a few seconds. "You're right, of course."

"Damn right, I am."

"All I'm asking is that you give me an hour to figure

things out, and if I do need your help, I can promise you'll be done by tomorrow afternoon."

Nate glanced at the bathroom where it sounded like Liz had decided to take a shower. "I'm not sure if this makes a difference, but one of Mr. Roberts's associates recognized me." He told her what had happened while the man was being carted out.

"I don't think that should be a hindrance, but I'll check. Can I call you back in an hour?"

He took a deep breath. "Fine. *One* hour."

CHAPTER
FIVE

BANGKOK

JUNG-HO KIM—JUNG to friends—shuffled into the bathroom and pawed through the cabinet for his bottle of aspirin.

Though he was not unfamiliar with a heavy night of drinking, the previous evening had been wild even by his standards. His childhood friend Woo-jin had flown in the day before, and it would have been bad form if Jung hadn't shown him a good time. After all, Woo-jin would have done the same for him in Seoul—if Jung were allowed to return to South Korea without being arrested the moment he stepped off the plane. The petty Seoul government took a dim view of its citizens skipping out on their required military service.

After downing four aspirin and two full glasses of water, he took a look at himself in the mirror and grunted in disgust at his bloated face. He turned on the shower and stepped into the water, the steam easing some of his aches and pains. By the time he stepped out again, he was feeling if not like a totally new man, then at least like one who might be able to face the day without puking.

Upon reentering the bedroom he heard a moan and glanced at the bed. A woman lay half under the covers, asleep. A blonde. Russian, probably. They were his weakness. What her name was or where he'd picked her up, he had no idea.

He pulled on underwear and pants before walking over to

the bed and leaning in for a closer look.

Nice, he thought. She wasn't bad looking at all. Might be worth seeing if she wanted to stick around for a day or two. At the very least he needed to find out where she worked so he could drop in again sometime.

He thought about slapping her on the ass and asking her right then and there, but decided to let her sleep. The happier she was, the more likely she'd be up for partying again. There would definitely be another party. Woo-jin would insist, and who was Jung to disappoint his friend?

He selected a shirt from his closet and donned it on his way into the hall. The door to the guest room was closed. As he passed it, Jung wondered if Woo-jin had brought someone home, too. Probably. Maybe even two. His friend liked multiples.

As Jung entered the living room, he paused long enough to touch the button that raised the blinds. The building he lived in was not a particularly tall one, but he hadn't bought the apartment because of the view. It was the wide, private terrace and swimming pool right outside his living room that had sold him.

He went into the kitchen, poured some food into the bowl for his cat Axel, fixed himself a Bloody Mary, and headed onto the terrace. It was midmorning and the temperature had already risen to Thailand's typical oppressive level. Fortunately, the sun shades and the water misters he'd had installed were more than enough to keep him from burning up. After sitting on his favorite lounge, he took a drink before retrieving the computer tablet he kept in a secret compartment of the chair's arm.

Like most mornings, he went first to his favorite news site and scrolled through the local headlines. He was starting to read an article about a new restaurant along the river when he caught a whiff of something pungent. He lifted his drink to his nose but it smelled exactly like a Bloody Mary should.

He sniffed the air again. Nothing. Probably a passing garbage truck, he decided.

He focused on the computer screen again, and had all but

forgotten about the disturbance when the smell returned, stronger this time. He put down the tablet and stood up.

The odor seemed to be coming from the outside edge of the terrace, just beyond the outdoor dining table where he often hosted parties. As he walked over, he was able to narrow down the source to the American-style barbecue that had cost a small fortune.

Cautiously, Jung snagged the long tongs hanging from the barbecue's handle and used them to open the top.

He screamed and jumped back. Axel lay flayed across the grill like he was ready to be cooked.

Jung doubled over and wrenched whatever was still in his stomach onto the deck. When his guts stopped clenching, he stood back up.

Whoever had done this to Axel was going to pay.

He knew Woo-jin wasn't responsible. But what about the girl in Jung's bed? Maybe, but from all indications she'd been at least as trashed as Jung had been and likely not moved from his side all night.

He headed back into the house and knocked on the guest room door. "Woo-jin. Woo-jin, wake up."

Not even a groan.

Jung knocked again, repeating his friend's name. When there was still no answer, he opened the door and entered. As he crossed the threshold, something on the floor caught his eye. He picked it up.

A knife.

A *bloody* knife.

Could his friend have killed Jung's cat?

He didn't want to believe it, but the evidence was right there in his own hand. Teeth clenched and eyes narrowed, he moved to the bed.

Woo-jin had indeed brought someone home. A woman with dark hair. Thai, probably. Like Woo-jin, she was facing away from Jung so he couldn't see what she looked like. Jung grabbed his friend's arm and pulled Woo-jin onto his back.

"Wake up!" He held the knife out in front of Woo-jin's face. "Is this yours? Did you...did you..." Woo-jin's eyes were still closed, his face slack. Jung slapped his friend's cheek. "Wake up!"

Not even a flutter of an eyelid.

What the hell?

Jung grabbed the sheet. "Wake up, you ass—"

The sheet was moist and sticky. With growing dread, he pulled it down.

Woo-jin had two wounds—a puncture in his chest near his heart, and a long deep cut across his stomach from which his intestines were spilling out. Jung could now see that blood not only covered the sheet but was smeared across the girl's back.

Not wanting to do it, he tugged on the girl until she fell on her back next to Woo-jin. One wound to the chest and the same cut across the stomach. Jung made it back into the hallway before the heaves grabbed hold of him again, but the only things that came up were bile and spittle.

How long had they been like that? All night? And why hadn't Jung been killed, too?

Whatever the answers, he knew he had to get out of there fast. Since he was a foreign resident with a dubious background, the Thai authorities would be more than happy to pin this on him.

He headed to his room to get his go bag filled with clothes and passports and money. He would go straight to the airport and catch the first flight out of the country. He should be long gone before the police knew anything had happened here. If he was lucky, it could be days before the bodies were discovered.

He pushed open his door and rushed in, so focused on getting away it didn't even dawn on him that he hadn't closed the door earlier.

But while that didn't stop him, the woman in his bed did. She lay on her back in the center, her arms flung out like she was being crucified. She, too, had a single wound to the heart and a slash across the belly.

She'd been alive when he'd left the room. He'd heard her breathing.

Which meant the killer was still in the apartment.

He whipped around, holding out the knife, but no one was there.

His go bag was in the closet. Where the killer might be hiding. Knife extended, Jung moved to the closet doorway, and then quickly reached in and turned on the light.

No one there.

He grabbed the bag, slung it over his shoulder, and quietly left the bedroom. Heading down the hall, he faced each doorway as he passed, ready to stab at anything that might emerge, but he reached the end unscathed.

He stopped for a moment to listen for the sound of anyone who might be waiting in the living room, but all he heard were the honks and drones of traffic drifting in through the open door to the terrace.

His heart was beating faster than he could ever remember. He took a few deep breaths to calm himself.

Get out of the building, Grab a cab. Go to the airport. Nice and simple.

He tightened his grip on the knife and moved into the living room.

With a boom, the front door shattered off its hinges. A dozen police officers rushed in, shouting, "On the ground! On the ground! On the ground!"

More officers poured in from the terrace, every single one pointing a rifle at Jung.

He froze, his go bag full of forged passports and ill-gotten cash over his shoulder, the bloody knife in his hand.

He dropped everything and lowered himself to the floor.

MEE NOI AND Chayan watched through the tinted windows of their sedan from across the street as a swarm of cops escorted a handcuffed and bewildered Jung-ho Kim out of his building and into a waiting police vehicle.

"Just as you wanted," Mee Noi said.

His boss grunted in agreement.

Kim had been the one who lured Chayan into the trap in Cambodia that had ended with Chayan's arrest. Though it would've been acceptable if Jung had been killed in the raid, it would not have been as satisfying as seeing the man thrown in prison for a while before his inevitable death sentence could be carried out.

"Shall we move on?" Mee Noi asked once the police car had driven away.

Chayan turned from the window and nodded.

Mee Noi leaned forward. "Thon Buri," he told the driver, and then settled back next to his boss.

CHAPTER
SIX

KOH SAMUI

BECAUSE OF ALL the travel Quinn did for his work, he rarely suffered from more than the subtlest of jetlag. Orlando was also good at adjusting quickly to new time zones. Unfortunately, the trait was not genetic. Claire was wide awake again after midnight.

Quinn carried her into the living room but kept the lights off, hoping the darkness would soothe her back to sleep. It worked, but not until five a.m., when they both knocked out on the giant couch listening to the waves, Claire on Quinn's chest.

The smell of sausage shook Quinn from his slumber. He cracked open his eyes to find the room bathed in sunlight. Claire was still out cold. He eased off the couch and put her down where he'd been lying.

Orlando hovered by the stove in the kitchen portion of the grand room, sausage frying in one pan, some kind of vegetable in the other.

"Morning," Quinn said as he joined her.

After they kissed, she said, "That didn't look comfortable."

His brow furrowed. "What didn't?"

She grabbed her phone off the counter and showed him a picture of Claire and him sleeping.

"Not as bad as it looks," he told her. "And it got her back

to sleep."

"How long did that take?"

"Too long."

"We should wake her. If she sleeps all day, we'll have the same problem tonight."

Quinn sighed. "Give me a few minutes and then I'll do it."

She cupped his cheek and kissed him again. "My turn," she said. "Why don't you put on your suit and go for a swim. I'll bring you and Garrett breakfast in just a bit."

"He's already up?"

"Since daybreak, I think."

Ten minutes later, Quinn arrived poolside to find Garrett throwing a coin into the water and then diving in to pluck it off the bottom.

"Have you gone down to the beach yet?" Quinn asked when the boy resurfaced.

"Mom won't let me go alone."

"Well, you're not alone now. Race?"

Garrett's eyes lit up. He hustled out of the pool and the two of them ran toward the sea.

Quinn let Garrett reach the water half a step ahead of him, but he still yelled, "First!"

"No way. I got here first."

"My foot hit the water before yours."

"You are such a liar," Garrett said.

"All right, I tell you what. See where that wave is starting to break?" Quinn pointed into the cove.

"Yeah."

"First one there and back wins. Deal?"

Garrett was sprinting into the water before he yelled over his shoulder, "Deal!"

This time Quinn let him win by a less controversial amount.

For years Quinn had been more like an uncle to Garrett than anything else, giving him advice when asked and teaching him some of the fun things in life. Not traditional things like how to throw a football or play poker. The tricks

54

Quinn taught Garrett were more like how to sneak up on friends without them knowing and how to pick any kind of lock. Even after Quinn moved in with Garrett and Orlando, he'd been careful not to take on the full role of parent. He didn't feel it was his place. Garrett wasn't his son. That distinction belonged to Quinn's mentor, Durrie. Never mind the fact Durrie would have been a terrible father if he wasn't dead. Quinn felt taking on the role himself would be disrespectful.

Since the birth of Claire, though, his relationship with the boy had started to shift. While Garrett truly loved his new sister and would do anything for her, he seemed unsure how to classify Quinn now. Sometimes Garrett almost seemed to resent Quinn's presence, and would respond angrily if Quinn asked him to do something like a parent would. But there were times like now when things were like how they had always been.

Quinn was well aware the kid was suffering from the double whammy of a change in the family dynamic brought on by Claire's arrival, and the fact he had recently entered that awkward, hormonal stage of life where he wasn't quite a child anymore but also not an adult. Quinn remembered what he'd been like at that age, and was always surprised he'd lived through it.

Though Quinn and Orlando had not openly discussed it, Quinn knew they were both hoping this trip would ease the on-again, off-again tension between him and Garrett. Things seemed to have gotten off to a fairly good start.

They played in the small waves, splashing and diving and goofing around. Like they'd seen the day before, powerboats and the occasional Jet Ski passed by the cove, most whipping across the water and quickly moving out of sight.

One boat, though, had dropped anchor about three hundred yards out. When Quinn noticed it, his first thought was that it was the same one he'd seen someone fishing from the day before.

Thai script took years to understand and read, but many

of the boats had English words painted on their hulls to appeal to tourists. The anchored boat boasted the name SAMUI FUN #3. Unfortunately, Quinn hadn't paid enough attention to what was written on yesterday's boat.

Knock it off, he told himself. He was on *vacation.* Besides, even if it were the same boat, the spot was probably just one of the pilot's favorites.

A whistle from the beach drew his attention away from the sea. Orlando stood on the sand, holding Claire in one arm and waving her other over her head.

"Time to eat, I think," Quinn said to Garrett.

"Can we come back out here after we're done?"

"We can do whatever you want."

A smile. "Race you to the beach."

Before Garrett could start swimming, Quinn grabbed him around the waist, tossed him backward into the water, and took off.

He couldn't let Garrett win every time.

THE REST OF the morning was spent by the water, Quinn and Garrett swimming in the cove, Orlando stretched out on a lounge chair under an umbrella reading a book—*Annihilation* by Jeff VanderMeer—while Claire played on a blanket beside her.

Every once in a while, Orlando would carry her daughter to the edge of the water and let her sit on the sand, with Orlando's hand on her back, as waves lapped against their legs. Claire loved it, laughing and surprising herself when she accidently flicked water into the air.

Around eleven a.m., Quinn carried Claire out into the water for a little while. Orlando took advantage of the break to go on a run down the beach and around to the end of the cove. Throughout her pregnancy she had stayed in shape. Claire had cooperated by being a small baby who took up little room. Still, Orlando had considered herself a blimp, though no one else would have said the same.

In the months since her daughter's birth, Orlando had worked double time to return to her excellent condition. She was surprised by how much harder it was this go-around than it had been after Garrett was born. If she hadn't felt the effects of age before, she was now.

But the hard work was paying off. The baby weight was gone, and her muscles were starting to feel that familiar toned and ready state. She still had a ways to go but the end was in sight.

She passed three more houses along the cove as she made her way out to the point. Upon reaching it, she stood on the jut of land twenty feet above the beach and looked out at the Gulf of Thailand. It was nice to get away from San Francisco and the routine of taking care of Claire while fitting in work whenever she could. She was hoping to get in some quality time with Garrett while they were here. She was sure he was feeling neglected, which no doubt contributed to the minor tension he and Quinn had been having. Though by the look of them out in the water, those issues had been forgotten, at least temporarily.

When she turned to head back, a boat that had been anchored near the cove's mouth began motoring north again. She'd seen a man fishing off the back, and wondered for a moment if he had caught anything. By the time she started running again, she had stopped thinking about him.

Daeng was standing next to her umbrella when she returned.

"I was thinking I'd take you guys out to lunch," he said. "There's some good restaurants back in Chaweng Beach. Unless you have other plans."

"My plans only go as far as sleeping at night and getting up in the morning."

"That sounds like a full schedule to me."

"I could fit in some eating."

"Great. In an hour, then?"

Orlando looked out at the water where Garrett was splashing his sister and Quinn, and Quinn was splashing him back while Claire laughed and laughed. "Make it an hour and a half."

PRAVAT SPENT THE morning spying on the compound from the boat. He would have probably remained there if not for the woman. When she'd come running down the beach, he thought she had made him. It wasn't until the anchor was up that he realized she was only exercising.

But his departure worked out for the best. No more than an hour after he'd rejoined Narong, the gate opened and the van reemerged with the target and his friends on board.

"Go, go," he said to Narong after the van passed their position. "Don't lose them."

"I won't." Narong swung the sedan around and eased onto the road fifteen seconds behind the van.

"A little closer," Pravat instructed, wishing he was behind the wheel.

"It's fine."

"Closer."

Narong grimaced, but at the first opportunity he passed the car in front of them so that there were now only two vehicles between their sedan and the van. "Better?"

"For now."

Not for the first time, Pravat thought about how simple it would be to take care of the target when the time came. In the week and a half he and Narong had been following the monk, they'd observed no guards whatsoever watching over him. Someone could easily sneak onto the property and slit the target's throat while he slept. Someone who wasn't Pravat or Narong, that was. They weren't killers. They were watchers. But it was nice to know what their efforts would achieve.

Fifteen minutes later, the van pulled into an open parking spot in front of a crowded section of businesses in Chaweng Beach.

"Let me out," Pravat ordered as soon as he realized what was going on.

Narong swung to the side of the road.

As he hopped out, Pravat said, "Find some place close to park, and message me where you are."

It was a hot afternoon, the sun beating down relentlessly on the island. He jogged over to the shady side of the street and headed toward where the others had parked. He nearly tripped when he realized they were walking in his direction.

He turned his back to the road and became suddenly interested in a street vendor's display of sunglasses. He listened as the others passed by, and then watched them enter a restaurant.

When they were out of sight, he headed after them. The café had a few tables in its small front room but all were empty. For a moment, he wondered if he'd made a mistake, but then he saw a sign reading BEACH PATIO RESTAURANT in both English and Thai, with an arrow pointing down a walkway that ran beside the building.

Pravat thought for a moment. He could go inside and take a seat, but he'd likely be seen. None of them would know who he was, of course, but he would have to avoid ever being seen again. No sense in wasting that card right now.

Three shops down he found another pathway to the beach. Once on the sand, he worked his way back until he could see the target and his friends at a table along the front rail of the patio. He noted that most of the surrounding buildings also had places to eat on the beach side. One of these occupied the property just south of the restaurant where the target was. A solitary customer sat at a table, nursing a beer, while the staff hung near the back under a fan.

Pravat nodded to the bored-looking waitress as he entered, and chose a table that allowed him to see the target without easily being seen.

He ordered *panang gai* and a beer. As soon as the server left him alone, he pulled out his phone. This was the closest he'd been able to get to his target since the airport, so he took pictures of the monk's friends and sent them to Virote.

After lunch, he followed the group at a safe distance as they perused the stalls and shops along the road. Shortly after three, they headed back to the compound.

Pravat and Narong took up watch again, but the gate remained closed for the rest of the day.

CHAPTER
SEVEN

BANGKOK

IF JUNG-HO KIM was the lure that had led Chayan into the Cambodian trap, Richard Maddox was the one who ensured the prison gate stayed barred.

Unlike Kim, Maddox did not make his living as a criminal. In fact, just the opposite. He was head of a nongovernmental organization whose sole aim was to prevent the human trafficking of girls and young women, specifically from the Isaan area. There, families would often be persuaded to sell their daughters just to get by. The story told to them was that these girls would work in factories or as domestics, but everyone knew most of the work the women would be doing was the kind performed on their backs. It wasn't only these sold women who were thrown into this life. Others would disappear without a trace after accepting rides from strangers or being dragged into a van.

It was a very lucrative business for someone like Chayan, one that had moved east into Cambodia, with plans for expansion into Laos and Vietnam.

Maddox's organization raised money used both to convince families they needn't sell off their own children and to set up schools for the girls to educate and help them find better work.

If the Englishman had left it at that, he wouldn't have drawn Chayan's ire. The work the NGO did was disruptive, yes, but ultimately affected only a small percentage of the business. Maddox, however, did not believe his responsibility ended with his group's cash-giving policies. He made it a habit of compiling information on the human trade, creating a damning trove of documents and pictures and stories.

Though he had not been a conscious part of the conspiracy that landed Chayan in trouble, he had nonetheless been tipped off to the arrest and had been more than happy to turn over reams of documentation to the Cambodian authorities, who used the information to temporarily seal Chayan's fate, and, without realizing it, permanently seal the fate of the Englishman.

Maddox lived in a modest apartment in an unremarkable building on the west side of the Chao Praya river. Chayan and Mee Noi had discussed in depth the plan they would employ to deal with the man. As with Kim, they would not kill him. That would be too merciful.

They would destroy him.

They arrived at Maddox's address at one p.m. One of Chayan's lieutenants had convinced the landlord to hand over a copy of the key to the Englishman's place. The landlord had been further persuaded that it would be a great time for her and her family to visit her brother in Hua Hin for a few days.

Chayan and Mee Noi then supervised the placement of the incriminating evidence, and the preparation of the other location they would be using.

The watcher outside Maddox's office called at 4:43 p.m. and said the Englishman had left for the nearby Sky Train station, where he was now waiting for the next departure.

Several minutes later, the lookout checked in again and told them Maddox was sticking to his normal routine, having boarded an eastbound train on the Silom Line. The next call came as the train approached Pho Nimit station, a few blocks from Maddox's apartment.

On the walk home, the Englishman stopped at a few food stalls to purchase his dinner, and finally arrived at the entrance to his building at eighteen minutes after five o'clock.

Before he could touch the door, a cloth bag was dropped

over his head and his arms were yanked behind him. When he started to yell, one of Chayan's men punched him in the jaw, silencing him. He was then carried into a waiting delivery van and whisked away.

They took him to a grimy room with a cheap bed and a toilet, separated only by a flimsy partition.

The first injection had been administered on the road and ensured that Maddox would be docile. Now that they were in the room, one of the men poked him with the second needle and gave him a large enough dose to keep the do-gooder knocked out for at least twelve hours. They arranged him on the bed and removed his clothes.

The girls were brought in next. They, too, were unconscious and unclothed. Most importantly, they were both underage. The girls had been schooled what to say once they came to. To guarantee their cooperation, they were told in no uncertain terms what would happen to them and their families if they did not perform as ordered. The carrot was that if all went according to plan, the girls would not only be free from their "obligation" to Chayan, they would also receive a small sum of money to start a new life. Though it would be easy for Chayan to renege on this promise, he had no intention of doing so. Sacrificing two of his assets was well worth the price of balancing the scales.

Chayan and Mee Noi made a last check of the room to make sure everything looked the way it should. When they were satisfied, they locked the trio inside and left the building.

In an hour, a phone call would be placed to the police, the caller a frightened girl who "got away." She would tell them about the *farang* and the girls and the drugs and the room. She would also say this was not the first time, and that he liked to take pictures he kept in his house. She would hang up without giving her name.

The script for the rest would write itself. News stories of the pedophile who had been masquerading as a champion of helpless women. Whether he was thrown in a Thai prison or exiled into a life of shame, it didn't matter.

Richard Maddox was done, and as a byproduct, his

organization would topple with him.

"So," Mee Noi said as they drove away, "the monk?"

Chayan smiled. "The monk."

CHAPTER
EIGHT

THE CALL WAS relayed through an automatic switcher buried in the wall of a cafe in Naples, Italy, to a router in Samarkand, Uzbekistan, that sent it on to its final destination, a small village in Pakistan a few kilometers from the border with India.

It was picked up after the second ring. "Yes?"

The caller repeated the appropriate code phrase and was told to wait.

Two minutes passed before the intended recipient came on the line. Instead of saying anything, he let the caller know he was there by clearing his throat.

"The handoff is to take place in the morning," the caller said.

"You're sure this time?"

"Yes. Our source is well placed." She described what she'd learned about the transfer. "If we time it correctly, I think we should be able to take possession ourselves."

"And if not?"

The caller described the secondary plan, and then said, "Either way, by this time tomorrow she will no longer be a threat."

The line disconnected and all information related to the call disappeared.

CHAPTER
NINE

BARCELONA

LIZ HAD BEEN annoyed when she found out Helen needed Nate for one more day, especially since his new task was a more active one that would not allow Liz to accompany him.

She couldn't get mad at him, though. She was the one who'd talked him into saying yes in the first place.

She didn't sleep well that night, worrying about what might happen to him the next day. The best rest she got came in the morning, but that ended with Nate shaking her awake.

"I just got the call," he said. "I need to head out right away."

"What? Wait. What time is it?"

"Eight thirty."

"You have to go now?"

He nodded. "I'm sorry."

"No, it's okay." She touched his cheek. "Be careful, okay?"

"Always am." It was the response he gave her every time she said that.

He leaned down and kissed her. She wrapped her arms around him and pulled him down on her.

Several seconds passed before he pulled his lips from hers. "If I don't leave now…"

He didn't need to finish. She knew his work needed prep time, and keeping him from it could get him hurt. But she pulled him in for one more kiss before finally letting him go.

"I won't be back until after lunch," he said as he headed for the door. "If you go out, just text me where you are and I'll meet up with you."

"Okay, sounds good," she said, trying to sound supportive and unconcerned. The former was true, the latter not so much.

"I love you," he said.

"I love you, too," she replied.

And with that, she was alone.

NATE'S CAB PULLED up in front of Barcelona Sants railway station at fourteen minutes after nine a.m.

As he moved inside the building, he fought a crush of people heading toward the exit, most likely commuters making their way from outlying areas to their city jobs. The crowds lessened the farther he went, but not by much.

From one of the orange self-serve ticket stations, he purchased a ticket for the ten a.m. train to Madrid, and then made his way through security to the waiting area near platform one. There, he procured a newspaper from a stand and picked out a suitable spot along the wall from where he could watch things. Opening the newspaper, he assumed the guise of a bored traveler.

Rafe Larson, Helen Cho's assistant, had messaged him photos of the two men with whom he was supposed to link up. One look told him what he'd suspected. They were the two men who'd been with Roberts at the stadium the previous night.

With the photos had come a recognition code Nate was to use upon contact. He hoped the men would give him a chance to say it before they tried to punch the crap out of him.

The two men arrived four minutes after Nate and scanned the room. As their gaze moved in his direction, Nate smoothly turned away and held up his paper. After a few moments, he flipped to the back page so he could easily peek around the edge.

The men were huddled together, talking. Then the one

who had chased Nate took a seat while his friend walked over to the coffee shop. The seated man scanned the room again and pulled out his phone. The instant he looked down at it, Nate began strolling along the side of the room. Not once did the man glance at him.

No wonder Roberts died, Nate thought.

A person with that lack of attention was not someone Nate looked forward to working with, but if everything went as smoothly as Helen predicted, their collaboration wouldn't last long.

From Nate's new position in the guy's blind spot, he watched the other man return with two cups of coffee and plop down next to his partner.

As departure time neared, Nate could see the men getting anxious. A few times they turned back and looked in his general direction. Of course, he always had the paper ready and not once drew their attention.

Whatever job they usually did, they weren't spies, not in the traditional sense. Their movements had no subtlety, which gave Nate the sense they were as out of place as he was on this mission.

An announcement in Spanish declared that platform one was now open and the train for Madrid was ready for boarding. Passengers rose from their chairs, grabbed their luggage, and headed toward the platform entrance. The two men, however, remained seated for a moment before moving toward the train. Nate waited until they joined the crowd, and then walked up behind them.

"I hate these midmorning trains. They're always so packed," Nate said. "Is this a business trip or pleasure?"

Both men stiffened upon hearing the recognition code.

Then the man who had chased Nate completed the dance with, "A little bit of both. It is Madrid, after all." The guy looked over his shoulder and stopped in his tracks, eyes narrowing. He then turned to Nate. "You?"

"Hey, relax," Nate said. "I'm not exactly excited to see you, either."

Up close, Nate could see something on the man's cheek

covering a bruise he must have received in his stumble down the stairs.

"Are you wearing makeup?" he asked.

The guy tensed, his forehead turning red as his lips pulled back from clenched teeth. He shot out a hand to grab the front of Nate's shirt, but Nate stepped out of reach.

"Whoa, there. You don't want to draw attention, now, do you?" Nate said.

The man glanced around as if suddenly remembering they weren't alone. When he looked back to Nate, he said, "What are you doing here?"

"You heard what I said when I walked up, right? I mean, you *did* give me the right answer, so clearly you know what I'm doing here."

"You're the replacement?" the second man asked.

"No way," the chaser said. "What did you do? Kill Roberts so you could have his job?"

"That would be no," Nate said. "Mr. Roberts dying came as much as a surprise to me as it did to you."

"If you weren't in on it, then what the hell were you doing there last night?"

"What do you think? I was watching you."

"Bullshit. You're a cleaner. That's not your kind of thing." He paused, eyes narrowing again. "*This* isn't your kind of thing, either."

The man had recognized Nate the night before, so it wasn't particularly surprising that he knew what Nate did. It was unsettling that Nate didn't know the same about them. But he kept his concern off his face as he said, "On that, I have to agree with you." He looked past them toward the platform entrance. "We should get going. We've got a schedule to keep."

"I'm not moving until you tell us what you're doing here."

"Are you an idiot? Or are you acting stupid on purpose? I've been sent to take Mr. Roberts's place. If that's going to be a problem, then I'll do this without you and let our employer know so I can pick up your fees as well as mine."

Nate easily caught the predictable right cross before it got anywhere close to him and used the momentum to twist the man's wrist until his temporary colleague grunted in pain.

When Nate finally let go, he asked, "Are you in or out?"

THE MEN'S NAMES were Leo and Ramon. After phone numbers were reluctantly exchanged—for Nate, an alias number that would forward to his phone for only the next six hours—they boarded a car near the middle of the train and took seats in different rows. Nate chose one close to the rear, where he could keep an eye on the other two. For the life of him, he couldn't understand why Helen had hired these guys. She usually had much higher standards. There must be a logical reason, but whatever it was, he was stuck with them for now.

The trip to Madrid was scheduled to last three hours and ten minutes. And though that was the destination on their tickets, they were only going as far as Zaragoza. There, they would take possession of the package and return to Barcelona. Leo and Ramon would help flush out any adversaries on the train trip and then shadow Nate as he took the package to a private marina, where he would turn it over to a contact on a boat named *Marea Alta*. At that point, Nate would be done and could get back to Liz.

About a half hour into the trip, Nate took a walk through the train to see if there was anyone suspicious enough to set off his internal alarms. To keep a low profile, he plugged his earbuds into his phone and pretended to listen to music as he walked, holding the phone in a way that looked like he was changing songs every now and then.

What he was really doing was video recording the other passengers, using a special setting that kept the image from displaying on his screen. When he returned to his seat, he scrolled through the footage and identified a handful of people who might be trouble. After a second look, he crossed off all but two from his list—a man and a woman, both in the next car up.

At the one-hour-and-forty-minute mark, the train pulled

into the station in Zaragoza. Nate let Leo and Ramon get off first, waiting until it was almost time for the journey to continue before stepping off himself. The first thing he did was scan all the passengers who had detrained and were now moving down the platform. The man he had pegged as a potential problem was not among them, but the woman was there, following a respectable ten meters behind Leo and Ramon.

Nate joined the back of the crowd and kept his eyes on her. It didn't take long before he knew for certain she was interested in the two men, and her status changed from potential problem to threat.

Their return trip to Barcelona was scheduled to leave in fifty minutes. The handover would occur just prior to departure, inside the train. Now was the time to deal with the woman.

Nate sent a message to the two bozos, instructing them to take care of her, and then did a sweep through the station for anyone else who might be an obstacle. The next time he spotted Leo and Ramon, the woman was no longer behind them. Perhaps they weren't useless after all.

Now that the real part of the mission was nearing, Nate's senses went into overdrive. He returned to the platform ten minutes before the train was to leave, and gave each of the waiting passengers an extra look to make sure there would be zero surprises.

Leo and Ramon were already there. While Leo acted like he hadn't seen Nate, Ramon gave him a slight nod. Nate quickly turned away without returning the greeting. He checked the faces behind him to see if any of them had made note of the connection. As far as he could tell, no one had.

Thank God for that. The jackass could have jeopardized the entire mission. This was why Nate didn't like this type of job. When he made bodies disappear, he always worked with a small team of people he knew and trusted.

A couple more hours and it will be all over, he told himself.

Leo and Ramon boarded the train five minutes before

departure. Nate waited to see if they were followed, and then did the same.

A man in a business suit stood in the aisle near Nate's seat, looking at his phone."

"*Disculpe*," Nate said, pointing at his seat. "*Ese es mi asiento.*"

The man looked up. "Oh, I'm sorry," he said, also in Spanish. He made a show of looking around. "I must be in the wrong car."

Handoff code complete.

As the man walked off, Nate dropped into the seat by the aisle. Occupying the spot at the window was the package—a dark-skinned woman, Indian perhaps, or Sri Lankan, somewhere between seventeen and twenty-five. Her loose fitting T-shirt and jeans didn't help narrow the range. Neither did the dark hair pulled into a ponytail, tucked out of the back of a baseball hat. To complete her ensemble, her eyes were obscured behind a pair of bulky black-rimmed glasses.

When Nate had sat down, she'd kept her eyes on the book in her hand. He knew she wasn't reading, though. The slight tremor in her hand told him she was far too nervous to focus on any of the words.

"Must be interesting," he said in English, following yet another one of Larson's scripts.

The girl jumped a little, and gave him a sideways glance before looking back at the book. Almost as if she were reading aloud, she said, "It is one of my favorites."

"It is? What's it called?"

"It is called, um…it is…uh..."

Nate leaned toward her and whispered, "It's all right. I think we've done enough to know who each other is, don't you?"

The girl nodded, relieved. "Yes."

"You can call me Nate," he said, holding out his hand.

She hesitated before taking it. "I'm—"

"Wait. Don't say it. Better for both of us if I don't know." He thought for a moment. "Why don't we call you Sonja? I've always liked that name. Is that all right by you?"

"Sonja? Uh, okay, sure."

"Nice to meet you, Sonja." Dropping his volume even more, he added, "This should go nice and easy, and soon you'll be on to your next leg."

Though she looked tired and scared, she said thank you in a way that made him think she meant it.

Sonja jumped again a few moments later when the train began pulling away from the station.

"Are you really reading that book?" Nate asked.

She shook her head.

"Then maybe you should close it."

"What?" She looked at him and down at the book again. "Right. Of course." She did as he suggested and leaned back in her seat.

Her accent was, for the most part, British, but there was something else there, too. If he had to guess, he'd say she'd lived part of her life in southern Asia, but had spent an extended period of time in England. He couldn't help but wonder what had caused her to need a multi-layered escort to get...wherever she was going. The effort wasn't a cheap one, but Helen Cho had apparently thought it important. So important, in fact, that Mr. Roberts's death couldn't delay it. Like most of the jobs Nate worked on, however, there was little chance he'd ever know the full story.

Once outside Zaragoza, the train picked up speed, zipping across the Spanish countryside in true bullet fashion. Nate busied himself keeping an eye on the other passengers, paying particularly close attention to anyone who entered their car.

Not long after they reached cruising speed, he texted his backups to do a walk around. Leo headed toward the front of the train, while Ramon turned and walked in Nate's direction toward the back.

Before the man reached Nate's seat, Nate said to the girl, "Head down and look at the wall."

"What?" she asked.

"Please, just do it."

She did as he asked. It wasn't that Nate didn't trust his

two colleagues—he was neutral on that subject—but he thought it best not to take any unnecessary chances. They could do their job just fine using Nate as their focal point. If things somehow went awry and the men were questioned about the girl's identity, they wouldn't be able to say much.

Ramon, unsurprisingly, looked over at the girl as he walked past, and then looked annoyed when he couldn't see her face.

Nate revised his previous neutrality. He didn't trust them.

The remainder of the trip was uneventful. Nate tried a few times to engage Sonja in conversation, but she seemed to prefer staring silently out the window.

As they pulled into Barcelona Sants, Nate said, "When we get off, I want you to put your arm through mine and stay tight to my side. Are you all right with that?"

She nodded.

"Do you have any sunglasses? Or do you need to wear those?" he asked, pointing at her glasses.

"I have sunglasses."

"Put them on."

She exchanged what she'd been wearing for a pair of Jackie-O sunglasses from her bag.

"Perfect," Nate said. Between the shades and the bill of her cap, her face was suitably cloaked.

When the train slowed to a crawl as the platform appeared out the window, passengers began filling the aisle.

Nate could feel the girl tense. "Just a moment," he whispered. "We'll let most everyone else get going first."

He waited until Leo and Ramon stood up before he finally stepped into the aisle. A few of the passengers behind him scowled while Nate waited for Sonja to ease out of their row. He mumbled his apologies as he maneuvered Sonja behind him and then guided the girl toward the exit.

Ahead, Leo stepped from the train, looked around, and made momentary eye contact with Nate, letting him know everything looked fine. At least there was no nod this time.

Upon reaching the platform, Nate was about to remind

Sonja to take his arm when she did just that. Being six foot tall, Nate could see over most of the crowd as it shuffled toward the exit. So far, he noticed nothing of concern.

"As soon as we get off the platform, we'll pick up the pace, get outside, and grab a taxi," he said.

"A taxi? You don't have a car?"

"Any taxi driver will know the city a lot better than I do. Besides, we don't have far to go."

Through the platform exit ahead, he could see people in the main part of the station going in all directions, some in a hurry, some not.

"We go left," he said before they passed through the doorway.

When they entered the large central terminal, Nate scanned the crowd. Ahead and to the right, he caught sight of a woman looking back toward them. And it wasn't just any woman. It was the same one he'd tasked his two companions to take care of in Zaragoza. Either they'd done a half-assed job, or they'd done nothing at all.

Nate had a feeling it was the latter.

"Change of plans," he whispered.

He made a U-turn, pulling Sonja with him and causing the people behind them to abruptly change course to avoid running into them. Ramon was five people back. He gave Nate a what-gives look that changed into an oh-shit-he-knows expression when Nate responded with a glare.

So they hadn't just done nothing. They were working with the woman.

Ramon made a clumsy attempt to push through the crowd and grab Sonja, but Nate snagged the collar of the guy's shirt and yanked hard.

As Ramon smashed to the floor, Nate grabbed Sonja's hand and took off through the mass of humanity, weaving as gaps appeared. Nearing the far end of the terminal, Nate chanced a look back. Ramon was hurrying after them with Leo at his side. Nate didn't see the woman, but he did notice at least three other men heading purposely in his and Sonja's direction.

"This way," he said, pulling the girl toward a lightly populated hallway between several stores. At the other end were glass doors to the outside.

People in the corridor veered out of the way when they saw Nate and Sonja running toward them. Some were probably wondering if they should be running, too.

Nate shoved one of the glass doors open with his shoulder while looking behind him. Leo and Ramon had entered the far end of the hallway with the other men.

After bursting outside, Nate spotted a bus pulling away. Earlier there had been taxis parked at the curb, but none were around now. He looked right, saw nothing, glanced left.

Bingo.

Several taxis were parked along the street that ran down the south side of the station. Still holding tight to Sonja, he made a beeline toward them.

Halfway there, parked in front of the station, was a police van, and standing beside it a cop in a helmet and bulletproof vest. The guy looked more bored than ready for a riot, however. In normal circumstances, Nate would have thought the cop's presence unfortunate, but today the man was a godsend.

"Help!" Nate yelled in Spanish as they neared the officer. "There are some men chasing us."

"What men?" the cop asked. "What are you talking about?"

Nate pointed back the other way just as Leo, Ramon, and their companions ran out the exit. "They took a swing at my friend. I don't know what they want."

"Stay right here." The cop headed off to intercept their pursuers, saying something into his radio.

The moment his back was to them, Nate whispered, "Come on," and he and Sonja started running toward the taxis again.

When they reached the curb, they jumped into the first vehicle in line.

"*Plaça de les Drassanes*," Nate told the driver. That would put them close to where he was supposed to drop off the girl.

The driver looked at them suspiciously from his rearview mirror.

Nate glanced out the window and saw that the cop had stopped Leo and Ramon, but the others were still running toward the taxis.

"*Rápido, por favor*," Nate said.

"*Yo no quiero problemas*," the cabbie said. He didn't want any problems.

"*No hay ningún problema. Solamente tenemos prisa. Por favor, nos podemos ir?*"

The man looked at them for a moment longer before turning on the meter and pulling into the street.

"Are you all right?" Nate whispered to Sonja.

"Who were they?" she asked.

"I'm guessing you know the answer to that better than I do."

Her eyes moved from his face to the floor, embarrassed as she realized he was probably right.

"Don't worry," he said. "You'll be on the boat soon."

"Boat?"

"That's where I'm supposed to take you. You didn't know that?"

"All I've been told is to follow whoever I'm with."

Nate came very close to asking her what was going on, but he checked his curiosity and said, "For what it's worth, next up is a boat."

Several minutes later, the taxi slowed as it approached a traffic jam, and within a few more seconds, they were stopped.

"*¿No hay manera de salirse de aquí?*" Nate asked the driver, hoping they could somehow go around the blockage.

But the driver said, "No."

Nate looked out the rear window. Traffic was building behind them, too. He was about to look away when the doors of a car about six vehicles back opened and two men got out.

"We're leaving now!" He threw twenty euros over the seat and opened his door.

"*¿Hey, a donde creen que van?*" the driver asked.

Nate scooted out and helped Sonja from the car, ignoring the cabbie.

Once more they ran.

From behind them came a shout of "Stop!" and then, off a building to the side, the metal ping of a bullet.

The traffic problem turned out to be larger than just a backup on *Carrer de Vilamarí*. The cross street was equally packed, and it looked like no cars would be getting through the intersection anytime soon. On foot, though, Nate and Sonja were able to wind their way around the stationary vehicles to the other side, where the road opened up again.

They ran all the way to the next intersection and turned right onto *Carrer de Sepúlveda*. Their lead on the others was up to about thirty seconds, maybe more if they were lucky, but they wouldn't be able to keep up this pace.

He scanned both sides of the road for a place they could dash inside before their pursuers came around the corner. He spotted several doors but most looked like they'd be locked, so he didn't waste any time checking.

Just then a taxi pulled to the curb a little ways ahead. As the passenger climbed out, Nate veered onto the street and reached the driver's window before the cabbie could pull away.

"*Necesitamos que nos lleve,*" he said and motioned Sonja to the back door.

She started to open it, but the driver, having taken a look at the state Nate and the girl were in, shook his head and started to press on the gas.

Nate jumped on the hood and glowered through the windshield, causing the driver to hit the brakes.

"Get in!" Nate yelled at Sonja.

Back at the corner, the others came racing around.

"*¡Coño! ¡Bájese de ahi!*" the driver yelled, waving for him to get off.

Nate waited until Sonja was inside, and then headed to the still open back door.

"No! No! No!" the driver said as he started to drive off

again.

Nate snatched the handle of the driver's door and yanked it open. The others were coming up fast and there was no time to argue with the man. He grabbed the driver's shirt, pulled him out of the car, and took his place behind the wheel.

The others came within a car's length of the back of the taxi before Nate slammed down the accelerator and sped away.

He turned down random streets, and when finally satisfied no one was following them, he headed toward the marina.

For the first time, he glanced at Sonja in the mirror. "You okay?"

"I-I think so. Are they gone?"

"For now."

"Do you think they'll find us again?"

A lie would make her feel better, but it wouldn't help them in the long run. "I don't know."

As far as he was aware, he was the only one who knew where the next handoff would occur, but given the betrayal of the men who were supposed to help him, it was better to not take any chances.

According to Helen's office, the *Marea Alta* was supposed to be moored at the dock closest to the sea channel. Unfortunately, a wide brick pedestrian zone separated the nearest road from the piers. Nate drove by twice. While he could see boats at the specified dock, he couldn't tell which one was the *Marea Alta*. Since there was no way to get any closer by car, he reluctantly parked the taxi on a neighboring street, shoved a hundred euros in the glove compartment, and he and Sonja made their way back on foot.

Upon reaching the main road, they dodged between slow-moving cars to get over to the pedestrian walkway. A lot of people were around, but they were spread over a wide area so it didn't seem crowded. All had the look of either tourist or local out for a stroll.

Nate headed for the fence that separated the walkway from a short slope that led down to the marina. He wanted to get eyes on the boat first to check for any trouble. He instructed Sonja to wait on a nearby bench while he raised his phone as if taking a scenic picture. Using his zoom function, he checked the names on the boats.

The *Marea Alta* was at the very end of the last dock. It probably wouldn't qualify for billionaire yacht status but it was pretty damn close. Definitely a lot more ship than Nate was expecting.

Three people were visible on deck, crew members, it looked like, getting ready for a voyage. The contact was probably wondering where Nate and Sonja were, since they were nearly a half hour overdue.

Nate swung the camera along the dock and confirmed that everything looked okay before lowering the phone and returning to Sonja.

"Is this the right place?" she asked.

He nodded. "We're almost done."

"You are, not me."

"You're right. Sorry." He smiled sympathetically. "The good thing is, it'll be really hard for anyone to grab you once you're on the ship."

He helped her up and led her toward the marina entrance at the west end of the walkway.

They had gone less than fifty feet when the air suddenly rippled with the concussion of a massive explosion, knocking them and all those around them to the ground.

Nate pushed back up as fast as he could.

Boats all along the waterfront were on fire. Except for the *Marea Alta* and the handful of boats that had been moored near it.

Because there was nothing left of any of them to burn.

CHAPTER
TEN

KOH SAMUI

A WARM BREEZE blew in through the open patio doors, carrying with it the sound of waves and the lingering smell of the rain that had fallen after sunset.

Quinn handed Daeng another Singha beer and took a seat on the couch.

"You were right," he said.

Daeng smiled. "Of course I was. But what specifically are we talking about?"

Quinn tipped the end of the bottle toward the window. "The view, this place. It's perfect."

"I couldn't let you go to some second-rate Bali resort when I had this at my disposal."

"It wasn't exactly second rate."

"Compared to this?"

Quinn looked around. "All right. You might have a point."

"*Chok dee, khrup,*" Daeng said, holding his bottle out.

Quinn tapped his against his friend's and repeated the toast.

As he took a drink, Quinn heard Orlando's footsteps in the hallway. He set down his beer, went into the kitchen to fetch the glass of pinot noir he'd poured for her, and met her with it when she entered the living room.

"Thanks," she said, taking it from him.

"Claire asleep?" Daeng asked as Quinn and Orlando joined him on the couch.

Orlando nodded. "Garrett, too. Knocked out with the lights on, still holding his comic book."

That wasn't surprising. Garrett had been going pretty much all day, alternating between the pool and the cove. That, combined with the lingering effects of jet lag, would likely keep him asleep for a good long time.

Orlando nestled against Quinn and shut her eyes. "Can we sleep right here tonight?"

"If that's what you want," Quinn said.

"Maybe." She took another sip.

"You two do realize it's only eight thirty, right?" Daeng said. "I could get someone to watch the kids and we could go out dancing. Maybe find a karaoke place. Play some pool."

The expressions on Quinn's and Orlando's faces remained unchanged.

"It was just a suggestion," Daeng said.

They watched the night for several minutes in comfortable silence. Finally, Daeng stood up and carried his half-finished bottle into the kitchen.

When he came back, he said, "You guys are making me feel old. Maybe I'll go for a jog while I still have some of my youth left."

He headed to the open back door.

"Daeng," Orlando said.

He stopped and turned back.

"Thank you," she said.

He smiled. "I'll see you in the morning."

Once they were alone, Quinn clinked his Singha against Orlando's glass. They took a drink and settled back against each other.

"I've been thinking," he said.

"Who said you could do that?"

"I've been thinking maybe we shouldn't have you go out in the field anymore."

She pulled away a few inches and looked at him. "Oh, really. How very 1950s of you to make that decision for me."

"I didn't say it was a decision. This is a discussion."

She smirked but said nothing.

"I mean, now that we have Claire," he said, "it would be better if—"

"You do realize I've been constantly working since Garrett was born."

"Yeah, I know." He paused, trying to get his words right. "It's just that Claire has made me see things in a way I hadn't before. I don't think we should both be putting our lives in jeopardy all the time."

"Fine. Then why don't *you* stop going into the field?"

"I'm open to discussing that option."

She sighed and leaned against him again. "Can we not talk about this right now? We've only been here a day and a half. I just want to…*be* for a while."

"Sure. Later's fine."

She laid her head on his shoulder. "When we get home."

PRAVAT STOOD BESIDE the car, looking at the night sky beyond Samui International Airport. The last Bangkok Airways flight landed seven minutes before ten p.m. After the final passengers had left the premises, the airport should have closed for the night. But arrangements had been made and the tower had remained open.

Pravat fidgeted with the keys in his pocket. He'd been called two hours earlier and told about the new plans. He knew he should be excited, but all he could think about now was that everything was resting on the surveillance work he and Narong had done.

A dot of light appeared in the distance. He watched it grow brighter and brighter as it neared the island on an intercept course for the airport's single runway. Three minutes later, the private jet was down, taxiing toward the plane holding area where Pravat waited with the sedan.

It pulled to a stop fifty feet away and the door opened. First out were six hard-looking men in dark clothing. Four of them fanned out around the plane while the other two headed straight to the sedan.

"You're Pravat?" asked the first one to arrive.

"Yes."

The second one looked at something on his phone and then said, "It's him."

"We were told there were two of you," the first one said.

"My colleague is keeping watch on the house."

A grunt. Pravat couldn't tell if it was approval or disdain.

Saying nothing more, the men searched the car inside and out. When they were done, the first one jogged back to the plane and went inside.

When he climbed out again, two new men exited the craft after him.

Though Pravat had never met either of the men before, he immediately knew who they were. Mee Noi, the number one lieutenant and Pravat's boss's boss's boss; and Chayan, the man himself, head of their organization. Pravat had been recruited while the two men were in a Cambodian prison, and had only seen pictures of them. But now here they were, coming across the tarmac toward him.

Pravat opened the back door and bowed in a deep *wai.* "*Khun* Chayan, *khun* Mee Noi, welcome to Koh Samui. I am Pravat."

Both men returned the *wai* with a slight tilt of their heads.

Mee Noi looked around. "Where is the vehicle for our men?"

"I have a van just on the other side of the fence." Pravat gestured toward the parking area. He had arranged for its delivery to the airport as soon as he'd been told the plans.

"It should be here," Mee Noi said.

"My apologies." It had been difficult enough for Pravat to convince the airport supervisor to allow the sedan into the restricted area. No way the guy was going to let him bring the van, too. But Pravat was smart enough not to say that.

While Chayan and Mee Noi climbed into the car, Pravat gave the van's key to the man who'd talked to him earlier, and pointed to where the vehicle was parked. After the man barked orders at his colleagues, three of them reentered the plane. They exited a few moments later with full-looking duffel bags and jogged toward the walkway that would take them into the parking lot.

Pravat drove the two big bosses out of the holding area and over to the van, where they waited until the other men were loaded into the vehicle. When everyone was ready, they headed out, the sedan in the lead.

"Pictures," Chayan said.

"Yes, sir. Here." Pravat picked up an envelope off the front passenger seat and passed it back. Inside were printouts of the better surveillance photos he'd taken.

"This house," Chayan said. "Is it the only one in the area?"

"Unfortunately, no," Pravat replied. "It is private, but there are a total of seven other houses around the cove."

"Does the monk own the house?" Mee Noi asked.

"Unclear. The name on the paperwork is not his, but it could be a cover," Pravat said, giving them information generated by Virote's staff in Bangkok. "After the photos, you'll find a list of all the other owners in the area and a satellite image of the cove."

The men studied the documents.

"He seems very close with his guests," Chayan said.

"Yes."

"Who are they?"

"Again, unclear, sir."

"Unclear? There's been plenty of time to run them down."

Pravat knew he had to be very careful with how he worded his response. "My colleague's and my particular assignment has been to watch the monk, see where he goes, and who he meets. I passed everything on to *khun* Virote so he could look into the details." He could see Mee Noi's expression sour, but before the man could chastise him, Pravat added, "When I checked with him earlier this evening, he said he believes the names they used to fly from Bangkok to Samui are false. They are going as the Millers, Harold and Elizabeth. The children are Garrett and Claire."

"Why does he think this?" Mee Noi asked.

"There's no record of the Millers entering Thailand, but Virote says security footage shows them exiting Immigration at Suvarnabhumi two hours before boarding the flight here. He's checking with his airport contact to see if he can find out what names they used to get into the country."

"Waiting for more information will be a waste of time." Chayan tapped the stack of photos. "It's clear they are close to the monk. That's all the information we need. If they are so important, they can be the down payment on his transgressions."

QUINN WOKE AND looked around, confused.

It took a moment before he realized he was still sitting on the couch. Orlando had slumped onto his lap and was breathing deep and even.

At first he thought it had been his awkward position that roused him, but then he noted a distant noise drifting in through the open back doors. A jet engine, fading now.

He checked the time and saw it was past ten thirty. Daeng had told them the last flights usually finished up around ten. Apparently someone was running a little late.

"Hey," he said, gently shaking Orlando.

She groaned, and parted her eyes only enough to peek at him.

"Let's go to bed," he said.

"Aren't we in bed already? I'm so comfortable."

"And I'm happy for you, but if I stay like this, you're going to end up having to give me back rubs all day tomorrow."

She stretched her neck. "Fine."

"Fine you'll give me back rubs?"

"Fine we can go to bed, jackass."

Once she was off his lap, he carried her half-empty glass and his beer bottle into the kitchen. He closed the back doors and checked that the front was locked.

"Ready?" he said.

She pushed herself to her feet, looking almost as if she'd

already fallen back asleep. "You're not going to carry me?"

"As you wish," he said.

He bowed his head and lifted her off her feet.

Immediately she curled up against his chest. "This is better."

"For you."

"Exactly."

"RED TEAM," MEE Noi said into the radio.

"Red Team in position."

"Yellow Team."

"Yellow Team in position."

"Blue Team."

"Blue Team in position."

Mee Noi looked at Chayan. "We're set."

"Then what are we waiting for?" Chayan asked.

Mee Noi raised the radio back to his mouth. "Begin."

CHAPTER
ELEVEN

BARCELONA

NATE PULLED SONJA to her feet, grabbed her hand, and ran north into the city. Having no idea if the threat extended beyond the explosion, he never stayed on one street longer than a block.

Distant sirens could be heard coming from almost every direction.

There were people on the streets everywhere, looking toward the column of smoke rising above the marina. Though most seemed content to stand and watch, a few were hurrying away from the spectacle. In this age of terrorism, Nate knew it wouldn't be long before more joined them.

But this was not an act of terror. At least not in the current definition. Nate was sure the bomb had been put on the *Marea Alta* with a timer set to go off after Sonja was scheduled to be delivered. No, this was an act of targeted murder, plain and simple, and if not for the traffic jam, the girl would be dead.

As Nate turned down another street, Sonja stumbled and would have fallen to the ground if he hadn't been holding on to her.

"Are you all right?" he asked.

She took a step and winced.

"What is it?"

"My ankle."

"Bad?"

She tried another step, less grimacing this time. "I think it will be all right, but can we rest for a moment?"

Nate spotted a small park ahead and nodded toward it. "Over there."

With an arm around her waist, he helped her to a bench in the middle of the park. The place was deserted, the explosion likely having cleared everyone out. Sonja leaned forward and rubbed her ankle.

"If you stay off it too long, it'll stiffen up," Nate said. "Plus, we should keep moving."

"Just give me a minute. Please."

He nodded and looked back in the direction from which they'd come.

The pillar of smoke was thick and high, telling him the fire was still raging through the marina. He couldn't for the life of him guess why the girl would elicit such a response. How many lives had been taken in the attempt to kill her?

He felt his phone vibrate and yanked it out. The name on the screen was HELEN CHO.

"I'll be right back," he told Sonja.

She looked up, scared. "Where are you going?"

"I need to take this call." He pushed ACCEPT as he walked away. "Helen?"

"I just received a report on a bomb in the marina. Are you all right?"

"I'm alive."

"The girl. She's dead, isn't she?"

Nate tensed. "Why? Was that your plan?"

"What? What do you mean?"

"For me to lead her to the bomb."

"Are you kidding? I was trying to keep her alive, not kill her."

"And yet someone blew up half a marina to make sure she was dead. If that wasn't part of your plan, how did whoever planted it know I was taking her there?"

"I don't know," she said.

"Are you sure? What about those two jackasses you had

me work with? They tried to take her from me when we got back to Barcelona."

Helen cursed under her breath.

"Are you mad they didn't succeed, or—"

"I didn't hire them!" she shot back. She took a breath before continuing in a slightly less agitated voice. "I've had to work with a few other agencies on this. Those weren't my men."

"So you didn't know their plans?"

"Of course I didn't. The job was to get the girl to the boat and then the next team would take over. That's it. No bombs. No kidnapping. Nothing else."

He wasn't sure but had a feeling she was telling the truth. He waited a beat, then said, "She's not dead."

There were several seconds of silence before Helen said, "Where is she?"

"With me."

"Oh, thank God! What happened?"

"You mean why didn't I get her to the boat in time to die?"

"You know what I mean."

Nate described what had happened since he'd taken charge of the girl.

"You need to get her someplace safe," Helen said when he was through.

He scoffed. "And where might that be?"

"I don't know, and I don't want to know. Hide her somewhere. I'll get back to you as soon as I can with instructions."

"Forget that! You need to send someone to take her from me right now. You promised I'd be through by now."

No response.

"Helen?" He pulled the phone away from his ear and saw the call had been disconnected. "Son of a bitch."

He almost rang her back but knew it would be a waste time. There was no other operative around but him. If there had been, Helen wouldn't have needed him that morning. He took a moment to compose himself before returning to the girl.

"Can you walk?" he asked.

"Yeah. I think I'm okay."

"Then let's go."

He grabbed her arm to help her up but she remained seated.

"We can't stay here," he told her. "We're too exposed." When she still didn't move, he leaned down. "Sonja, we need to keep going."

In a ragged voice, she whispered, "My name's not Sonja."

She was staring at the ground, stunned.

He crouched beside her. "It's going to be all right. We just—"

"Don't say that. Don't say it's going to be all right." She glanced briefly at the smoke. "There's no way to know that."

"Sure there is. You're with me. I've been in a lot of tight places, but look, I'm still here."

She stared at him.

"And let's be honest," he continued. "I'm doing a pretty good job so far today. You're still here, too."

Her shoulders sagged. With a defeated nod, she stood up. "Which way?"

LIZ SPENT THE morning at the Barcelona Museum of Contemporary Art, hoping it would distract her. By noon, though, she was in a cab on the way back to the hotel, worried about Nate and wanting to be in the room when he returned.

It was easier when she was at school and he was out in the world on assignment. She didn't know when he might be in a dangerous situation, so she didn't worry as much. Being this close to it was much different. How would she ever handle it if they ever moved in together? But moments after she thought it, she pushed the question from her mind. That was something to be resolved in the future.

In the room, she tried to watch a movie on TV, but it wasn't long before she was flipping through the channels. She was just starting a second trip through the available choices when a loud boom rattled the hotel's window.

She hurried to the French doors and threw them open. As soon as she stepped onto the balcony, she spotted a column of smoke to her right, northeast of the hotel. It was thick and black and coming from somewhere along the shoreline.

There was no way to stop herself from thinking it had something to do with Nate. Not that he'd set off a bomb—she could never believe that—but that he might have been caught in it.

A million different images of his burning corpse began spinning through her mind.

"No, no, no, no, no," she said under her breath as she walked to the edge of the balcony.

She lost all concept of time, her only reality the smoke rising into the Barcelona sky. She didn't even hear her phone when it started to ring. By the time it finally registered and she'd rushed back inside, the call had disconnected. She exhaled in joy when she saw the name on the screen:

NATE

She hit REDIAL.

"Come on, come on, come on."

Just when she thought her call would go to voice mail, the line clicked. "Liz?"

"Nate, my God. Are you all right? Tell me that wasn't you."

A pause. "You mean the explosion?"

"Of course I mean the explosion! I've been going out of my mind here since it went off."

"We were close, but...I'm fine."

"Are you sure? You're not hiding something from me, are you?"

"No, I'm not hurt."

She let out a breath. "Where are you? When are you coming back?"

"That's why I called. We need your help."

"We?" she said, suddenly realizing this wasn't the first

time he'd used the word.

"I'll explain when I see you. But you need to get out of the hotel fast. Pack as many changes of clothes as you can fit into your backpack. There are also a few things I need you to get out of my suitcase." He told her what he was talking about. "Leave everything else and call me as soon as you're away from the hotel."

"What's going on?" she asked.

"Later. I promise. Just hurry. And Liz, be careful."

She'd been around Nate and her brother enough to know when it was better to act than talk. "I'll call you in a few minutes."

She dumped everything out of her backpack and shoved in five changes of clothes, her passport, Nate's computer, and the other things he had asked for. Before opening the door to leave, she checked the peephole. The hallway was clear. She exited and hurried down to the elevators.

As she reached out to press the call button, she stopped herself. She could hear Nate's voice in her head. "Be careful." She didn't know if he meant there might be another bomb or there were people looking for them. Whatever the case, the elevator was a contained box from which there might be no escape.

She hadn't even thought about where the hotel's emergency staircase was located, so it took her a few moments to find it tucked around a corner farther down the hall. She went down, taking the steps two at a time until she reached the ground floor. When she pulled the door open, she was relieved to see it didn't let out straight into the lobby but into a quiet hallway. A hallway, she realized after she entered it, that she'd been down before.

To the right was reception and the main hotel entrance, and to the left Barcelona 2020, the hotel's nightclub. She went left.

A Gaudiesque archway led into the club. This being daytime, the entrance was blocked by a set of portable wooden screens. Liz was easily able to slip around them and hurry through the deserted dance club to a metal door along the back wall marked SALIDA—exit.

The narrow alley the door opened onto smelled of trash and piss and rotted food. Holding her breath, she ran to the closest end and headed into the city. When she thought she'd put enough space between herself and the hotel, she found a quiet spot and called Nate.

Two rings. Three, four, five. Voice mail.

Frowning, she tried again, but had the same result.

Where is he?

She called again.

And again.

And again.

AS NATE AND the girl walked away from the park, he finally had some time to think about something other than escape. That's when he began to wonder how much the girl's pursuers knew about him.

Leo knew Nate was a cleaner. Was that info right now being used to learn more about him? Perhaps even where he'd been staying? That's when he knew he needed to reach Liz. His first thought was to tell her to go back to Paris as fast as possible, but he needed things only she could bring him. He had no choice but to pull her into his plan.

He and Sonja paused while he called, but were soon on the move again.

Emergency sirens continued to wail through the city. It seemed at every turn they were confronted by police cars racing down the streets toward the sea.

Nate had no reason to think the pulsating lights reflecting off the buildings they were approaching would be any different—until he turned onto the road.

He cursed under his breath.

A roadblock had been set up in the middle of the street, right before the next intersection. A queue had already formed of people wanting to get through. Apparently, law enforcement was trying to set up a perimeter in hopes of snaring those responsible for the bomb.

Nate could have told them it was a wasted effort.

Whoever had placed the device on the *Marea Alta* was a pro and had likely left the city hours ago.

"Do you have a passport or some other ID on you?" he asked the girl. "Not in your real name."

"I do," she said hesitantly. "But I was told to only use it in an emergency."

"I'm pretty sure this qualifies. What's the name on it?"

"Um…" She dug a British passport out of her purse and opened it. "Reeva Mahal." She showed him the information page.

"Okay." He tapped his pocket to make sure the fake passport he'd brought for the job was still there. "My ID says Mark Plunkett."

She raised an eyebrow. "Not *your* real name?"

"No. I told you mine already."

She looked at him, surprised. But before she could say anything, he put a hand on her back and gently pushed her toward the roadblock.

She looked nervous. "I don't know if I can do this."

"Everyone's a little freaked out right now, so it's okay if you're not calm. Calm would be suspicious."

They joined the back of the queue. As Nate suspected, IDs were being checked and faces scrutinized. Once the police were satisfied, they'd wave each person through and gesture for the next to approach.

A woman about ten places in front of Nate reached the front, but when asked for her ID, she said in Spanish, "It's at home." She gestured toward a building beyond the barricade. "I'll bring it right back. I promise."

"*Señora*, I can't let you through without identification," the officer said.

"My building's right there. I can be back in a few minutes. Please."

"If you don't have it, please wait over there," the officer said, indicating some kind of makeshift detention area.

"Let me through! I want to go home!"

The cop didn't even tell her to move away a second time. Instead, he nodded to a couple of his colleagues, who moved in and grabbed the woman.

"What are you doing?" she screamed. "Let go of me! Let go!"

They hauled her to the side and slapped cuffs on her as the officer at the opening waved the next person forward.

Sonja slipped her arm through Nate's and squeezed tight. He gave her a couple of reassuring pats with his other hand, but the look on her face remained tense.

They were only one person away when Nate's phone vibrated in his pocket. He knew it was Liz but couldn't answer with the cop a few feet away, so he let her go to voice mail. Almost immediately his phone vibrated again.

"*El que sigue,*" the cop said, signaling for Nate to come forward.

"Come with me," Nate whispered to the girl.

They walked toward the cop arm in arm. The man took a step toward them, wagging his palm back and forth in the air. "*No, no, no. Uno a la vez.*" One at a time.

"I'm sorry," Nate said in English. "I don't understand. You want our passports? Is that it?"

"*Uno a la vez!*"

Nate kept moving, pulling the girl with him, and then said in his best ugly American tourist impression, "Can you tell us how long this is going to take? We're supposed to meet—"

"*No, no. Solamente usted. No los dos.*"

Good, Nate thought. The guy didn't speak English.

"I think he wants our passports." With his free hand, Nate retrieved his fake one and held it out to the cop. "Sweetie," he said to the girl, "he needs to see yours, too."

"No problem," she said, and pulled hers from her bag.

The cop, exasperated, gave up trying to separate them and took both their passports. As he looked at the documents, Nate casually scanned the other officers. Most were standing along the line of cars that blocked the road. There were three, however, at another car parked behind the temporary barrier. One of them was reading something off a piece of paper to the other two. When he finished, all three turned and looked directly at Nate and the girl.

Not moving his lips, Nate whispered, "I think we've been spotted."

The girl looked nervously around. "Who?"

The three cops started walking toward the roadblock.

"Them?" she asked.

"Get ready to run."

He took her hand.

The cop who had their IDs was about to hand them back when one of the three approaching officers called out to him. Nate really hated the idea of leaving the passports behind. Though all the information was false, the pictures were accurate.

The cop told them to stay where they were, and then seemed to remember they didn't speak Spanish, so he held out a palm to convey the message before heading over to meet his friends. As he joined them, one of the men held out a hand for the passports. That was all the confirmation Nate needed of their cover being blown.

"Follow my lead," he whispered.

She nodded.

He started backing away from the checkpoint, Sonja matching his steps. When they reached the head of the line, Nate turned as if he were simply taking a look around. The crowd had grown, and the line, while single file at the front, had quickly bulged into an amorphous beast that almost reached the curbs on either side.

Still holding tight to Sonja's hand, he started walking down the line.

"*Con permiso*," Nate said as he slipped into the crowd.

At almost the same moment, one of the police officers must have noticed they were gone. Shouts rang out from the barricade. The crowd, unsure what was going on, surged forward, helping to hide Nate and Sonja.

The shouts continued and the already frightened onlookers became even more agitated.

As the crowd thinned out a bit, Nate said "This way," and guided her over to a narrow driveway.

It let out into a large central courtyard between the buildings that lined four separate streets. The courtyard was divided up between a parking area and several smaller structures that might have been for storage.

Sticking as best he could to the shadows, he escorted Sonja to an open back door of the building catty-cornered from the narrow alley they had used. It was basically a straight shot through the place to the front door.

From there, Nate surveyed the new street. All appeared calm so he led Sonja across the road and into the courtyard of yet another set of buildings. Trying doors, he found one that was unlocked, but instead of being a passage to the front lobby, it opened onto a stairwell. He thought for a moment, and then decided to go all the way up to the roof.

When they reached the final landing, they discovered the roof door was propped open. There were people already outside. They stood in clusters of threes and fours, all looking southeast toward the smoke. A few of the gawkers glanced back at the new arrivals, but they didn't seem concerned. It was only natural, after all, that people would want to get a good view of a catastrophe.

Nate claimed a spot along the north wall well away from the others. The smoke was no longer a thick black column but a gray billowing cloud that had already lost much of its density. He checked the north and west, and saw flashing lights playing off the sides of buildings on roads where more of the police barricade had been erected.

The cops seemed to be constructing an arc that started at the beach in the south and circled around the city back to the water north of the marina.

The whole thing was a massive manpower effort that had probably necessitated calling in all off-duty officers and perhaps even the army. Given it had barely been an hour since the bomb went off, Nate doubted there were enough personnel available yet to get all the desired roadblocks up.

He surveyed those he could see, and noted a wide area to the southeast that showed no signs of emergency lights. That would be their way out, but they'd have to hurry.

"Time to go," he whispered.

"Can't we stay until you hear back from your contacts? The police aren't going to find us here."

"That's not true. At some point, they're going to start checking roofs. When that happens, there will be no place for us to go."

She waved a hand out at the city. "There are hundreds of buildings, maybe thousands. They can't search through them all."

"All it would take is for one person to have seen which way we went to help the police narrow their search." He nodded at the others gathered on the roof. "And what if one of them goes down in a little while and IDs us to the cops?"

She was lost in thought for a moment, as though trying to come up with another reason to stay.

"I don't think for one second that you want to give up, but that's what you'd be doing if we stayed here. I mean, if *you* stay here. You can make that choice, but I have zero desire to spend any time in a Spanish jail, so I'm leaving." He paused. "We can relax a little once we get on the other side of the barricade."

She took a breath, and gave him a halfhearted okay.

When they reached the ground floor, they paused in the lobby so he could call Liz back.

"Where were you?" she asked, panicked. "I kept calling but you didn't answer."

"Because I couldn't."

"Are you all right?"

"I'm fine. Did you get out?"

"Yeah."

"No one saw you?"

"I don't think so."

"You don't think so or they didn't?"

"They didn't."

He took a breath. "Okay. Sorry I didn't answer before. The cops have set up roadblocks, and I think someone gave them descriptions of me and...the package. Now the police have our pictures, too."

"They have your pictures? How?"

"I'll tell you later. Where are you?"

"In a park a mile or so east of the hotel."

"What's it called?"

"Hold on." The line went silent for a moment. "*Parc del Centre del Poblenou.*"

Nate checked its location on the map. It was outside the police perimeter.

"Okay, stay there. We'll get to you as soon as we can."

"Please hurry."

"That's the plan." Nate hung up.

"Who was that?" the girl asked.

Though he heard the question, his attention had been drawn to a line of mopeds parked outside the building.

"Stay here until I signal you," he said, then slipped outside.

Near the middle of the pack, he picked out a Vespa that had half a tank of gas. He quickly disabled the steering lock and hotwired the motor.

He waved for Sonja to join him. "Hop on."

The first three streets they checked had roadblocks already in place. The fourth, however, was still clear. Nate gunned the Vespa down the street and whizzed through the intersection into the free part of the city.

INSTEAD OF BENCHES, *Parc del Centre del Poblenou* had chairs grouped in threes, separated by armrests. Liz sat on a seat with a direct view of the entrance she guessed Nate would use.

Twenty minutes had passed since their phone call and she was getting nervous again. What if the police had caught him? How would she even know?

If worse came to worst, she'd have to call her brother. He would know what to do.

She heard footsteps on the walkway behind her and looked over her shoulder, expecting to see a local out for a walk, but it was Nate and a young woman.

Liz jumped up and ran to him. They wrapped their arms

around each other and kissed long and deep.

When they finally separated, Liz said, "What's going on?"

"I wish I knew," he said.

"Who's the girl?"

"The package I was supposed to deliver." He turned to the other woman. "This is…" He looked perplexed. "What do you want us to call you?"

"Dima," the girl said. "It's my real name."

"All right, Dima. This is Liz. My girlfriend."

She looked at Liz. "Your boyfriend is quite brave."

"He's also an idiot sometimes," Liz said.

"My grandmother used to say all men are."

"I think I like her."

"She was easy to like."

Liz looked back at Nate. "What was that explosion all about?"

"It was the drop-off point," he said.

"The drop-off? You mean you were supposed to be there?"

"Dima was, but thankfully we were running late. Were you able to bring everything?"

Liz led them back to the bench and showed Nate the bag.

"You and Dima are about the same size," he said. "I was hoping you wouldn't mind letting her use some of your clothes."

Liz raised an eyebrow. "So that's why you wanted me to meet you?"

He pulled her back into his arms. "Yes, that was the only reason."

She pushed away from him and pulled some clothes from her bag.

In a quiet section of the park, up against the hedges, Nate and Liz stood shoulder to shoulder to shield Dima while she changed.

"Better," Nate said when she was done. "But keep your hat and glasses on."

For his part, he'd donned the hoodie Liz had brought

him. Liz thought it wouldn't be enough to deter the curious, but the casual observer would likely look right past him.

"So what now?" she asked.

Nate looked around. "Helen should be calling soon with new instructions. Until then, I think we should find someplace less exposed."

Donning the backpack, Liz said, "Let's go."

CHAPTER
TWELVE

THIS TIME THE call traveled the other way around the world, through Peru, South Korea, and Singapore before arriving at the house in Pakistan.

"There has been a complication," the fixer said.

Her client remained silent, waiting.

Trying not to sound nervous, the fixer said, "The transfer occurred on schedule, and an attempt was made to obtain her at the Barcelona train station, but her new escort was able to get her away."

"Then I assume the more permanent solution was employed."

"It was, but..."

She told him about the bomb going off before the girl was on the boat, blaming the delay on the escort. In truth, she was well aware it was her own fault. If they had not tried to grab the girl at the station, the escort would not have taken the extra precautions he obviously had on the way to the *Marea Alta*, and the girl would have been delivered on time. But telling her client that would seal her own fate.

Quickly, she added, "I believe they are still in the city. I've used one of my contacts to provide the police a description of them."

"The police? I don't want her in custody. I want her dead."

"I am to be immediately notified if she is picked up. And arrangements are in place for the girl to be transferred to me.

They've already been seen trying to get through a police checkpoint. We will find them."

CHAPTER
THIRTEEN

SAMUI

SINCE PRAVAT WAS most familiar with the villa, it was
decided he would accompany Red Team while Narong stayed
with the van, where Mee Noi and Chayan had moved for the
duration of the operation. The vehicle had repositioned a
quarter kilometer down the road to the south, where they were
out of harm's way but could keep an eye on the villa's gate
via the camera.

Red Team approached the villa through the jungle
between the monk's place and his immediate neighbor to the
south, their first task to scope out the house and assess the
situation. Since Pravat had told them the easiest way to get
into the building would be through the sliding doors on the
ocean side, they worked their way through the jungle and
finally stopped parallel to the swimming pool. The house
looked quiet and dark, the only illumination coming from a
light inside the pool that cast an eerie undulating glow onto
the palm trees towering above the surrounding deck.

On the cove the tide was low, the waves small and
gentle, lapping almost soundlessly against the sand. Louder
was music drifting over the water from a house around the
south end of the cove. Pravat sneaked a look through the
brush and across the bay at the offending home but saw no
lights. Maybe someone was sitting out on a deck, having a
drink and enjoying the stars, or maybe someone had passed

out with the music still playing.

Whatever the case, the man in charge of Pravat's team—introduced only as One—had noticed the music, too. He reported the sound and its general location over his radio, and said someone should check it out.

One motioned for Pravat and Two to follow him to the edge of the jungle closer to the house. On their way, they discovered a wooded pathway leading from the deck around the side of the house and up the slope.

One looked at Pravat, silently asking where it led. Pravat had seen the monk head up this way a few times, but he had no idea where the path went so all he could do was shrug. The group leader pointed at Pravat and Two, and then motioned up the path, instructing them to check it out.

Sticking to the sand, the men headed up the slope, Two in the lead.

After they were past the house, the jungle closed in again, until there was only a meter of space on either side of the path. Two seemed unfazed by this, but Pravat had to slow so he wouldn't trip, and didn't catch up to his companion until the point where the jungle fell away again. The path had brought them around to the island side of a clearing just big enough for the guesthouse and the deck that occupied it.

That explains where the monk has been going, Pravat thought.

The place was constructed to match the house below, but was nowhere near as large. Pravat guessed there couldn't be more than a single bedroom and perhaps a little living space.

He tapped Two on the shoulder, cupped his hands, and whispered in the man's ear. "I think this is where the monk is staying."

The man raised an eyebrow and looked at the house anew. He signaled Pravat to go around the right side while he went around the left.

There were three windows along the side of the house, none covered. If Pravat were very careful, he could probably get up on the deck and take a look through one of them, but that was a task he'd rather leave to his companion.

THE UNLEASHED

Better he step on a creaky board than me.

Pravat continued to the ocean side of the house, and stopped when he rounded the corner. At the other end, Two had done the same thing. Like the corresponding side of the villa, this side of the guesthouse was all glass doors.

Two signaled for Pravat to approach the window and peek inside. Pravat wanted no part of that. As far as he was concerned, he shouldn't be out here at all. But with Chayan and Mee Noi actively monitoring the situation, it would do his career no good if he refused.

With reluctance, he mounted the deck as quietly as he could and worked his way over to the window. Leaning in close to the glass, he could make out several dark shapes—a dresser along the left wall, two chairs near the windows, and a bed against the far wall, its foot nearest Pravat. He rose until he could see the lump of a person lying under a sheet.

The size seemed right for the monk, but Pravat couldn't see the sleeper's face. It was clear, though, that the person was alone.

Pravat tiptoed across the deck and joined Two.

"Is it him?" the man asked.

"Maybe."

They rejoined One at the big villa, where Pravat described what he'd seen. One reported the discovery to their bosses, and included information from the scouting he'd done around the big house while the others were gone.

"Yellow Team. Status?" Mee Noi asked over the radio.

A pause, then a hushed voice said, "Just completed a sweep around house at point 2A. Music is coming from speakers mounted on the outside wall. The house is dark. No movement detected. We can disable the speakers if you'd like."

"Not necessary," Mee Noi said. "Reposition to the target house. Blue Team, you move in also. We stick to the original plan."

"Blue Team moving in."

"Yellow Team on the way."

106

QUINN'S EYES CRACKED open. In the crib, Claire cooed and giggled, wide awake. He groaned, dislodged himself from under Orlando's arm, and slipped out of bed.

"Shh, quiet," he whispered as he approached the crib.

Claire reached her arms out toward him, ready for the morning that was still hours away.

He rubbed a hand across her back. "It's the middle of the night. You need to sleep."

She laughed again.

"Shh."

Orlando stirred behind him. "I think it's my turn," she mumbled.

"It's all right. I'm already up."

"You sure?"

"Yeah.

She laid her head back down, eyes already closed.

Quinn returned his attention to their daughter. "How about we get you something to eat?" He lifted her out of her crib, hoping a little food in her belly might put her back to sleep.

Claire shoved a hand in his face, feeling his nose and lips and chin, and laughed again.

"I'm up, I'm up," Orlando said, rising a few inches off her pillow.

"Sleep," Quinn told her. "I've got her."

"Right. Thank you. I wu ee..." She fell back asleep, mouth half open.

Quinn carried their daughter into the hall and down to the living room.

His eyes were accustomed enough to the dark that he could make his way into the kitchen without turning on a light. He set Claire in the high chair Daeng had provided, and then grabbed a bottle of juice out of the refrigerator. He poured some into Claire's sippy cup and screwed on the top. She babbled and reached for it.

"Don't drink it all in one gulp," he said, giving it to her.

She kept talking until the spout was in her mouth.

With her needs dealt with, he headed back to the fridge

to see what he could drum up food-wise for himself, but before his hand touched the door, he heard a faint scraping sound. He looked back at Claire, thinking she might have caused the chair to move a bit across the floor. But she was leaning back, contentedly sucking on her cup. It couldn't have been the chair anyway, he realized. The floor in the kitchen was tile and the chair had rubber caps on its feet. The noise he'd heard had been more like grit rubbing against wood.

Though he was no expert on Samui wildlife, he thought perhaps a stray dog had walked across the deck.

His caution radar kicked in, though. The house was a nice place, after all, and would likely have nice things—a tempting target for a thief.

He walked over to the back windows but noted nothing that might have caused the sound.

An animal, then. Already moved off. Probably scared away by the sounds of Quinn and Claire.

He was starting to turn back toward the kitchen when a shadow along the path to the pool moved. It was low to the ground, but his years of experience told him it was not an animal. It was a human trying to remain unseen.

Quinn scanned the land between the house and the cove, looking for similar shadows, but there was only the one.

He was starting to think through his options when the sippy cup fell to the floor behind him and Claire cried out. As he turned, he heard the groan of a board on the deck, as if someone standing just outside had reacted in surprise to Claire's outburst.

Not as if, he thought.

Under normal circumstances, Quinn would have slipped out a side door and worked his way around the house to surprise the intruder from behind, but that would mean leaving Claire in harm's way.

Abandoning stealth, he hurried back and picked up his daughter. As he spun back around, he spotted the knife rack on the counter. If they'd been here on a job, he and Orlando would have secured weapons upon arrival. But this being vacation, they had none.

Holding Claire in one arm, he grabbed a carving knife and raced out of the kitchen.

RED TEAM WAS to enter the villa through the glass doors overlooking the main deck, while Yellow Team would use one of windows at the north end of the house. Blue Team was tasked with watching the guesthouse in case the monk realized something was going on and attempted to assist his friends. If all went well, *Khun* Daeng wouldn't wake until morning, when he would find the presents they left for him.

Red Team leader assigned Pravat a position as backup on the deck just beyond the glass wall. Pravat reached his assigned spot without a sound. The same couldn't be said about Two, who lightly scraped a foot against the wooden path on his way to the house. The man immediately dropped into a huddle.

"See anything?" One whispered over the radio.

"No," Two said.

Though he wasn't sure if the question had also been meant for him, Pravat said, "Nothing from here."

One craned his neck to get a better look through the window. "I think someone is in there. No one move!"

Pravat pressed himself tight against the wall. Several tense seconds went by before a bang came from beyond the windows. Pravat rocked back in surprise, a board under his foot groaning in protest.

He could hear a child crying and then the sound of feet hurrying across the floor.

"I think we've been made," Pravat said.

"Look inside and check," One ordered.

Pravat moved up to the edge of the window and peeked into the house.

A shadow ran across the back end of the room and disappeared into a hallway on the left.

"Our cover's definitely blown," Pravat said.

"*Khun* Mee Noi, abort or execute?" One asked.

The pause lasted no more than a second. "Execute."

"Yellow team, go!" One ordered. "Two, window, now!"

One and Two converged on the back window, no longer worried about staying hidden or quiet. One whipped a short crowbar out of his pack and jammed the end between a pair of sliding doors. With a pop, the sections parted. He shoved them open and whispered over the comm, "Seven, which way?"

It took Pravat a moment to remember he was Seven. He moved over to the other two and pointed toward the hallway. "There."

"Follow us," One said to Pravat. With guns raised, he and Two moved into the house.

Pravat reluctantly moved after them.

AS QUINN RACED across the living room, he shot a glance back at the windows and saw someone peeking in from the deck. Still operating under the assumption they had burglars, his plan was to get Claire to Orlando and return to take care of the assholes.

But as he entered the hallway, Garrett stepped out of his room and headed toward the bathroom. The moment the boy realized he wasn't alone, though, he stopped.

"Quinn? What's going on? Why are you running?"

"Get back in—" Quinn stopped himself. He could wrap things up a lot faster with Orlando's help. He put Claire in her brother's arms. "Take her into the bathroom, lock the door behind you, and try to keep her quiet."

"What's going on?"

"Someone's trying to break in."

"What?"

"Garrett!"

"Sorry. I'm going."

While Garrett took his sister into the bathroom, Quinn rushed to the master bedroom.

Shaking Orlando's leg, he said, "Get up."

She groaned but didn't move.

"Orlando!"

She sat up in a bolt, eyes wide open. "What is it? Claire? Is she all right?"

Quinn had moved back to the bedroom entrance and closed the room's double doors until only a slit was left to peek through. "Not Claire." Before he could say anything else, a pop echoed down the hall from the living room. "We've got visitors."

Orlando jumped out of bed and hurried over to him.

"Who? Did you see them?" she whispered.

"Just a shadow."

"No one knows we're here," she said, no doubt wondering if this had anything to do with their jobs.

"They're probably just looking for something to steal."

She nodded and looked back at the crib. "Where's Claire?"

"With Garrett, locked in the hall bathroom."

"Okay. Good." She glanced down at the knife in his hand. "You got another one of those?"

"No."

She headed toward the other side of the room. "I'll check if there's anything in the bathroom."

"YELLOW TEAM INSIDE," the leader of the second team reported.

One clicked his radio to acknowledge as Red Team moved down the hallway. The first doorway on the left was open. He stopped short of it and motioned for Two and Pravat to check inside.

Pravat was not pleased with any of this. He was not a gunman. He was a watcher, damn it. He should not be in the house at all. But again, the choice was not his, so he followed Two through the doorway.

A bedroom. Twin beds, both empty, but one with ruffled sheets indicating someone had been using it.

Two moved over to the bed and put a hand on it. "Warm," he whispered.

They checked under the beds to make sure no one was hiding there before rejoining One in the hallway.

There were four more doors, two on the right, two on the left, the farthest of which was a set of double doors, presumably to the master bedroom.

They moved to the next room. The door was closed. One carefully wrapped his fingers around the knob and turned it.

When it didn't move, he placed his ear on the door and listened.

QUINN WATCHED THROUGH the crack as three men entered the hallway.

He'd been wrong. The intruders weren't ordinary thieves. They were armed with pistols equipped with high-end sound suppressors. But even without the top notch gear, he could tell by the way the men moved that they weren't the type of people who'd waste time snatching trinkets from tourists.

Orlando watched from under his arm and tensed as she also realized the situation was not what Quinn had thought.

The men stopped in front of Garrett's room and two went inside. When they returned, the trio continued down to the bathroom door.

Quinn tapped Orlando to move out of the way, and then switched his grip on the knife.

Down the hall, the man who seemed to be in charge tried the knob, but Garrett had done as instructed and locked it. The guy turned, his back to the master bedroom, and leaned toward the door.

Quinn checked the others. Their attention was also on the bathroom so he eased the master bedroom door open, raised the knife, and let it fly.

THIS WASN'T THE first time Garrett had found himself in the middle of the action. That had occurred when he was five years old and kidnapped by a man who he later found out was his biological father. His memories of that time were hazy at best—guns and snow and wanting to be home, that was about it.

The events from the previous summer, however, were still very clear in his mind. It had been right before Claire was born. He and his mother and the Vos—the couple who helped take care of him and Claire, and whom he considered to be his grandparents—fled San Francisco just ahead of some people who were trying to capture his mom and Quinn. He hadn't been there when the threat was finally taken care of, but he had been around long enough to experience plenty of tension and fear and—though he hadn't admitted it to anyone— excitement. When Quinn shoved Claire into his arms and ordered him to hide in the bathroom, he felt those same sensations again.

After locking the door, he climbed into the tub, thinking it would be the safest place if any gunfire erupted, something he knew was all too common in his mother's and Quinn's world.

Claire pouted, and her eyes took on that sad look indicating she was about to cry.

"Hey, hey, hey, it's okay," he whispered and rocked her in his arms. "Shhh. No crying. Everything's fine."

She whimpered, and he knew if he didn't do something, she'd be wailing soon. As he'd seen his mother do, he slipped a finger between her lips, hoping it'd distract her. Sure enough, she began to suck it. What Garrett hadn't taken into account were the three baby teeth that had sprouted in the front of her mouth. He winced as she pinched his finger between them, so he wiggled it over to the side where she was still all gums. The discontent on her face faded.

Just as he was beginning to relax, he heard the doorknob jiggle. He wasn't all that great at picking locks yet, but even he could get through that door in a heartbeat.

No scratches of metal in the keyhole, though. Maybe they were moving—

Suddenly all hell broke loose.

PRAVAT WAS LOOKING directly at One when the knife plunged into the side of the man's neck. The Red Team leader dropped to the floor, blood pumping out in rhythmic gushes.

Pravat stared, too stunned to do anything. But Two fired a shot down the hall and yelled into the radio, "One's down! One's down!" He fired two more shots toward the master

113

bedroom and then glanced at Pravat. "Check him!"

Pravat shook off his stupor and dropped down next to One. The gushing continued, though not quite with the same vigor as before. Pravat yanked the knife out and clasped a hand around the man's neck.

"You'll be okay," he said. "Don't worry."

He was lying. There was far too much blood on the floor, and despite his efforts, more continued to leak out around his hand.

He heard steps pounding the floor back toward the living room and turned in a panic, thinking maybe the monk's friends had somehow gotten behind Pravat and the others. But it was Yellow Team, coming from the other wing of the house.

They dropped down behind Two and Pravat, and glanced at Red Team's leader.

"Shit," Four said. "Is he...?"

Pravat looked back at One. He could no longer feel the blood pumping under his palm. With his free hand, he searched for a pulse but found none. Even if the man was somehow still clinging to life, he'd need a transfusion right that very second.

Pravat removed his hands and crawled away from the body.

"Shit," Four repeated.

"Who shot him?" Three asked.

"Not a gun," Pravat said, pointing at the knife lying in the puddle of blood. "Came from the end of the hall."

Three looked incredulous. "Someone threw that from *there* and hit him in the neck?"

"Yeah."

Turning an accusatory eye to Pravat, Three said, "I thought these people were supposed to be tourists."

"It wasn't my job to check who they are," Pravat said. How many times did he have to tell someone that?

Two motioned toward the body and said to Pravat, "Stay with him." He shifted his gaze to Yellow Team. "Three, outside. Make sure they don't escape out the windows. Four, with me."

Three headed back the way he'd come.

Before the other men moved out, Two flicked on his radio. "Blue Team, what's your status?"

"All quiet here."

Two nodded to Four and they headed toward the master bedroom door.

Afraid that someone might come from the other end of the house, Pravat's gaze jumped back and forth from one end of the hall to the other.

A *thunk* came from beyond the locked door One had been checking before the knife hit him. As Pravat twisted around, he heard what sounded like something sliding. He looked toward the master bedroom as Two and Four pushed open the door and moved inside.

Almost immediately, flashes of gunfire spilled from the room, each accompanied by the dull spit of a suppressor. Then, as fast as it had begun, it was over.

"Two, this is Seven," Pravat said into his mic. "If you've cleared that room, I think there's someone behind the door over here."

Dead air.

"Two, do you read me? There's someone over here."

Still nothing.

"Two? Four?"

Another pause, then, "What's going on?" Not Two's voice but Mee Noi's.

"Two and Four went to engage the targets. They're not responding."

"Then check on them!"

Pravat hesitated. "Yes, sir."

He had the foresight to grab One's gun before starting out, but as he crept toward the double doors, he couldn't help feeling he should turn and run the other way. Talk about this not being his job.

A meter away from the door, he flicked his mic on again. "Two?"

Silence.

He didn't bother with another attempt for fear of incurring Mee Noi's wrath. He silently counted to five, and then slowly curled around the edge of the open doorway.

It was his cowardice, not superior reaction time, that saved him. He had just about cleared the door frame when panic gripped him and he pulled back into the hallway. A bullet ripped through where he would have been if he'd kept going.

Screw this, he thought.

He rushed down the hallway, slowing only long enough to send a couple of bullets flying back toward the bedroom to discourage those inside from chasing him. He repeated the action when he reached the end of the hall, and then raced across the living room, out the open glass door, and across the deck, not slowing again until he was well into the jungle.

THE MOMENT THE knife hit its mark, Quinn shut the door.

He knew the remaining two would be coming this way soon. He whispered to Orlando what he wanted to do. After a nod, she hurried off to set things up while Quinn crouched beside the lounge near the door.

It was nearly a minute before he heard faint footsteps in the hall heading their way. The steps stopped just outside, and then the door swung open.

As soon as the men crossed the threshold, Orlando flicked on a flashlight and threw it from the master bathroom toward the bed, in a steady arc that kept the beam pointing toward the bedroom door.

The men stepped toward the light, raising their guns, but stayed their trigger fingers when they realized no one was holding the light. The moment they passed the lounge, Quinn launched himself at the closest man and wrapped an arm around the guy's neck. With his other hand, he grabbed the intruder's gun, aimed it at the man's partner, and squeezed his captive's trigger finger twice. The first bullet struck the other guy in the shoulder, but the second hit right above the ear and killed him instantly.

Quinn's captive tried to get the gun free, but Quinn

increased the pressure around the guy's neck until the man went limp.

As he laid the unconscious guy on the ground, he whispered, "We're clear."

Orlando stepped out of the bathroom.

"I need something to tie this guy up with," he said.

She pulled the cloth belt from a robe draped over a chair and secured the man's hands behind his back. While she did this, Quinn moved to the doorway and listened. Since these intruders were pros, he'd be a fool to assume there weren't more of them.

Sure enough, he could hear a whisper down the hall, something he couldn't make out. The speaker was male, and from the occasional pauses, Quinn knew he was hearing one side of a radio conversation.

He returned to the two downed shooters and examined the one still breathing, finding a radio attached to the guy's ear. Quinn ripped it out, but there was no time to don it before he heard the voice in the hall again, this time right outside the bedroom door, saying something in Thai.

Quinn grabbed one of the guns, and then he and Orlando moved quietly to the other side of the bed, where he rested his wrist on the mattress and aimed the gun at the doorway.

The first thing he saw was a pistol moving into the opening. It was soon followed by the outline of a man. Quinn held his fire, waiting until the intruder was completely visible, but when he finally pulled the trigger, the man had ducked out of sight.

Quinn heard rapid footsteps moving away down the hall. He rushed over, but before he reached the door, two bullets ripped into the jamb. He slammed back against the wall.

A few seconds later there was another *thup*, the bullet smashing into the end of the hall.

Quinn moved low out of the bedroom, ready to shoot. Seeing no targets, he continued toward the living room. Upon reaching it, he found the back doors wide open and could see the silhouette of a man running across the deck. He tried to take a shot, but the man disappeared into the brush before

Quinn could pull the trigger.

Quinn ran to the back door but had no desire to play a game of hide-and-seek in the jungle. The man had fled because he was smart or scared. Whatever the reason, Quinn doubted he'd be returning.

He took a breath and started to lower his gun.

A bullet passed through the space between his dropping arm and his ribs, missing him by less than an inch. He dropped to a knee as he spun around and sent off three quick shots.

A groan and the thump of someone hitting the deck.

Quinn got to his feet and approached carefully, ready to put another shot into the still mound. There was no need. Two of his bullets had hit center mass.

Three intruders in the house, one in the jungle, and this guy made five. Was that it? Or were there more?

As Quinn scanned the area, Orlando shouted his name from inside.

He rushed back into the house and down to the hallway, his gun raised.

"Quinn!" she yelled again. Her voice wasn't coming from their bedroom, but from the now open doorway to the guest bathroom.

He crossed into the room and almost ran into Orlando as she was heading out.

"What is it?" he asked. "Are they okay?"

"I thought you said they were in here!" She turned back to the room. "Where are they? Where are the kids?"

CHAPTER
FOURTEEN

CLAIRE JERKED AT the muted *thups* from the other side of the door.

"It's okay," Garrett whispered. "It's okay."

But it wasn't okay. Not even close.

Garrett knew that sound, had heard it before. Gunfire, the type made by what his mother called suppressors. The type of equipment used by people who worked in her and Quinn's world.

Dangerous people.

Garrett's everyday life was pretty typical for a kid his age. He went to school, was on a swim team, played videogames with his friends when he should be doing homework. But he knew he wasn't typical. None of the other kids had a spy for a mother.

Though Quinn—and sometimes Daeng or Nate—had shown Garrett some of the fun tricks of the business, it was his mom who'd taught him things she said were more practical. Things like observation skills, specialized self-defense, and most importantly, what to do in an emergency. Not earthquakes or house fires or car accidents. No, an emergency just like this.

"The most important thing is to remain calm," she had said. "If you're not calm, you'll make mistakes. And mistakes can get you hurt."

That one was easier said than done, but he did have her DNA, so while he was definitely agitated, the activity in the hallway—a grunt followed by hushed panicked voices and then the gunfire not long after—had not stunned him into helplessness.

"Next, assess the situation."

The situation was that there were some really bad people right outside the door. Bad people with guns.

His mom had also told him that if he was already someplace safe, he should stay there. If not, find somewhere that was.

The bathroom had seemed fine at first, but someone had already tried to open the door once. And now he knew they were armed. One shot would take out the lock. Plus, he had Claire, and he was responsible for keeping her safe.

The only other way out of the room besides the door was a window above the tub. It was small, but he was pretty sure he could fit.

As he stood up to check it out, he removed his finger from his sister's mouth. Instantly her pout returned.

"No, no," he whispered. "Don't cry. It's okay."

He grabbed a washcloth off a shelf next to the tub and put one end between her teeth. She wasn't happy at first, but after a moment it seemed to satisfy her.

He slipped the window lock loose and pushed the pane open. He'd worried there might be a screen on the other side, but there wasn't. Maybe he should take that as a sign he was doing the right thing.

Getting through the window with Claire proved to be a challenge. Holding her against his chest, he pulled his torso through the opening, and then swung out a leg so that he was straddling the window frame. Holding her with one hand, he was able to grab a lip at the top of the window, swing his other leg out, and drop to the ground. His arm ached like crazy but they'd made it.

To throw off any potential pursuit, he closed the window so no one would know they'd used it, and then looked around to assess his options.

They were on the island side of the house. Off to their right was the entry bridge that led to the looping driveway where the van was parked. He momentarily considered following the road to the gate, but he feared running into more intruders that way. As he looked to the left, it dawned on him he was being stupid.

Uncle Daeng.

He was staying in the guesthouse just up the hill. Not only could Garrett and Claire hide there, Daeng could help Mom and Quinn.

With Claire still sucking on the cloth, he moved into the jungle. Thankfully, the brush consisted mostly of palms and scattered bushes so he could easily move around.

Nearing the guesthouse, Garrett began to worry Daeng had also been attacked. He didn't hear any noise ahead, but maybe that just meant the gunmen had visited Daeng before they hit the main house.

Garrett slowed, his mother's voice in his head telling him to be cautious. The guesthouse had a deck that went all the way around. Daeng's bedroom was on the beach side.

Garrett snuck around until he found a sheltered spot from which he could see the glass doors to the bedroom. While it was too dark inside to see anything, the back doors were closed and there were no signs of trouble. Had the intruders entered some other way?

He scanned the area behind the house, looking for something he could sneak behind to get a better vantage point.

What's that shadow there, near the back of the deck? he thought. *Is that a rock?*

Whatever it was, he could crouch behind it and—

The shadow moved.

Garrett nearly fell backward as he realized it was no rock, but was a man. Not Daeng, though. This person was too short and stocky. He was facing the house, staring at the same window Garrett had been trying to see through.

Claire made a gurgling sound. It was soft, but loud enough to cause the shadow to twitch again.

Before she could make another sound, Garrett slunk back among the trees.

Okay, so Daeng was out. The only thing Garrett could

think of doing now was to hide in the jungle.

"Everything's going to be fine," he whispered to his sister, though he was really saying it for himself.

He tried to reorient himself. In his retreat from Daeng's place, he had become turned around. He thought he was facing south so he continued in that direction, but when he came upon the main highway, he realized he'd been heading east.

That was fine, though. There were some restaurants and shops to the north. It would mean walking past the gate to the villa, but he could always move back into the jungle at that point if anyone was waiting there.

If the businesses were closed, he could hide behind them until the sun came up, when he should be able to tell whether or not it was safe to return to the house.

"You're doing great," he said to Claire. "Hang in there for a little longer. We'll rest soon."

She pulled on a clump of his hair and smiled as he started down the road.

PRAVAT WAS DEEP in the jungle north of the house when he finally stopped. Somewhere along the way, his earpiece had fallen out and was dangling from its cord on his shoulder.

He took a few deep breaths before putting it back in.

"—eam report!" Mee Noi was yelling. "What the hell's going on? Red Team, Yellow Team, do you read me?"

Pravat turned on his mic. "This is Pravat, uh, Seven. Two and Four are dead, I think. I don't know about Three."

"You told us the place wasn't guarded!" Mee Noi said.

"It wasn't guards. It was the monk's friends."

"The monk's friends? Are you saying the man and woman took down three of Chayan's men?" Mee Noi asked, then added sarcastically, "Or was it the boy and the baby?"

Pravat decided it was best not to reply.

"Did you actually see Two's and Four's bodies?" Mee Noi asked.

"Someone shot at me before I could get a look. I barely got out." The last was stretching the truth, but he didn't think by much.

"Blue Team, report," Mee Noi said.

"No movement here," Five said. "The monk is still asleep."

The pause that followed was long. Pravat had no doubt Chayan and Mee Noi were contemplating whether or not Blue Team should attempt to take out the monk.

But it wasn't Mee Noi who finally broke the silence. It was the man from Blue Team again. "I just heard something in the brush behind me. I think someone is coming. What do you want us to do?"

A briefer silence. "Abort," Mee Noi ordered. "Meet at the rendezvous. Five minutes."

Pravat sighed in relief and headed toward the van.

"MAYBE THEY WENT into Garrett's room," Quinn suggested.

Orlando threw out a hand toward the bathroom door in frustration. "It was still locked! I had to kick it in."

If they hadn't left through the door...

Quinn moved past her, farther into the bathroom.

"I told you, they're not *here*," she said.

"I know."

He stepped into the tub to get a good look at the window. It was the only other way out. Sure enough, the latch was undone. He lifted the window and stuck his head out. The kids weren't there, but in the sandy ground below were a couple of indentations that could have been made by Garrett. It was too dark to know for sure.

Pulling back inside, he said, "They must have gone out this way." He moved toward the hallway. "Come on."

Outside, he and Orlando hurried along the front of the house to the bathroom window. The indentations had definitely been made by feet, but the sand was too soft to hold a print. Quinn looked around and then pointed at similar imprints leading into the jungle. It was only the one set so it didn't appear anyone had forced the kids out of the bathroom.

"Garrett must have been trying to get Claire away from the gunfire," he said.

They followed the tracks. When they were among the trees and bushes, the prints became intermittent and then disappeared completely. It was clear, though, that Garrett had been heading toward Daeng's guesthouse. A sensible move for a boy of thirteen, but both Quinn and Orlando thought it likely Daeng's place had also been attacked. So the kids might be running from one set of trouble to another.

They hurried quietly through the jungle, and stopped just inside the tree line near the guesthouse.

"Looks undisturbed," Orlando whispered.

Quinn nodded, noting that none of the doors he could see had been pried open like the ones at the villa.

"Cover me," he said.

Keeping low, he crept from the brush and made his way onto the deck. Through the glass door he could see someone lying on the bed. What Quinn couldn't tell was whether the person was sleeping or dead.

He scanned for any sign of the intruders, but since he hadn't been shot at yet, he thought it likely they had cleared out.

He tried the door handle. Locked. He tapped the barrel of his gun against the glass. "Daeng!"

The lump on the bed jerked in surprise, and then Daeng raised his head and looked around. Like most people in the business, he slept and woke easily.

"Quinn? Why are you—"

"Have you seen the kids? Are they here?"

"The kids?" Daeng pushed out of bed, hurried to the door, and pulled it open. Like Quinn, he was wearing only boxer briefs. "What happened? What's going on?"

"Someone broke into the house. Garrett made it out with Claire, but we don't know where they went."

Daeng raced back into the room and grabbed a pair of shorts and a T-shirt off a chair. As he pulled them on, he asked, "Broke in? Why?"

"They weren't there to steal the TV, I know that much." Quinn raised his newly acquired pistol.

Daeng looked at it in disbelief. "Who was it?"

"No idea."

"Did anyone get hurt?"

"You mean except for the three we killed and the one we've got tied up? No."

Daeng joined Quinn outside. "There were four?"

"At least five. Probably more."

"Do you think they took the kids?"

Quinn shook his head. "I think Garrett's just doing what he's supposed to and had gone looking for someplace safe to hide. I'd rather he didn't bump into any of these assholes so we need to find them quick."

Orlando emerged from the jungle as they hopped off the deck.

"We'll split up," Quinn said. "Daeng, you go south. Orlando, you continue north. I'll go east until I reach the highway. We'll meet back at the villa in fifteen minutes."

PRAVAT REACHED THE rendezvous point with two minutes to spare.

"Get in," Mee Noi ordered.

Pravat moved toward the seats in the back row, but Mee Noi said, "No, here," and pointed at the seat beside him.

Feeling bile rising from his stomach, Pravat did as ordered.

He was sure they were about to accuse him of being responsible for all that had gone wrong, but neither Mee Noi nor Chayan said a word. Chayan didn't even look back at him, making Pravat feel as if the big boss had decided Pravat no longer existed. Mee Noi, however, spent several seconds staring at Pravat in disgust before turning his gaze away.

The two members of Blue Team showed up a minute later. As soon as they entered the van and the door was shut, Mee Noi said, "Go."

Narong pulled onto the road.

This isn't my fault, Pravat thought as a tense silence filled the van. How could he have known the monk's visitors had those kinds of skills? They looked like an average family to him. If anyone was to blame, it was Virote for not finishing the background checks in time.

It's not my fault. I did everything—

A splash of color and movement along the right side of the road.

Pravat sat up. "Stop!"

Narong looked nervously at Chayan, but Chayan and Mee Noi had both turned to look at Pravat.

"Narong! Stop! Didn't you see them?"

"See who?" Chayan asked, his words underlined with contempt.

"The kids along the road."

Mee Noi frowned. "What about them?"

"It was their kids! The *tourists'* kids!"

Mee Noi swiveled in his seat and looked out the back window before returning his gaze to Pravat. "Are you sure?"

"I'm positive. I recognized the boy."

"Turn around," Chayan ordered Narong.

Narong made a Y-turn in the middle of the highway and began retracing their route.

"There they are," Pravat said after a moment.

At the very far reaches of the headlights, the boy's red shirt stood out against the night.

"Slow down," Chayan said as he lowered his window.

GARRETT REALIZED HE and Claire must have come out on the main road a little farther south than he had intended.

They should've passed the gate to the house by now, but there'd been no sign of it—or much of anything else. The only bit of civilization he'd seen was a van passing by. Otherwise the road was quiet.

At some point after he had started following the blacktop, Claire had lost interest in the towel. Her eyelids grew heavy, and for a minute or so, she tried to fight off sleep, but finally she slipped under, her head resting on Garrett's shoulder.

He rubbed her back like his mother would do, hoping it would help her fall more deeply into her slumber. If he could keep her that way for a while, it would certainly make his life easier.

He heard a vehicle coming down the road ahead of them a few seconds before its lights lit up the night. Tired from all the exertion, it took him a moment before he remembered he should hide. He moved into the jungle and crouched behind a thick bush.

The vehicle slowed as it approached and stopped when it was parallel to Garrett's position.

"*Sawadee, khrup*," the man sitting in the front passenger seat said out the open window.

Garrett held perfectly still, sure the man couldn't see him.

"I know you hear me," the man said in English. "Come out, please. We not hurt you."

The side door opened and two men climbed out. When Garrett saw their guns, he realized these people must be connected to those who had broken into the house.

He backed away from the bush, intending to head deeper into the jungle, but a branch that had been caught on his arm flicked free, snapping against Claire's leg.

Her eyes flew open, and a cry escaped her lips before he could get a hand over her mouth.

He looked back at the vehicle and saw the two men heading toward the bush he and Claire were behind. He jumped to his feet and ran.

"You're okay," he said to his sister over and over, trying to calm her down.

He could hear the others enter the jungle behind him, so he increased his speed and followed the terrain down a shallow ravine that had a small stream running along the bottom.

He almost went up the other side but then wondered if the stream led to a storm pipe he could use to get to the other side of the road. He turned down the ravine and followed the water, staying as quiet as he could. Claire's cry had become a whimper.

His plan fell apart when he reached the end of the ditch. While there was indeed a pipe under the asphalt, it wasn't wide enough for even Claire to fit through.

Adjusting his plan, Garrett moved up the side of the culvert until he could peek over the edge and see how far he was from the van. Fifty yards at least, maybe more. He was positive he could cross the road unseen.

Claire let out a whimper, louder than the others.

"Shhh," he whispered.

He rubbed her back again as he climbed out of the ditch and started across the highway in a crouch.

Another loud whimper.

"Shhh."

Middle of the road. No sign of the van moving or the men who'd been following him and Claire.

"Unh, unh, unh."

Claire was winding up for another all-out cry.

He turned her so he could cover her mouth with his hand, but she twisted her head away.

When the cry came, Garrett was able to muffle it but not silence it completely. He gave up on the crouch and ran. Before he reached the other side, someone emerged from the brush behind him and shouted toward the van.

Garrett reentered the jungle to the sound of footsteps pounding across the road toward him. Claire was in full breakdown mode now, wailing beneath his palm. He knew his attempts to suppress her cries were failing, but he kept his hand over her mouth. "Please, be quiet."

Without a free hand to push away branches, he had to twist and turn to keep from getting slapped in the face, leaving his ears and the rest of his head to take the brunt. Roots on the ground were another problem, and twice he tripped and nearly fell.

All of a sudden, the jungle fell away, and he found himself on another road. Not another highway, though. The blacktop was too narrow and there were no lines painted on it. What it reminded him of was the driveway to the villa. He knew it couldn't be that, though, because he'd run in the opposite direction. A driveway to one of the other houses? If so, maybe he and Claire could hide there, or perhaps someone could help them.

But as he turned down the road, a man rushed out of the jungle thirty feet in front of him. Garrett whipped around to go the other way.

Another man was there.

Garrett pivoted toward the jungle and disappeared again into the brush.

THEY COULD HEAR the muted cries of the baby ahead of them. Blue Team leader indicated that he and his partner would each circle wide while Pravat, who had volunteered to join the chase, would follow the boy.

Thirty seconds later, there was a change in the sound coming from ahead. No more moving branches, but feet running on a hard surface.

Pravat increased his speed, wanting very much to catch the boy himself to improve his situation with his bosses. Just ahead, the jungle seemed to be thinning.

I've got you now.

With a burst of energy, Pravat shot out of the jungle onto what turned out to be a road. The boy was in the middle of it. The moment he saw Pravat, he turned the other way. But Six had moved onto the road behind the kid.

Pravat sneered, and started to tell the kid it was over. But the brat rushed back into the jungle.

Dammit!

Pravat took off after the boy, entering the jungle at exactly the same spot the kid had seconds before. Within a dozen steps he could see the back of the boy's head. Another burst of speed and the kid was right in front of him. Pravat grabbed the boy's shoulder and jerked him to a stop.

Twisting the boy around, he said, "No more. Finished."

"Let me go!" the boy yelled as he tried to squirm away. "Let me go!"

"I not let go, so no more move. Understand?"

The boy continued struggling as Pravat hauled him back toward the main road.

The baby's cries grew louder as the boy's hand slipped

from her mouth.

"Shut her up," Pravat said in Thai. He tried to remember the right English word. "Quiet!"

The boy dug his feet into the dirt. "No!"

Pravat raised a hand to strike him, but was saved from having to do so by the arrival of Blue Team. Both men had their guns aimed at the boy. He looked as if he would remain defiant, but then put his hand over the girl's mouth.

"Good," Pravat said. "Now you come."

QUINN PUSHED THROUGH a thick wall of brush as he continued east.

So far he'd discovered no signs of the kids. The urge to shout their names was strong, but if there were more intruders about, he couldn't risk it.

A cry, distant and low, but one he'd become acutely attuned to over the past six months.

Claire.

He listened a moment longer, homing in on its position, and then ran.

The jungle whipped at his body, slicing at his bare torso and legs, but he felt none of it. He tried to pick up Claire's voice again, but either she'd stopped crying or her sounds were masked by the noise of the bushes he was racing through.

A row of short palms forced Quinn to circle to the right. Upon reaching the other side, he saw that the jungle ended not far ahead, at what he thought was the highway.

A motor roared.

Dread pouring into every inch of his body, he covered the remaining distance to the road as fast as he could. Bursting from the jungle, he turned north toward the noise and could see a receding pair of taillights. The vehicle looked like a van, the kind used to ferry tourists to different attractions on the island.

Orlando shot out of the jungle fifteen yards in front of him.

"Garrett! Claire!" she shouted.

Quinn ran toward her. When she heard his footsteps, she twisted around, her gun raised.

"It's me," he said.

She lowered the weapon. "I heard Claire."

"So did I."

"Garrett!" she shouted again.

"I don't think they're here anymore."

CHAPTER
FIFTEEN

BARCELONA

WHEN NATE SPOTTED the scaffolding-covered stone building on the corner of a narrow street, he knew it would be a good hidey-hole.

He, Liz, and Dima made their way in through a boarded-up door in the back of the building, and took the stairs all the way to the roof. From there they could see the last remnants of smoke rising above the marina.

Dima stared toward the water, hugging her arms to her chest. Nate was thankful when Liz put an arm around the girl's shoulder. Though Dima jumped a little at the touch, she soon relaxed and gave Liz a quick smile.

Nate wandered out of their earshot and pulled out his phone. Still no call from Helen, which was pretty damn annoying. He tried her again.

When the line was answered, he gave his personal ID code, and then said, "I need to speak to Helen Cho. Now."

He was put on hold for nearly half a minute before Rafe Larson came on the line.

"She's still not ready to talk to you," Helen's assistant said.

"Well, that's too bad, because if she isn't on the line in the next few seconds, I'm walking away from the package."

"Threats aren't going to help."

"Who said it was a threat? Put her on."

An exasperated sigh. "Hold."

Helen picked up a few moments later. "Nate, I'm so sorry. I know you're in a tight spot, but believe me, I'm trying to get everything worked out."

"A tight spot would be putting it mildly. The city isn't safe. You need to get us out of here now."

"What do you think I'm working on? I'll call—"

"The police have our pictures."

She said nothing for a moment. "How?"

He told her what had happened since they last talked.

"How secure is your current location?" she asked when he finished.

"Secure enough, but I don't think we should stay anywhere too long."

"I'm working on getting a plane. I should have more details soon, but any rendezvous probably won't happen until this evening. You'll have to find a way to get the package out of the city."

"No, *you* need to get her out of the city."

"Nate, please."

He took a moment to calm his frustrations before saying, "Can you at least give me a direction we'll need to head in?"

"When I know it, I will."

"How long until that happens?" he asked.

"Not long."

"If I don't hear from you in an hour, I'm calling back."

"Understood. The package—is everything all right?"

"You mean is *she* unharmed?"

"Yes."

"I guess it all depends on your definition of the word. Physically she's fine."

"Is she giving you problems?"

"No."

"Then what—"

"Some people aren't used to seeing a bomb go off that was meant for them."

"Of course. But she's cooperating?"

"She's fine."

Pause. "I'll be in touch."

The line went dead.

When Nate returned to the others, Liz said, "So?"

"You two are going to have to stay here alone for a little bit."

"Why? Where are you going?" Liz asked.

"To get us a ride." He looked out at the sky and noticed a couple of helicopters circling the marina area. "It'll be safer if you stay inside. Top floor, away from the windows. If you hear someone come into the building, find a place to hide and don't come out unless you know it's me." He leaned in and gave Liz a kiss. "It shouldn't take too long."

OBTAINING A VEHICLE wasn't the only thing Nate needed to do. He hadn't mentioned the second task because he knew it would make Liz even more concerned.

After pulling the hoodie over his head, he moved through the city, adopting the persona of a man hurrying to get home.

It was crazy how quiet the streets were. It felt like a scene from an apocalyptic movie where the people had disappeared but all their belongings remained. As far as checkpoints, he encountered only one, but heard police radios echoing down the road in plenty of time to find alternate routes.

Finally, the hotel where he and Liz had been staying came into sight.

When he'd had Liz bail out earlier, he'd assumed she could return to the hotel after things settled down. But that had been before the police obtained his photo. If they decided to broadcast it on TV, inevitably a hotel employee would identify Nate as one of the guests. The cops would storm in, search their room, learn about Liz, and label her a potential terrorist, too. Nate needed to make sure no clues to his and Liz's identities were left behind.

He made a complete circle of the property and spotted no police cars. Though he took that as a good sign, it still didn't mean he could just walk through the lobby. It was possible his picture had already made its television debut but no one at the hotel had made the connection yet. Seeing Nate live and in person might trigger the association. So he used a side entrance and took the stairs up.

Once in the room, he gathered all items of identification—luggage tags, receipts, tickets, and anything that could provide DNA samples—and stuffed them into his duffel. He then went through Liz's things and put a few items she particularly liked into his bag. Everything else went into Liz's suitcase, which he set by the door with the duffel.

Next, he undressed, took scissors from his toiletries bag, and got into the shower, where he cut his hair as short as he could. When he finished, he turned on the water and flushed all the hairs down the drain. He then grabbed his razor and shaving cream and shaved his scalp. A quick shower sent the remains down the drain also.

Dressed again, he wiped down the entire place before stuffing all the trash into an old shopping bag. He would toss it in a rubbish bin somewhere in the city.

He scanned the room to make sure he hadn't missed anything, and then headed out with the duffel over his shoulder, the suitcase and bag of trash in his hands.

He dumped the suitcase in the bin behind a restaurant two blocks away. As he walked back to the street, four police vehicles—lights flashing but sirens off—sped by, heading toward his hotel. Perhaps it was a coincidence, but he wasn't sticking around to find out.

After disposing of the trash bag several blocks later, he started checking car doors.

Sedan number nine was the winner.

LIZ CHECKED HER watch again. Nate said he wouldn't be long, but he'd already been gone over an hour.

Dammit, she thought, wishing her heart would unclench.

She glanced at Dima. While she knew she shouldn't blame the woman for any of this, she couldn't help but feel some anger. Whatever Dima was mixed up in had pulled Nate into its whirlwind, and now Liz, too.

Dima must have noticed Liz's look because she said, "I

haven't thanked you for your help yet."

"It's not me you need to thank." It came out snarkier than it probably should have, but Liz didn't apologize.

"Are you…" Dima paused. "I'm not sure what to call what Nate does, but do you do the same thing?"

Liz laughed. "No. I'm…just a student."

Dima's eyes lit up. "A student? I'm a student, too. What are you studying?"

"Art history."

"Really? That sounds fascinating."

Liz shrugged. "What about you? What do you study?"

Dima opened her mouth to respond, but paused, her expression darkening. "Nothing at the moment."

They fell back into silence.

Finally Liz asked, "Why are you here?"

"What do you mean?"

"I mean, why do you need Nate's help? Why did someone try to blow you up? What are you doing here?"

"I-I-I'm not supposed to talk about that."

Liz shook her head and turned away. "Of course not."

Quiet again.

"My sister," Dima said, almost in a whisper.

"What about your sister?"

"She's getting me out."

"Out of where?"

Pause. "A bad place."

Whatever anger Liz had been holding on to evaporated. "Were you…hurt?"

A faraway look took hold in Dima's eyes, and on her face a blend of anger and fear and shame. "Not any worse than others."

Liz wanted to probe further, but instead placed an arm around the woman's back. "Nate will take care of you. He's good at that."

Dima blinked, coming back to the now. "I hope so."

From one of the floors below them came the sound of a door opening and shutting. Dima looked at Liz. "Nate?"

"Wait here," Liz whispered.

She made her way through the offices to a window. All the glass had been removed from the top several floors, so she started to lean out and look down at the road.

"Oh, crap."

Two police cars were parked in the middle of the street. Though the angle didn't allow her to see inside them, Liz doubted the officers were still in the cars. She leaned out a bit more to see the sidewalk. Empty.

They're in the building.

She hurried back to Dima. "Come on. We need to hide."

"It's not Nate."

Liz shook her head.

"The police?"

A nod. "We need to hurry."

She led Dima to the hiding place she'd found when she did her initial inspection of the floor. The nook was concealed behind a loose sheet of wood and was just large enough for the two of them. She let Dima crawl in and then followed. With the board back in place, the space was almost pitch-black.

"If they move that, they'll find us right away," Dima said.

"We're not staying here." Liz pulled out her phone, turned on the flashlight app, and shined it toward the ceiling.

The walls of the space were finished but the ceiling was open, exposing the building's infrastructure. There would be plenty of room for both of them there.

"You first," Liz said. She set her phone on the floor and laced her fingers together.

Looking doubtful, Dima stepped into the cradle.

IF NOT FOR Nate's years of training, he would have slammed on the brakes the moment he turned the corner and saw the two police cars in front of the building where he'd left Liz and Dima. Instead, he let his newly obtained Peugeot hatchback roll to a less dramatic stop.

The officers who'd come with the cars were nowhere to be seen.

He backed around the corner, then circled the block to the next street over and parked.

A narrow alley took him to the rear of the stone building. From his previous check, he knew there was no way in back here. He moved down the right side and peeked around the front corner.

The cop cars were still there and unoccupied, so he strode down the sidewalk along the front of the building as if he did the same every day. Then he went up the steps toward the entrance, making no attempt to hide.

A cop standing in the middle of the large lobby whirled around as Nate opened the door.

"You can't be in here," he said in Spanish. He took a step toward Nate and pointed back at the door.

"I want to know what's going on," Nate replied in the man's language. "My friends and I saw you arrive, and we were—"

"Sir, you'll have to leave." The cop was walking toward Nate now.

"Does...does this have something to do with that explosion? My God. It does, doesn't it?"

As Nate had hoped, the cop reached for Nate's arm.

Nate thrust his elbow into the cop's jaw. As the officer staggered back, Nate whipped around behind him, put an arm around the guy's neck, and cut off the blood flow to the brain. It was only a few seconds before the cop passed out. Nate dragged him into one of the nearby rooms, found a discarded electrical cord in a pile of renovation debris, and tied the man's wrists and ankles together.

Two police cars meant likely no more than four men.

He cocked an ear at the entrance to the stairwell and moved inside when he heard nothing. At each landing he paused only long enough to listen at the doorway. It wasn't until he reached the second-to-last floor that he finally heard something.

A crunch, or perhaps the crinkling of paper.

He reached for the door, intending to crack it for a peek.

Another noise. Footsteps this time, right on the other side

of the door.

Nate squeezed against the wall next to the door's hinges. A moment later the door swung open and two cops rushed through. Nate tensed, ready if either man turned and saw him, but they continued across the landing and started up the stairs to the top floor—where Liz and Dima were.

Quick and quiet, Nate swung around the door and into the corridor before the cops reached the point where the stairs doubled back He waited until he heard them exit onto the top floor before following them up.

At the next landing, he eased the door open and peeked out. The stairwell exited at the midpoint of the floor's long central corridor. The cops had split up, one man going in each direction. Though Nate knew the women were on this floor, he didn't know their exact location. He did a mental coin flip and went left.

The cop he was trailing entered the last set of offices on the street side of the building. Nate checked the other way to make sure the second policeman was out of sight, and then hurried to the end of the hall.

The officer had propped the door open, allowing Nate to slip across the threshold into a reception area. There were two exits along the back wall, each missing its door. Beyond them was what appeared to be a corridor running side to side. The cop was to the left, his footsteps pinpointing his position. It wasn't long, though, before he headed back Nate's way.

As the man reentered the lobby, Nate slid through the doorway on the right, and then came back into the lobby through the door the man had used.

A piece of trash on the floor betrayed Nate as he moved in behind the cop. But as the guy swung around, Nate's hand was already in flight. His palm strike to the man's cheek sent the cop staggering across the room. Before the man had a chance to snap out of his shock, Nate slammed a knee into his gut. The cop started to fall, but Nate grabbed him around the neck and repeated his choke hold until the officer blacked out.

An old phone cord worked as the tie this time, and half a minute later, Nate was headed down the main corridor toward the suite the other cop had entered.

The other set of offices had no lobby, the entrance leading into a hallway that ran back several dozen feet before T-boning into another corridor. When Nate reached the intersection, he could hear the cop somewhere to the right.

He used his camera to check around the corner. When he saw it was empty, he snuck down to the doorway where the sounds of the cop were coming from.

Crouching low, Nate leaned around the edge of the jamb.

A long room. Empty.

He leaned out a little farther and spotted a door to another room. He could see the beam of a flashlight swinging around inside it. He entered the front room and moved over to the wall just outside the other doorway.

He flexed his fingers and waited.

LIZ WAS SURE she'd made a mistake.

They'd used the open ceiling of the nook space to crawl into the concealed area above the adjoining room. The space was narrower than she'd thought, however, making it necessary for her and Dima to wiggle into place. But that wasn't the real problem. Though the boards had appeared sturdy enough when she did her initial inspection, they'd creaked and moaned as she and Dima shimmied on top of them. She was now convinced if they stayed there too long, the whole thing would collapse and send them on a ten-foot drop to the floor.

Trying not to think about it, she concentrated instead on listening for the police officers.

For several minutes there was nothing at all, and she wondered if they had left. Then all of a sudden, footsteps crossed the floor directly below them.

Dima slipped her hand into Liz's. Liz gave it a gentle squeeze, hoping it would reassure the woman. It would be nice, she thought, if someone could do the same for her.

Next came the worst sound she could possibly imagine— the *thunk* of the board covering the nook being removed.

A flashlight beam seeped up through the nook and into

their hiding place. It moved and disappeared and came back again a couple times. Finally the light went out and the board was put back into place.

Her plan had actually worked.

But her euphoria lasted only a few seconds, as strange sounds drifted up from below.

Dima heard them, too. And the hand that had started to relax squeezed Liz's again.

NATE MADE A sweep of the building but encountered no other officers besides the three he had disabled.

The question now was, where were Liz and Dima?

Returning to the top floor's main corridor, he yelled, "Liz! Where are you?"

Nothing.

It was a large floor, so perhaps she couldn't hear him from where she was. He ran as far right as he could go. "Liz!"

No response.

"Liz, it's me! Where are you?"

As he jogged to the other end, a thought occurred to him. What if the police *had* found them and taken them away? Maybe the cops he'd knocked out were simply making sure no one else was here?

He shouted his girlfriend's name again.

Still quiet.

"Liz! *Liz!*"

He cocked his head. Was that a voice?

He took a few steps toward the sound. "Is that you?"

There it was again. Definitely a voice, coming from the same set of offices where he'd encountered the final police officer. He rushed back in.

"Liz!"

"Over here," she called, her voice muffled like she was behind a closed door.

He followed the sound into the room the cop had come out of. "Where are you?"

"Here," she called. This time her voice seemed to be coming from above him.

"How did you—"

"Help us down," she said.

"Um, okay. How?"

"Do you see the board against the wall?"

He swung around. "Yeah."

"Move it out of the way."

Nate was impressed. The hiding place Liz had picked out was superb, especially since the cop had searched the space and not found them.

Nate helped Dima down and then Liz.

His girlfriend hugged and kissed him before suddenly pushing away. "What the hell did you do to your hair?"

He rubbed a hand across his scalp. "What? You don't like bald?"

"I didn't say that. *Some* men look good bald. Is that why you took so long?"

"That, and taking care of a few other things."

"Did you see the police? You must have. They were here just a few minutes ago."

"They haven't exactly left yet, but they won't be a problem." He turned to Dima. "How about you? You okay?"

She nodded. "Your girlfriend took very good care of me."

He smiled at Liz. "I'm not surprised."

Liz sniffed at him. "You took a shower, too, didn't you? You little—"

"I think it's time we get out of here," he said.

Liz turned serious. "You know where we need to go?"

"Yeah." After he'd procured the Peugeot, Helen had texted him the GPS coordinates of a location northeast of the city. They had exactly an hour and forty-five minutes to get there. "Come on. The car's not far."

CHAPTER
SIXTEEN

SAMUI

QUINN SPOTTED FOOTPRINTS on the shoulder of the road and
knelt down for a closer look. The sand was not as fine here as
on the beach, allowing the barefooted prints to form.

He wasn't sure they belonged to Garrett, but they were
about the right size and were top layer—not having been
driven over or walked on yet. Given the amount of people
who used the road, Quinn knew the prints were created after
traffic had died for the night. The troubling part was, there
were other prints, too—belonging to shoes that appeared to be
walking alongside the barefooted person.

He followed them until they stopped at a set of fresh tire
tracks.

"Over here!" he called to Orlando.

She ran over. "What is it?"

He showed her the footprints and the tire tracks.

"We have to get back to the house," she said. "Whoever
picked them up might be taking them there."

Sure, that was a possibility, Quinn thought, but the
evidence was telling him that was wishful thinking. Returning
to the villa *was* a good idea, however, for an entirely different
reason. There was information that should cut down their
search time for the kids.

They raced through the jungle to the back deck of the
house and ran in through the still-open doors. Orlando

continued straight on to the front door and flung it open. Quinn came up behind her a few seconds later, but the only thing in the driveway was their vehicle.

"The gate," she said. "If they tried to buzz in while we were out, no one would have answered." She turned to Quinn. "Open it!"

Quinn punched the button on the intercom box by the door to open the gate. Orlando raced outside, across the bridge, and down the driveway toward the main road.

"Come back!" Quinn yelled.

As he moved onto the bridge to yell again, Daeng emerged from the jungle near where their van sat.

"Did you find them?" Daeng said.

"No," Quinn said, then yelled, "Orlando! Come back!"

Daeng ran over to him. "What's going on?"

"I found what could be Garrett's prints along the highway. I think someone put him in a van."

"You think it was the people who broke into the house?"

Quinn looked at him but didn't have to answer. They both knew it was the only logical possibility.

"What's Orlando doing, then?" Daeng asked.

"She's hoping whoever took them is bringing them back here." Quinn turned for the house. "I need your help with something."

AS SOON AS the water hit the intruder's face, he sputtered and blinked.

It was another moment before he seemed to realize Daeng and Quinn were standing in front of him. He tried to stand up, but found he was tied to a chair.

Quinn leaned forward. "Who do you work for?"

Daeng translated, and the man answered with a spit that landed just short of Daeng's face.

Quinn thought it odd the man hadn't aimed his response at him.

Quinn repeated his question, his tone the same as before.

This time the man grumbled something under his breath.

"He isn't in the mood to cooperate," Daeng said.

"Is that how he put it?" Quinn asked.

"Something to that effect."

They'd set up in the large master bathroom in the unused wing of the house. The chair the man was strapped to was pushed up against a claw-foot tub. Orlando was there, too, having returned from the gate after accepting the fact no one was bringing her children back.

"Ask him again," Quinn said to Daeng.

Daeng did as requested. The intruder smirked and kept his lips shut.

"We don't have time for this," Orlando said.

She grabbed Quinn's new gun off the sink counter and jammed it into the intruder's thigh. "He asked you a question. Answer him!"

This time the man said something.

Daeng frowned.

"What?" Quinn asked.

"He says it doesn't matter what we do to him. He's already a dead man."

The intruder spoke again.

Daeng looked surprised and confused, but didn't immediately translate the man's words.

"What did he say?" Orlando asked.

Daeng blinked and said something to the man. The conversation lasted several seconds, most of it coming from Daeng's side, with the intruder adding a word here and there. Eventually, though Daeng continued to pelt him with questions, the intruder stopped talking.

Clearly agitated, Daeng headed out of the room.

Quinn looked at Orlando and nodded at their prisoner. "Watch him."

"Gladly," she said.

Quinn ran out of the room. Daeng was already at the far end of the hall, moving into the main room. He stopped inside and looked around.

Quinn caught up and grabbed his friend's arm. "Daeng. What is it?"

"I need a minute," Daeng said, without looking at him.

When his gaze locked onto the house's landline, he hurried over to it and punched in a number.

"Daeng, what did he say?" Quinn asked. "Does he know where they are?"

Daeng glanced at him, and then looked past him toward the bathroom. When he spoke, his words came out low and tense. "He called me monk."

It took a moment for the meaning to sink in. The intruder knew who Daeng was, knew that at one point in Daeng's life, he'd been a Buddhist monk. Quinn had never heard anyone call him that.

The call connected and Daeng spoke rapidly in Thai. The conversation lasted less than two minutes.

Daeng hung up, looking tense. "I don't think you're the reason the intruders came."

"Then what is?" Quinn asked.

"Me."

"They thought you were staying here?"

Daeng said nothing for a moment. "No. I'm sure they knew I wasn't."

"I'm not following you."

Again, Daeng looked back toward the bathroom. "He asked me how I was enjoying my payback."

"What?"

"I think he and his companions were sent to kill you."

"Why?"

"Because you are important to me."

"So who are they?"

"That, I don't know yet. My associate is checking into it right now."

"Are you saying they're going to kill Garrett and Claire?"

"I don't know that, either. But they could have easily done that at the side of the road. So I think the kids are probably safe for now."

"We need to get back in there," Quinn said, motioning toward the bathroom. "He knows where the others are going. We need to find them before they do decide to hurt the kids."

"I'm not sure we can get him to talk."

Quinn narrowed his eyes. "Oh, we'll get him to talk."

CLAIRE STARTED TO cry right after they sped past the entrance to the villa. Garrett rocked her in his arms until she quieted down again. He then looked out the window.

Both sides of the street were crowded with businesses, all but a few of the restaurants closed for the night. It looked a lot like the part of Chaweng Beach where they'd gone for lunch.

"Where are you taking us?" he asked the man in the front passenger seat. He seemed to be the one in charge.

The guy looked back but said nothing. It was his friend, the one on the bench seat in front of Garrett and Claire, who turned and said, "No talk. But you not worry. Everything going to be okay." He grinned and nodded as if that should be enough of an answer.

As terrified as Garrett felt, he knew he needed to stay ready in case a chance to get away presented itself.

"Shhh," he whispered to Claire when it looked as if she might cry again.

The man next to him—the creepy-looking guy who'd caught him in the jungle—nudged Garrett's arm and held out a piece of fruit.

"For baby," the guy said. He pointed at his own mouth and mimed putting the fruit in it.

Reluctantly, Garrett took the offered piece. Since it wasn't a fruit familiar to him, he tasted it first. The skin was a little tough, but the fruit inside was soft. He held it up to Claire's mouth and let her suck on it. After only a few seconds, the tears that had been brimming her eyes receded.

The man nudged Garrett again. "See. I right." He laughed softly.

After a few minutes, Claire started drifting off again. Once she was asleep, Garrett leaned down and whispered in her ear, "I'll get you out of this. I promise."

Less than ten minutes later, the van slowed to a stop. Garrett looked through the windshield and saw the road was

147

blocked by a chain-link gate. Beyond it was a large dark space. Not jungle, but a meadow or field that was lit here and there by dim points of light low to the ground. A farm?

A man in a uniform rolled the gate out of the way and the van drove through.

Garrett noticed a few buildings off to the left, and several more on the other side of the clearing. The van zigzagged over a series of paved roads around the field. When it slowed again, Garrett realized the open space was no farm.

Sitting directly in their path was a private jet.

QUINN UNTIED THE intruder's right arm. Not surprisingly, the man struggled, but the attempt was in vain as he was no match for Quinn and Daeng. They maneuvered the arm on the stool they'd brought in from the kitchen, and Orlando secured it in place with a generous amount of packing tape.

"One more time," Quinn said.

Daeng translated the original question, and the intruder replied with a tremor in his voice.

"He says we can ask all night but he'll never answer," Daeng said.

"Is that so?" Quinn leaned down so that his face was directly in front of the intruder's. "You seem to be unclear on the situation here. Your people have taken our family. That is unacceptable. We *will* get them back. And you *will* help us. So here's what I'm going to do." He leaned back. "Every time I ask a question and am not satisfied with your answer, I'm going to take a little bit of you."

He separated the man's pinkie finger from the others, and then held out his hand to Orlando. She gave him a carving knife. Quinn gave the blade a once over before resting the tip on the stool.

"Who do you work for?" he asked.

The intruder looked at him, scared, but pressed his lips together.

Quinn chopped down, cutting off the tip of the pinkie at the top knuckle.

The intruder screamed.

Quinn repeated his question.

The man writhed in his chair, not seeming to have heard the question.

Quinn brushed the dismembered fingertip onto the floor, isolated the man's ring finger, and cut its tip off.

More screams, this time with a few pleading words thrown in.

"Who do you work for?"

Before Daeng could finish translating, the man babbled something.

"He says, 'Please stop.'"

"How very polite," Quinn said. He isolated the man's middle finger. "That's not the answer we're looking for."

He brought the knife back down. When the man started to pass out from the pain, Daeng slapped him in the face and repeated Quinn's question.

A single word passed over the man's lips, one that seemed to stun Daeng.

"What?" Orlando asked. "What did he say?"

Daeng said, "Chayan."

"Does that mean something to you?" Quinn said.

"Unfortunately."

"Who's Chayan?" Orlando asked.

"Trouble."

"If he has our kids, then he's the one in trouble," Orlando exclaimed.

Quinn was about to ask Daeng more about this Chayan, but their prisoner was starting to pass out. He grabbed a handful of the guy's hair and jerked his head back up.

"Not yet." He slapped the man's cheek and said to Daeng, "We need to know everything. The vehicle they were in. Where they were going. What their next move is."

Daeng asked the questions without translating the answers. There was no need for the knife anymore as the intruder answered in a progressively weaker voice. When he finally slumped unconscious in his chair, Quinn cut away the tape holding the man's hand to the stool and said to Orlando, "Can you get him some ice?"

"Let him bleed," she said.

"Tempting, but this asshole's our only resource at the moment. We may need him again."

She hesitated a moment longer before walking out of the room.

As Quinn wrapped tape around the guy's fingers to stanch the flow of blood, he asked Daeng, "What did he tell you?"

"Just like you thought. They came in a van that matches the description of the one you saw."

"Did he say where their hideout is?"

Daeng shook his head. "Apparently there's been two men watching us but he didn't know where they're staying. The rest of them flew in a few hours ago on a private jet."

Only a few things had ever made the hair on Quinn's arms stand on end. The thought of Garrett and Claire being loaded on a plane and flown off to God knew where had just rocketed to the top of that list.

He jumped up. "We need to get to the airport right now."

"What's going on?" Orlando asked, reentering the room with a bowl of ice.

"They have a plane."

"What?"

"Put his hand on ice, tie him up, and then you and Daeng collect the guns and meet me at the car."

Quinn ran across the house to the bedroom he and Orlando were using, washed the blood off his hands, and pulled on some clothes. The others were waiting for him when he reached the van, Daeng behind the wheel and Orlando in the front passenger seat. The moment Quinn was inside, Daeng hit the gas. Quinn slammed the door shut and dropped into the forward most bench seat, centering himself between the two chairs in front.

The gate was still open but after they passed through, Daeng touched the remote control clipped to the visor and the barrier closed behind them.

"We need someone at the house in case our source wakes up," Quinn said. "We also need the bodies gone and the place sanitized. At the very least, the guy on the deck needs to disappear before the sun comes up."

"I can arrange that, but my phone's still in my room," Daeng said.

"Use mine." Quinn handed the mobile forward, but Orlando grabbed it before Daeng could.

"Keep your eyes on the road. I'll dial," she said. "What's the number?"

Daeng gave it to her. She turned on the speaker.

A woman answered in English. "Yes?"

"It's Daeng. I'm in need of your assistance."

"What can I do for you?" The woman had a mix of accents, mostly American but with a light British touch and even a bit of Australian thrown in.

It was a voice Quinn knew.

Christina, an ex-pat who'd lived in Thailand since around the end of the Vietnam War. She had a hand in a lot of different things, few of which were entirely legal. But she used those resources to do good work where she could, and lived—mostly—by the rule of not taking advantage of those less fortunate than herself. She was, in fact, the one who had introduced Quinn to Daeng.

Quinn touched Daeng on the arm, indicating he would do the talking. "Christina, it's Jonathan Quinn."

"Quinn? How are you?"

"I've had much better nights."

"Then perhaps business first."

"Orlando is here with us, too."

"A pleasure to finally meet you."

"Yeah," Orlando mumbled. "Same.

"What's going on?" Christina asked.

After Quinn finished outlining the situation, Christina promised to have a full team at the house by first light, and at least two people there within an hour to get things started.

"Thank you," Quinn said.

"Is there anything else I can do?"

Daeng said, "The guy we've got tied up told us Chayan is responsible for this. But Chayan's in prison."

"He *was* in prison. They've tried to keep it quiet but he and Mee Noi escaped sometime in the last couple of months. Since then they've been busy fixing the damage to Chayan's businesses that occurred while they were away."

"What about the people responsible for putting him in jail?"

"I would think he'd want to deal with them at some point, too."

"Why didn't anyone tell me?" he said.

"I guess probably because you've been in the States a lot. And I don't believe anyone thought you needed to know." She paused. "You didn't have anything to do with him."

"Sure, I did. I was the one who made sure he went away."

THE CREEPY MAN who'd been sitting beside Garrett climbed out of the van first, and then stood by the door and waved for Garrett to follow.

Garrett tried to swallow but his throat was dry. He could see the door of the plane from his seat, a retractable staircase hanging below it.

The man in the seat in front of him, the one who'd said everything would be okay, smiled. "Better you go out yourself then our men pull you out, I think."

Garrett wasn't so sure about that. He knew he and Claire were in deep trouble, but their situation would become even worse once they were inside that airplane. How would his mom and Quinn ever find them then?

The creepy man pulled out his gun. Though he didn't point it at Garrett, his message was clear. "Out now," he said.

Garrett scooted to the end of the seat and stepped out of the van, Claire asleep against his chest.

Creep motioned toward the plane with his gun. "Go."

Garrett's mother's voice whispered another one of her lessons: *Always be aware of your surroundings.*

Trying not to move his head, Garrett checked his peripheral vision. If there was somewhere nearby he could get between him and his captors, maybe he could lose himself in the night before they could grab him again. But it was a wide-open area with too many lights. He'd be tackled to the ground or shot dead before he could even reach the shadows.

He stopped a few feet short of the stairs to the plane.

"In," Creep said.

"Where are you taking us?"

"In."

"Not until I know where we're going."

"In."

Creep tried to grab Garrett's shoulder, but Garrett ducked under his grasp and stepped out of range.

The boss and the smiling man arrived a moment later. They said something to Creep in Thai. By the look on the gunman's face, Garrett guessed he was being reprimanded—a feeling that was reinforced when the man climbed into the plane without looking in Garrett's direction.

The smiling man said, "Please. Step inside. Food for you and drink. You are hungry, I am sure."

"Where are we going?"

"You are boy very brave."

At the moment, Garrett felt anything but, yet he held his ground, keeping his expression as stern as he could. Naturally, that was the moment Claire chose to stir.

When the man directed his next smile at her, Garrett reacted without thinking, twisting his body so the man couldn't see her.

"Sister you?" the man asked.

Garrett didn't answer.

The man exchanged a few words with his boss, then said to Garrett, "I cannot tell you where we go, but can say is someplace safe. If everything okay, you and sister you see family again. Everyone happy."

Garrett wanted to believe the last part, but knew he couldn't. "Tell me where."

The man grinned a little wider, showing more teeth. "If not get on plane, we take girl from you and you not see her again. You want or no want?"

Garrett was out of options.

QUINN, ORLANDO, AND Daeng were racing through Chaweng Beach toward the turnoff to the airport when they heard the roar of a jet. The lights of an aircraft appeared above the beach, heading out over the ocean.

"No!" Orlando exclaimed.

It had to be the plane the intruder told them about. No aircraft were supposed to take off from the island in the wee hours of the night. Someone was trying to get away in a hurry.

Quinn watched the plane's lights move away from the island. Right before they faded into the night, they began to turn.

"It's heading north," he said.

To the north was the bulk of Thailand, which meant the likely—though not certain—destination was Bangkok.

Were the kids on the plane or had they been left at the airport? Quinn knew the chances of the latter were next to zero, but they had to check so they continued on.

The gate to the airport parking area was closed, the lot itself mostly empty. Daeng drove down the road that paralleled the facility for another minute before pulling off to the side and parking.

"The plane holding area should be right over there," he said, pointing between two buildings as they all climbed out of the van. It was where the intruder had said his colleagues' plane was.

Keeping low, they snuck between the structures to a concrete slab fence with barbed wire across the top. The slabs were only a bit over five feet high, so Quinn and Daeng had a good view of the holding area below them, while Orlando had to find an old crate to stand on before she was able to see over it, too.

Two planes were parked there. Both, however, were commercial jets probably scheduled for the first flights out in the morning. As Quinn had feared, no private aircraft was in sight.

There was something unusual in the plane area, though. A parked van.

"Is that the one you saw?" Orlando whispered.

"I didn't get that good a look at it," Quinn said.

"But it has to be it, right?"

"I don't know." Quinn looked at Daeng. "Is there a quiet way in?"

"Easily checked," Daeng said. "May I use your phone again?"

Quinn handed it to him.

Daeng moved back into the gap between the buildings. A few seconds later, they could hear him talking in a low voice.

Orlando looked down at the van. "We have to find them." Though her voice was controlled, there was no hiding the panic underlining it.

"We will," Quinn said.

"You promise me? You promise we'll get them back and they'll be okay?"

Her question was both unfair and impossible to truthfully answer, but he said, "I promise."

She stared at him, making it clear she expected him to deliver on his words.

When Daeng returned, he said, "There's an access gate on the other side of the field that should serve our purpose."

They hurried back to the van.

THE ACCESS GATE was in a quiet portion of the airport, and they were able to quickly scale it without raising any alarms.

Sticking to the shadows, they approached the runway and crossed it in the darkness between sets of lights. From there it was a sprint to the edge of the plane holding area, where they paused. Scattered flood lamps created pools of light on the concrete. The dim areas in between were not as dark as Quinn would have liked, but they didn't have much choice.

He pointed out the best path, and they crept over to the van. Orlando climbed in first, moving quickly from one end to the other.

"They're not here," she said as she finished searching the last row. There was both relief and fear in her voice. If this Chayan guy had taken the kids, they might be far away, but at least they would be alive. "They've got to be on that plane."

They returned to where Daeng waited.

"We need Christina to find out where the plane's going," Quinn said. "We also need a way to follow them."

Daeng nodded and held out his hand. "Phone."

As Quinn handed the mobile over, Orlando said, "That'll take too much time," and headed left down the grassy divider that paralleled the runway.

"Make the call," Quinn told Daeng before rushing after Orlando. It took several seconds before he caught up to her. "Where are you going?"

Without stopping, she motioned at the terminal. "We can get the flight info from the tower."

"You do realize the tower is the other way, right?"

When she looked back at him, he pointed across the landing strip. There, very near where they'd sneaked into the airport, was the control tower.

CHAPTER
SEVENTEEN

ABOVE THE GULF OF THAILAND

MEE NOI GLANCED at the seat in the rear of the cabin where the boy sat with the baby, staring back at him, eyes narrow and angry.

Impressive, Mee Noi thought, though he was sure beneath the mask of defiance the kid was terrified.

Turning back to Chayan, Mee Noi said, "When the monk comes for them, he won't be alone."

"If we cannot handle a few hired thugs, then we are the ones who should suffer."

If Pravat had not been lying, and the monk's friends *had* picked off Chayan's men, then it would be more than hired thugs they'd have to deal with. Angry parents could be so unpredictable. While Mee Noi was confident their men could deal with the problem, there was something they could do to improve the odds.

"Do you think *Krung Thep* is the best place to confront him?" Mee Noi asked. *Krung Thep* was what the Thais called Bangkok, the plane's destination. Though the capital would provide Chayan and Mee Noi with many resources, it would also do the same for the monk and his friends.

"You have a better plan?"

"Perhaps," Mee Noi said. "I was thinking we could arrange for one of our vans to meet us at Suvarnabhumi. When we arrive, we will make it look as if our guests have gotten off. I will also get off and lure the monk into a trap, then join you as soon as he's taken the bait."

Chayan raised an eyebrow. "Where will I and the brats be while you're doing all this?"

"If I'm not mistaken, we have recently come into possession of some suitably comfortable accommodations outside the country."

For the first time since Mee Noi started describing his plan, Chayan smiled.

GARRETT MAY HAVE appeared angry when the man looked back at him, but in truth he was assessing his captors. The more information he gathered, the better his chances of keeping Claire from harm.

He watched as the men talked. Though he couldn't understand what they were saying, he was able to learn more about the two men's relationship. Such as the way Mr. Smile always spoke to the boss with a deferential tone, like he was constantly trying to please the man. As for the boss himself, he gave off a sense he was superior to everyone else, not just in the job but in everything.

Claire stirred, but didn't wake. When she settled back down again, he looked out the window at the night, and wondered what his mother would be looking for if she were here.

"Knowing your opponent's weaknesses is always your greatest strength," she had once told him. She'd been training him in some self-defense moves, and had shown him exactly what she meant. The bruises from that lesson lasted for several days.

All right, had either man revealed a weakness?

They were both probably around fifty. Mr. Smile was smaller than his boss, and older. He wore glasses, so maybe that was something Garrett could use. Other than that, Garrett couldn't see anything else.

About the only weakness he could detect in the boss was the flash of anger he'd directed at Creep right before they boarded the plane. It was an emotion that always made people stupid. Garrett didn't need his mother to tell him that. He saw it at school all the time. But he wasn't sure how he could exploit that without the risk of having the man's rage turned on him and Claire.

When he could come up with nothing else for either man, he turned his thoughts to figuring out why these people had kidnapped him and his sister in the first place. All the kidnappings he'd ever heard about were motivated by money. But if that was the men's goal, wouldn't there have been much easier ways of taking Garrett and Claire than storming the house? They could have just grabbed them when they were walking through town, or, if the kidnappers were going for the dramatic, raced into the cove on Jet Skis and plucked him and Claire off the beach in front of the house.

He couldn't help but feel something else was going on here. He thought and thought but came up with no explanation that made any sense. He knew the reason didn't really matter, though. The only important thing was getting Claire free.

He had no idea how to accomplish that, but he would find a way.

He was, after all, his mother's son.

CHAPTER
EIGHTEEN

CATALONIA, SPAIN

IT TOOK A little creative driving, but Nate was able to get them out of Barcelona without encountering another roadblock. From there, they headed northeast.

The tension and fear the explosion had caused in the Catalonian capital lasted into the countryside. The towns they passed through would usually be teaming with life, but the sidewalks were all but empty, and many of the restaurants and other businesses were shuttered.

Nate worried that more checkpoints had been set up outside the city, but despite plenty of police cars on the road, there were no barricades.

It was well after eight p.m. when they reached the small town of Riudellots de la Selva. Per Helen's instructions, they left the car parked on Avinguda del Mas Pins, an industrial area, and walked two blocks to a machine shop named Maquinaria Guerrero.

Inside a young woman sat behind a counter, working at a computer. Without looking over, she held up a hand, letting them know she'd be right with them, and continued with what she was doing.

When she finally looked up, she said in Spanish, "Good evening. How can I help you?"

"I believe the owner is expecting us," Nate said. "Oscar Guerrero?"

"Of course. You must be *Señor* Garner."

"I am."

She picked up a phone and spoke quietly into the receiver. When she finished, she said, "He'll be right with you. Would you like a coffee or something else to drink?"

"Water would be great," Liz said.

The woman exited through a door in the back wall and returned moments later with three bottles of water. As she handed them out, the door opened again. A middle-aged man—thin with salt and pepper hair—entered the room.

"*Señor* Garner?" He held out his hand to Nate. "I'm Oscar." After they shook, he nodded his welcome to Liz and Dima, then said, "This way."

He led them into a large shop. Many of the lights were off, and the machines that filled the space sat silent, their work for the day apparently done. The group zigzagged around presses and drills and cutters and routers and other devices Nate didn't recognize, to an open area at the back of the building. Here, along with boxes awaiting shipment, sat a cargo van with the shop's name and contact information painted on the side.

Guerrero said, "Please, wait here," and retreated the way they'd come.

A few seconds later, they heard the door at the front of the room open and close again, leaving them alone.

Per Helen's instructions, Nate opened the back of the van and waved Liz and Dima inside. After he joined them, he shut the doors. A solid wall separated the cargo area from the driver's cabin, so they were unable to see the person who climbed behind the wheel two minutes later.

They heard the machine shop's loading-area door roll up with a rattle, and then the van's engine fired to life and they were on the move.

Nate automatically noted every turn and stop and speed adjustment. If he'd had time to study a map of the area ahead of time, he could have followed along in his head. Among many other things, this was another benefit of training under Quinn.

The trip lasted twenty-seven minutes, their arrival heralded simply by the van stopping and the engine shutting off. Nothing happened for well over three minutes.

"What are we waiting for?" Dima asked, anxious and confused.

Nate touched a finger to his lips.

Ninety additional seconds passed before a soft knock sounded on the wall between them and the front cabin.

Nate opened the back door and scanned the dark field behind them. He motioned for Liz and Dima to wait, and climbed out to check both sides of the van. When he was satisfied no one else was there, he motioned for the women to join him.

The moment he closed the van doors, its engine started again and the vehicle drove off, disappearing seconds later into a break in the trees surrounding the field.

Liz looked around but said nothing.

"What are we supposed to do now?" Dima asked, confused.

"Wait for our next ride," Nate replied.

"Here?" she said in disbelief.

The word was barely out of her mouth when several dozen dark blue lights flicked on, creating two parallel lines running down the length of the meadow.

Dima jumped in surprise. "What is that?"

Nate pointed into the sky, downwind of their position, where one of the stars was growing brighter as it descended. Moments later, a Gulfstream G650ER landed on the private runway and rolled over to where they were waiting.

When it stopped, the door folded out, turning into a set of steps. Nate hurried over as a man about his age exited the aircraft.

"Ah, hell," the guy said when he saw Nate. "If I knew it was you, I would have asked to be reassigned."

"I don't see how I'm making out any better in this deal," Nate said.

They stared at each other for a moment before both men suddenly grinned and hugged.

"Good to see you, Nate."

"Back at you."

The man's name was Magnus Herlin, a Swedish pilot who had started off doing contract work for the Office, a defunct organization that had also employed Quinn and Nate occasionally. Nate had not been aware Helen used the Swede, but he was glad she did.

"It's my understanding you have someone in need of a ride," Magnus said.

"Three people, actually."

The pilot raised an eyebrow. "I was told only one."

"My associate and I will also be joining you."

Magnus studied him for a moment. "Problems?"

"More like trying to avoid them."

"Then let's get you on board and out of here."

Four minutes later, the jet's wheels left the ground and the plane rose into the Catalonian night.

CHAPTER
NINETEEN

SAMUI

BREAKING INTO THE airport tower would have been a snap if they'd had the right equipment. But working had been the last thing on their minds when they'd come to the island, so the device that would have quickly dealt with the pass-coded lock on the main door was sitting in their storage unit back in Los Angeles.

Quinn surveyed the structure for an alternate method. Since the airport had only a single runway, the tower was not a tall one, the equivalent of three or four stories high.

"There," he whispered, pointing at a doorway on the observation level at the top. It let out onto a small deck, where a ladder was attached to the side of the building, providing access to the roof.

That door, too, would undoubtedly be locked, but unlike the one at ground level, there was a window in the top half.

The tower was encased in a decorative metal frame that went all the way from the bottom to the observation level, with half-inch-thick rods providing a makeshift ladder to the top.

Quinn grabbed a palm-sized rock off the ground, wrapped it in his T-shirt, and went up. The window in the door cracked on the second tap. From there, it took only a steady push on the glass for it to give way and fall inside. Though the act had not been silent, most of the sound had been contained within the building. Judging by the lack of lights, Quinn thought it unlikely someone was inside to hear it.

The possibility of an alarm concerned him more, but all remained silent. He reached inside, unlatched the lock, and opened the door. Once inside, he checked the frame for alarm sensors and was happy to see none.

He waved for Orlando to join him.

She shot up the side of the building as if she were trying to set a record. Upon joining him in the control room, she rapidly assessed the equipment.

"This should work," she said, taking a seat at one of the computer stations.

While she hunted down the information, Quinn kept watch out the tower windows. Several minutes passed before he detected movement on the other side of the runway, near the terminal area.

A guard. No, two guards, walking just outside the passenger area.

Quinn tensed. They seemed to be in no rush, but their current route would take them into the plane holding area where the van sat. Did they know the abandoned vehicle was there? Or would they be surprised and raise an alarm?

He watched them, willing them to reenter the terminal, but the guards didn't deviate from their course. When they reached the end of the terminal and the holding area came into full view, they came to a sudden stop.

"Well, that answers that question," Quinn muttered under his breath.

After a short pause, they continued forward, their previous leisurely stroll now a cautious approach—one that included drawn weapons.

He looked back at Orlando. "How much longer?"

Instead of answering the question, she said, "Look at this."

He moved over to her. On the computer screen was footage from a security camera, a wide shot of the plane holding area. Just off center was a private jet, and in front of it the van.

People were walking from the van to the plane. Though the shot was from a distance, there was no mistaking Garrett. In his arms was his sister.

Quinn could feel Orlando's tension build as they watched. When Garrett reached the plane, he seemed reluctant to go inside. It wasn't until after two others walked up and talked to him that he mounted the steps.

"All right, so we know for sure they're on that plane. Where did they go?"

"I'm going to find out. I just need a few more minutes."

"You need to hurry. Airport security just found the van, and I don't think they expected it to be there."

"All right, all right. A minute, all right? Maybe two."

"A minute, okay. Two, I'm not so sure."

"I'm not leaving until we know where that plane is going."

Quinn watched the security guards as they separated and closed in on the van from different directions. When they were about twenty feet from the vehicle, they stopped. It looked like one of them was shouting something. After a few seconds, they started forward again. One approached the driver's door, while the other headed for the main passenger door. The one at the driver's door hesitated a second and then yanked it open and jumped back.

A sudden flashing light drew Quinn's attention back to the terminal. A sedan topped with blazing emergency lights raced down the road in front of the buildings.

Dammit.

Back at the van, the two guards were huddled together, talking near the driver's door. The million-dollar question was whether they thought the occupants had all boarded the private jet, or that someone was illegally wandering around the airport. Logic would dictate the first, but if the security men were cautious, an all-airport search would begin.

"We're out of time," Quinn said as he turned away from the window.

Orlando glanced at him and then back at the computer,

saying nothing.

Striding over, he said, "If we stay any longer, we'll be caught."

"Thirty seconds."

He frowned, but said, "Just hurry."

Orlando worked the keyboard for another moment before exclaiming, "Got it!"

She ripped the top sheet off a pad of paper from the neighboring workstation, grabbed a pen, and jotted something down. She then turned off the machine and wiped down the keyboard and counter with the end of her shirt. The pen she stuck in her pocket.

Without a word, they slipped back out the way they'd entered.

AS SOON AS Quinn and Orlando headed for the control tower, Daeng found a hidden spot beside the adjacent airport fire station and called Christina.

After telling her what he needed, she said, "Give me a few minutes. I'll call you back." The line went dead.

Daeng peeked from his hiding spot and scanned the airport. All was quiet. He leaned back against the wall, the thoughts he'd been trying to hold at bay finally breaking free.

Chayan.

Daeng had all but forgotten about the vicious lowlife. He had moved on with his life, and trusted that if Chayan didn't die in prison, by the time the animal finished his sentence, he would be a weak old man.

What a huge mistake that assumption had been. Daeng had no doubt whatsoever Chayan's men had been sent to kill Quinn, Orlando, and the kids. That kind of retribution was the man's signature. Daeng's failure to keep tabs on Chayan had turned his friends into victims.

In the eyes of humanity, Daeng's orchestration of the events that had put Chayan away would be seen as undeserving of any payback. The man's prison sentence was an inadequate payment for the evil he had wrought. The final straw had been the death of Daeng's cousin after she disappeared into Chayan's flesh factory. If Chayan had been flailed and left in the sun to be eaten alive by birds, it still would have been too mild a punishment. He and his people—Mee Noi in particular—should have been sentenced to death a thousand times over.

But Chayan wouldn't care about that or what humanity thought. Revenge would be the only thing that mattered to him. Daeng should have seen it coming. He should have been prepared. And he definitely should never have exposed his friends to danger. If anything were to happen to Garrett and Claire, Daeng would be the one who deserved a million deaths.

The phone buzzed in his hand.

"We're in luck," Christina said. "A friend has a jet in Krabi that he won't need until the end of the week. It should be off the ground in ten minutes and to you thirty after that."

"Clearances?" he asked.

"They'll be taken care of."

"Thank you."

"Whatever you need, I'm here for you."

BANGKOK

CHRISTINA SET THE phone on her desk and stared across the room.

There had been a time when she had high hopes for Chayan. She'd taken a special interest in cultivating his talents not long after he joined her organization.

He'd been what then? Eighteen? Nineteen?

Her memory wasn't what it used to be, but he'd been young, that's for sure.

He took to the business like he'd been bred for it. She seldom had to explain the workings of her various operations more than once, no matter how complicated they were. He'd get it right away, and was able to step in at a moment's notice and assume control of whatever she needed him to handle.

It wasn't until he'd been with her for a year or two that she began to realize something was off with him. She hadn't been able to put her finger on it at the time. It was just a sense that he was hiding something from her. It eventually concerned her enough that she'd tasked one of her advisors to take a deeper look into Chayan's background. Mee Noi had reported back that he'd found nothing unusual. Which, it turned out, was a lie.

Later she found out what Mee Noi had really learned was that Chayan had a history of ruthlessness that stretched back through most of his teenage years. And he was off-the-charts smart, way smarter than Chayan ever let Christina see. Mee Noi had apparently recognized Chayan's potential and aligned with him when Chayan broke off from Christina a few years later to start his own organization.

Daeng had entered her world a few years after Chayan and Mee Noi departed. And though the former monk had never officially become a member of her group, he was like a son to her.

And now that son needed her assistance in dealing with the monster she'd helped create.

She checked the time.

If Chayan was indeed heading to Bangkok, he would be arriving soon. It was highly unlikely she could get a team to Suvarnabhumi before his plane landed, but she'd send one anyway on the off chance the aircraft was delayed. A quick call got things moving. As she hung up, she realized there was another potential option she could enlist. This wasn't the kind of thing she would usually ask of him, but he'd have to suck it up.

She picked up her phone, hoping he was still at the airport.

PATAWEE SUENG SHOULD have been home two hours ago, but a late arriving flight from Abu Dhabi had kept him at his post an extra ninety minutes. That would have been annoying enough, but as he was collecting his things, Christina had called with one of her "requests" that were never really requests at all.

His position and the security clearance that came with it

allowed him to move freely throughout the airport. He took pride in this status, but knew it was the reason Christina had taken a special interest in him.

With her request this time came a warning to cover his tracks. It had been unnecessary since he was always careful when doing anything for her, but the fact that she'd thought it prudent to tell him was disturbing.

Using a passkey no one knew he had, he let himself into the office of one of the airport engineering supervisors and turned on the man's computer. When prompted for a username and password, he used a set belonging to a senior colleague from Immigration. Within a minute, he verified a private jet was on approach to the airport, a flight from Koh Samui.

He called Christina to give her the information, thinking he could then be on his way. But no, the woman had more for him to do. Though he protested after she explained things, she wouldn't take no for an answer. He hung up, logged out of the computer, locked up the office, and took the elevator down to ground level.

There he took possession of one of the airport management sedans, and drove through the winding paths around the terminal buildings to the access road leading to where all private jets were kept.

Christina's instructions had been clear—observe only. Do not engage. Do not interfere. Do not let them know you are there. So, instead of approaching the area from the front, he took a route that brought him in behind the buildings that lined the holding area, and parked.

His heart was racing as he exited the vehicle. Most of the help Christina asked him for involved only a phone call or computer search. Spying on someone in the middle of the night was a first. And, he hoped, a last.

He reached the front corner of the building just in time to see the jet make its final approach. He was so used to seeing commercial airliners come and go that the tiny plane looked like a mosquito in comparison.

Nearly a dozen other private jets sat on the concrete pad,

separated into two parallel lines. All were dark. The area was not completely deserted, however. Two vehicles—a sedan and a white delivery van—were parked together at the far end of one of the rows. It didn't take a genius to guess they were there to meet the incoming aircraft.

The problem was, they were too far away for Patawee to really see anything. Against his better judgment, he eased out from the building and crept over to the nearest jet. From there, he moved from plane to plane until he was as close as he dared go.

He'd barely situated himself by a jet's nose gear when the noise of the approaching aircraft began bouncing off the buildings. When the plane was about ten meters from the vehicles, it stopped and the engines wound down.

Patawee watched as the plane's door opened. Unfortunately, before it was halfway to the ground, the van moved forward and blocked his view.

He winced and looked around for a better angle, but if he wanted a clear view, he'd have to move into a position where he might be seen. He stayed where he was.

He could hear the cargo doors of the van open, and then the sound of feet and voices, but the low rumble of the jet engines made it impossible to discern what they were saying. Less than a minute passed before the cargo doors slammed shut again.

The van idled for several more minutes and then pulled away, heading toward the exit. Now that the jet was back in view, Patawee saw that its door was closed again.

A man who'd been standing on the tarmac near the plane started walking toward the waiting sedan, which was in Patawee's general direction. There was something familiar about his face. Patawee was sure he'd seen him before. But not in person. A picture, or maybe on TV. Was he an actor?

Patawee narrowed his eyes. The guy didn't look like a movie star. He looked more like a—

A name clicked into place.

Mee Noi, brutal henchman of the former criminal boss Chayan. Older, but the pictures Patawee had seen of him were all from several years ago.

But hadn't Mee Noi been locked up somewhere? Chayan, too, for that matter?

Patawee shuddered. If the guy really was Mee Noi and Patawee had known that ahead of time, he would have never agreed to do this for Christina. To hell with what she would have done to him for refusing. What Mee Noi could do if he knew Patawee was there would be ten times worse.

A hundred times, even.

Patawee held his breath as Mee Noi climbed into the sedan, and he didn't release it until the car had driven out of sight. When he was sure no one else was around, he made his way on shaky legs back to his car.

It took four fumbled tries before the call to Christina went through.

"Tell me everything," she said.

He wanted to say no, and that she should never call him again. But as satisfying as that might be, when she needed him she would call, and he would do what she asked.

He took a breath and, in the calmest voice he could muster, gave her his report.

SAMUI

QUINN AND ORLANDO met Daeng at the van. They drove back around to the terminal side of the airport to wait for the plane Christina had sent.

They hurried aboard when it arrived, Daeng confirming with the pilot that their destination was Bangkok. As they taxied to the end of the runway, Christina called.

Quinn put her on speaker.

"The plane you're looking for landed at Suvarnabhumi ten minutes ago," she told them. "The good news is, I had someone there to watch it when it arrived."

"Please tell us they were able to get our kids back," Orlando said.

"Unfortunately the individual I had available is not cut out for that kind work."

Orlando closed her eyes for a second, exasperated.

"What did he see?" Quinn asked.

"The plane was met by a cargo van and a car. But the only person we know for sure got off was Mee Noi."

"What about Garrett and Claire?" Orlando said. "Are they still on the plane?"

"We don't know. My observer's view was blocked so he couldn't see everyone who got off. After the vehicles left, the plane taxied to the refueling area. My source called again a few minutes ago. The pilot has filed a flight plan for Chiang Mai and should be taking off any moment now."

"Don't let them go," Orlando said. "You've got to keep them on the ground."

"I have many resources, but even if I could get the tower to order a takeoff hold, we're talking about Chayan. He would order his pilot to ignore the tower."

"What about the van and sedan?" Quinn asked.

"I have people following them. If your children are in one, we'll know soon."

The LearJet's engines began powering up for takeoff.

"Since we'll be in the air, it makes sense for us to follow the plane," Quinn said.

"I agree," Christina said. "I'll have someone monitor the radar to make sure they're headed for where they say they're headed. I'll call back as soon as I know more."

"Thank you," Quinn said.

A moment after he disconnected the call, their plane roared down the runway.

Once they were in the air, Quinn said, "We may need more help."

"Christina will give us whatever we want," Daeng said.

"And we'll take her up on that. But with all due respect, I've never really worked with her before and I don't know her men."

He snatched up his phone and opened his speed-dial list.

CHAPTER
TWENTY

THIRTY THOUSAND FEET
ABOVE THE IBERIAN PENINSULA

NATE STARED DOWN at the lights of villages dotting the countryside, thankful they'd soon be out of Spanish airspace.

He had checked the news feed on his phone as Magnus and the copilot—a guy named Dan Barbier—readied them for takeoff. A handful of organizations had already taken credit for the Barcelona "attack," chief among them the latest ISIS splinter group.

He knew the world would never think of the bombing as anything but a terrorist act, despite its actual intent. And because of that, Spain would be on high alert and diligently search for anyone who had even a tangential connection to the event. So until one of Nate's contacts could remove Nate's and Dima's pictures from the police records, Spain would be off limits to them.

"Your phone," Liz said.

Nate blinked and turned from the window. "Huh?"

The plane was equipped with four sets of seats facing each other, with tables between each set. Liz was sitting next to him, with Dima on the other side.

His girlfriend nodded at the table. "Your phone."

He checked the screen and pushed ACCEPT. "Quinn?"

Liz looked at him, surprised.

"Where are you?" Quinn asked.

"Exact location? No idea. Somewhere over northern Spain, I believe."

"You're in the air? Dammit. When will you land?"

"I haven't been told our destination, but I'm guessing it'll be several hours. Why?"

"You haven't been told? What are you talking about?"

"Helen dragged me into a little mission that's snowballed into something bigger. Currently I'm escorting someone out of the country."

"So you're in a private jet?"

"Yes."

A pause. "What do you think the chances are of rerouting?"

LIZ WATCHED NATE'S face and listened as he talked to her brother. It wasn't long before she could tell something was wrong. When Nate hung up, much of the blood had drained from his face.

"What is it?" she asked.

"The kids," he whispered.

"Garrett and Claire?"

He nodded.

"What happened?"

"I promise I'll tell you, but I need to do something first." He headed to the back and opened a storage bin near the bathroom. When he walked by Liz toward the cockpit, he was holding a gun behind his back.

NATE KNELT JUST behind the two pilot seats. "Magnus, do you have a moment?"

The pilot looked back. "Sure. What can I do for you?"

"In private, if you don't mind."

"Um, okay." Magnus glanced over at his companion. "I'll be back in a moment."

"Grab me an orange juice while you're up, would you?" Barbier asked.

"No problem."

Nate stepped out of the way to give Magnus room to

maneuver out of his seat, and then told the pilot, "The back would be best."

He led the way, moving the gun in front of him so Magnus wouldn't see it. Liz and Dima looked at him wide-eyed as he walked by, but thankfully neither said a word. Upon reaching the rear of the cabin, he turned to Magnus, again slipping the weapon out of sight.

"What is with all the secrecy?" Magnus asked.

"There's been a change of destination."

Magnus's brow furrowed. "I have not received any information about this."

"You're receiving it now."

"From you."

"Correct."

"And you got this from Helen."

"No."

"No? Then who's initiating the change?"

"I am."

Magnus smiled as if Nate were making a joke. "You know I can't do that. I don't answer to you."

"I know you don't. I'm asking this as a friend."

"As a friend, I'd expect you to give me a little more to go on."

Nate hesitated. "Quinn needs my help."

"Quinn? Well, then, he should go through Helen."

"He's not on a job for her."

Looking sympathetic, Magnus shook his head. "You know there is nothing I can—"

"His and Orlando's kids have been kidnapped."

Magnus froze. "What?"

"The place where they were staying was attacked and Garrett and Claire were taken. He needs my help getting them back. And I need your help to get there."

"Jesus. Where did this happen?"

"Thailand."

"Thailand? We don't have enough fuel for that."

"Then we fill up on the way."

"Helen will never go for this."

"That's why I'm not asking her. I'm asking you."

Silence.

"So?" Nate said.

"If I say no, will you shoot me with that gun you're hiding?"

The corner of Nate's mouth ticked up. "I could never shoot you, Magnus. I'd just pistol-whip you a few times and tie you up."

The pilot thought for another few seconds. "Dan will be a problem. He's very by the book."

"Give me two minutes and then send him back here. I'll deal with him."

"He's a good guy. Don't shoot him."

"No one's getting shot."

Magnus started to turn away but then stopped. "Don't pistol-whip him, either."

Two minutes later, Barbier made his way back to where Nate was waiting.

"Magnus said you needed to brief me on something."

Nate nodded. "Do me a favor and grab that bag, would you?" He pointed at the seat nearest Barbier.

Barbier turned toward the chair. "What ba—"

Nate jabbed the needle into the copilot's arm and depressed the plunger. The contents of the syringe he'd taken from the storage locker took effect almost instantly. As Barbier turned back to see what had happened, he stumbled and threw out a hand in an attempt to grab the chair.

Nate caught him before he hit the ground and eased him into the empty seat. "Easy there, buddy. It's going to be fine. Think maybe you just need some sleep."

Barbier looked at him through unfocused eyes. He tried to say something, but only a short string of slurred sounds came out.

Nate eased the chair back until it was prone. Barbier tried to fight his sagging eyelids but a few seconds later he was out.

As a safety precaution, Nate secured him with prisoner restraints specifically designed to be used with the jet's seats. He then covered the man with a blanket.

When he started moving forward, he could feel the plane banking in a turn that would soon have them traveling in the opposite direction.

He knelt in the aisle when he reached Liz and Dima and told them what was going on.

"Where are we going?" Dima asked.

"Bangkok."

Dima tensed. "Bangkok? No! This is supposed to be over. You're taking me to America where I'll be safe. Bangkok isn't *safe*!"

"It's going to be fine. No one has any idea where you are, nor will they. I promised to protect you, and I will. But this is family, and I don't ignore family."

Liz glanced at Nate and silently told him she'd take care of Dima.

If he could have loved her any more than he already did, he would have in that moment. With a quick smile of thanks, he headed up to the cockpit and climbed into Barbier's seat.

Magnus looked at him suspiciously. "Where's Dan?"

"Sleeping."

"I told you not to hurt him," Magnus said.

"Relax. Chemically induced, that's all. He didn't even know it was coming. You'll have to replace one of the knockout syringes in your supply cabinet, though." Nate looked at the instrument panel and saw they were heading east-southeast back across Spain. "You have the route figured out?"

"With the fuel we've got, we could make it to maybe about seven hundred miles off the west coast of India."

"I'd rather avoid ditching in the ocean if you don't mind."

"Not my preference, either. That's why we'll be stopping at a field outside Doha to refuel. It's not US controlled, but I've used it a few times and we should be okay even if Helen issues a warning to be on the lookout for us."

His mention of Helen brought up something Nate hadn't had time to consider yet. "What if she tries to track us?"

"Way ahead of you," Magnus said. "Before I made the

turn, I disabled both the standard transponder and the one Helen's group uses to keep tabs on the plane."

That was a start, but not a perfect solution. "She can still track us by radar data."

"Not if we do a little low threshold flying every now and then."

"Won't that eat up our fuel?"

"Already calculated in."

CHAPTER
TWENTY ONE

CENTRAL WASHINGTON

THE FIXER'S PHONE rang, the number indicating the caller was one of her Spanish sources.

"You have news for me?" she asked.

"Perhaps. I'm not sure."

"Tell me."

"A private jet left an airfield about ninety kilometers northeast of Barcelona about an hour ago. It filed a flight plan for Toronto, Canada."

That's got to be the girl, she thought. Toronto was likely a false destination to explain the plane's westward path.

Her mind already working up a list of North American contacts she could use, she said, "Thank you."

"That's not all," the man said.

"Go on."

"Fifteen minutes ago, the plane executed a one-eighty course change and is now heading east. At least I think so. Four minutes ago it dropped off the radar."

"What do you mean, dropped off the radar?"

"It made a rapid descent until we could no longer pick it up."

"Are you saying it crashed?"

"The descent was more controlled, and it made no emergency call."

"Did it land somewhere?"

"Unlikely. There are no landing strips, public or private, in that area."

"Then what is likely?"

He paused. "Their last position put them near the Pyrenees. If I had to guess, they're using the mountains to shield themselves from radar so that when they show up again, no one will realize it's the same plane."

If the fixer still had any doubt the girl was on the jet, it vanished now.

CHAPTER
TWENTY TWO

BANGKOK

THE MEN CHRISTINA had sent to the airport were still en route when she retasked them to follow the van and sedan that had met the plane. It was touch-and-go for several minutes whether they would be able to locate the other cars, but thanks in part to the reduced number of vehicles on the road near Suvarnabhumi at that hour, they finally caught up to the van and the sedan containing Mee Noi. By the time the vehicles exited the Sirat Expressway and headed south on Ratchadamri Road, three more cars carrying Christina's people had joined the chase.

Over the years, Christina had accumulated a gigantic database of information on friends and foes alike. She used it now to search for known Chayan properties in the direction the cars were heading and came up with a handful of buildings southwest of Lumphini Park.

Seven minutes later, her lead car reported that the van and sedan had turned south on Chareon Krung Road, narrowing the list of possibilities down to two—an apartment building one kilometer south and a commercial building near the Shangri-La Hotel.

"Turning east on Charoen Krung 44," Kiet, her senior man, reported.

The building near the Shangri-La, then.

She passed on the information.

The phone line stayed quiet for another thirty seconds, then, "Brake lights...they've stopped.... Someone's getting out of the van...he's opening a garage door on a building on the south side. It has to be the one you gave me.... Okay, they're pulling inside."

"Both vehicles?" she asked.

After a pause, Kiet said, "No. Just the van. The sedan has stopped in front of the entrance but is still on the street. The man in the backseat is talking to one of the people who got out of the van.... Okay, the guy from the van is going into the building...the garage is closing...and...the sedan is driving off. What do you want us to do?"

"Two cars stay with the sedan. The rest of you see if you can find a quiet way into the building. I need to know if the kids are inside that van."

"Yes, ma'am."

MEE NOI'S PLAN for the diversion in Bangkok depended heavily on his little convoy being followed from the airport. Though he had not seen any evidence of a tail, the two men on motorcycles he'd assigned to follow a discreet distance behind them had easily spotted the vehicle. At first there had been only one car, but by the time they were into the city proper, three more had joined in. It had then been a simple matter of leading the followers to the mechanic's shop by the river.

Outside the shop, he confirmed his instructions to the men in the van, and then told his driver to go. Once the men at the shop had done what Mee Noi ordered, they would sneak away through a secret tunnel that led to a basement room at the Shangri-La.

As his sedan moved down the street, he contacted the motorcyclists, putting them both on the line. "Did they take the bait?"

"Yes, sir," one of them said. "Two cars have parked and the occupants have gotten out. Four people total."

"And the others?"

"Still tracking you," the second cyclist said, the sound of

his bike's engine growling around his words.

All as expected. "Report any changes immediately." He hung up and said to the driver, "The route we discussed."

"Yes, sir."

They would lead the cars tracking him across the river, where, in a way that would look completely natural, they would lose them.

AFTER FINDING A way onto the roof of a place near the end of the street, Kiet led his team from building to building until they arrived on the one the van had driven into.

A metal hatch in the back corner opened onto a narrow staircase. Kiet went first, his pistol out and ready, the others only steps behind. When they were sure no one was on the top floor, they descended to the next and repeated the process.

While the building was tall enough to have four floors, it turned out the ground level—a mechanic's shop, by the look of it—was two stories high. The men learned this when they opened the door to the final set of stairs and found it ran against the wall to the floor seven meters below.

Kiet motioned for the others to stay back. He then lay on the ground and very slowly lowered his head until it was almost resting on the first step. He scanned the shop. The van was parked in the middle of the room. He had a good view of the driver's side, and could just see the top edges of open double cargo doors on the other side, but saw no one.

Did the van's occupants know Kiet and his men were here? Were they waiting inside the van to spring a trap? It was either that or they'd left, but as the team had made its way across the roofs, it had monitored the streets below and hadn't seen anyone sneaking away. After the operatives entered the building, they'd spent no more than thirty seconds on each floor, and Kiet was confident they would have heard something if the others had departed within that narrow time frame.

He sat up, whispered what he'd found to the others, and then said, "We'll hold here for another five minutes. See if they show themselves."

He lay back down and focused on the van again, but each minute passed without a sound. There wasn't even a creak from the van indicating someone shifting position inside.

When the waiting period had elapsed, he said, "Stay here. If I get into trouble, don't come after me. Get out through the roof and call *khun* Christina for further instructions."

He crept down the stairs, his gun out and ready. Upon reaching the bottom, he checked under the van. No feet standing on the other side. He eased over to the vehicle, moved around the back, and peeked down the passenger side. He now had a narrow angle inside through the open doors, but still saw no one.

He inched over to the doors and swung into the opening, his pistol sweeping back and forth.

The van was unoccupied.

Where the hell are they?

He checked the small bathroom—the only other room on the entire floor—and then moved over to the back door. No way they left that way. The door was padlocked on the inside. So they must have gone out the rolling door, but why hadn't he and his men heard it open?

"Come down!" he yelled up.

While his team descended the stairs, he searched inside the van and found a baby's sock. He tucked it in his pocket.

"Kiet," one of his men called.

He hopped out of the van and went over to the rubbish bin the guy was standing next to.

The man pointed inside. "Look."

Sitting on top of the trash was a used disposable diaper.

He pulled out his phone.

ABOVE THE GULF OF THAILAND

QUINN, ORLANDO, AND Daeng were more than halfway to Bangkok when Christina called again.

"I have news. Not long after the jet took off, it went dark."

"So we don't know if they're actually going to Chiang Mai?" Quinn said.

"Correct."

"Where was it heading before its signal was lost?"

"North-northwest."

"In the right direction."

"Yes, but given Chayan's and Mee Noi's nature, I suspect it was a ruse."

"Then where would they be going?"

"I have people working on possibilities, but at the moment I don't know."

No one said anything.

Finally, Quinn leaned forward. "What about the van?"

"My people followed it from the airport to an auto shop. When they got inside the building, they found that the van had been abandoned. They also discovered a white baby's sock and a recently used diaper."

"Diaper?" Orlando said. "What brand?"

"I don't have that information. But I'd be willing to bet it was one your daughter was wearing."

"What do you think the chances are it was a plant?" Quinn asked.

"Same as with the plane. Chayan and Mee Noi are well schooled at manipulating information."

"What's your gut say?"

He heard her take a breath, then, "That Chayan still has them on the plane."

That jibed with what Quinn was thinking.

Unfortunately, they didn't know where that plane was headed, so they could either circle around and wait for more info to come to light, or they could land and at least do something.

"We're coming to you," he said. "Can you send someone to pick us up?"

"Consider it done."

BANGKOK

A SEDAN AND driver were waiting for them at the private aircraft debarkation area when the jet arrived.

Daeng climbed into the front passenger seat while Quinn and Orlando got in back.

As they made their way out of the airport, Orlando asked the driver, "Where are you taking us?"

"*Khun* Christina tell me bring you to home."

"No," Orlando said. "We want to see the van first."

The driver looked confused until Daeng explained in Thai. The man shook his head and said something.

Orlando leaned forward. "Tell him to take us to the van, or drop us off in front of the terminal and we'll take a taxi."

Daeng spoke to the man again, and after the driver made a call to Christina, Daeng turned around and said, "The van it is."

Traffic was light as they made their way into the city and down near the Shangri-La Hotel. They parked around the corner from the building where the van was, and were met by a man named Kiet.

"Can show you where the building is, but only way in through roof."

"Why?" Quinn asked. "Did they come back?"

"No. I have a man watching room from above. No one returned yet."

"Then they're not going to. They probably know you've been there already. Did you sweep the place for cameras?"

"I...uh...no."

Quinn took a breath. "Show us the building."

Kiet led them halfway down the *soi* and pointed at a building with a closed roll-up door. "They drive van inside and shut door behind them."

"How did they leave?" Daeng asked.

Kiet looked uncomfortable. "Don't know."

"Let's go take a look," Quinn said, heading straight for the door. Orlando and Daeng fell in behind him.

"Wait," Kiet said, following them. "Cannot go that way.

Might get caught."

"I already told you," Quinn said without stopping. "They know you've been there."

He didn't have any proof yet but it was a classic trap situation, the purpose of this one: to plant what he was sure was a false trail.

The first piece of supportive evidence came a moment later when he grabbed the metal door and shoved upward. The door rolled open without a struggle, the metal squealing and rattling all the way up. Not locked. Chayan's men wanted this place to be found.

Quinn glanced at Kiet.

Kiet looked embarrassed. "I not check before. Sorry."

Orlando hurried inside to the van.

"Where's the diaper?" she asked.

"It wasn't in van," Kiet told her. "We found in a bin. Is still there if you want to see it."

"What about the sock?"

Kiet pulled it from his pocket. "I found near where you standing."

Orlando snatched it from him. "It's hers. Were there any fingerprints? Maybe footprints, too? Garrett wasn't wearing any shoes. If they were here, there would be prints."

"Prints? No, I don't know how to do that."

Orlando looked at Quinn. "Can you see if there's any powder? As fine a grit as possible."

Quinn, Daeng, and Kiet searched the shop. The interior of the van was a scuffed-up creamy white so darker powder would be best. The closest thing any of them found, however, was a container of white talcum powder. Quinn did discover an air compressor that would help with the job.

As Orlando got to work, Quinn motioned Daeng over to the front of the van and said in a low voice, "Did you see them?"

A nod. "I counted five."

"That's what I got, too."

Five small wireless cameras were scattered around the room, all high enough to take in an overview of the whole space.

"Do you want me to look for the hub?" Daeng asked.

Somewhere, probably within a hundred-foot radius, would be a router that was collecting the camera feeds and sending them somewhere else.

"It would be a waste of time," Quinn said. "They already know we're here. No sense in letting them know we're aware of that."

Inside the van, Orlando had finished sprinkling the powder across the floor and had turned on the compressor at its lowest setting.

The loud motor echoed through the space, forcing Quinn to lean toward Daeng when he said, "What I'm really curious about is how the people from the van got out of here."

The roll-up door was too loud not to have been heard by Kiet and his people, even if they were on the third floor. The padlock on the inside of the back door meant that wasn't an option, either. There must be a third exit.

They split up, both men making it look like they were checking out the room in general, with no particular goal in mind, so that whoever was watching the feeds wouldn't know what they were doing.

Their charade turned out to be unnecessary. Quinn found the secret entrance in the bathroom—where there were no cameras—behind a cabinet that swung out from the wall on noiseless hinges. Behind it was a narrow staircase leading down to a dark tunnel that appeared to run almost due west from the building.

While it was tempting to see where it led, he knew it wouldn't produce any useful information. The discovery did, however, put a ribbon on the fact this had been a setup from the very beginning. So he wasn't surprised in the slightest when, a few minutes later, Orlando announced she'd found no children's prints—from fingers or feet—in the van.

CHAPTER
TWENTY THREE

"TIME TO WAKE up, sir."

A hand gently rocked Mee Noi's shoulder.

"Sir? It's 6:15. Would you like me to come back later?"

"No," Mee Noi groaned. "I'm getting up."

He took another moment before opening his eyes. In the semidarkness of his room, he could see Lek, his maid, standing by the bed expectantly.

"I don't need you this morning," he said as he threw back the sheets and swung his legs off the bed. Sometimes it was nice to have her wake him in other ways, but there was no time for that today.

She gave him a deep *wai*, said, "Your coffee is on the dresser," and left.

He couldn't tell for sure, but she seemed happier as she walked out the door.

Perhaps a little discipline was in order. Or maybe it was time for someone new. He could always do both.

But that would have to wait until after the monk was dealt with.

The good news was that Mee Noi hadn't been woken earlier, which meant everything was going as planned. After showering and dressing, he headed into his study and shut the door so Lek would know not to disturb him.

He received a report on what had happened at the mechanic's shop after the van was left behind. Of the two incursions into the facility, the second was the most interesting. The monk had been there, as had the parents of Chayan's guests. Mee Noi had his man send him links of the pertinent camera feeds and time frames, and then watched the footage himself. He would have really liked to know what the woman was doing in the van with an air compressor, but none of the cameras had an angle through the open doors. It was an oversight someone would hear about.

Nevertheless, the man and the woman were becoming more intriguing by the hour. He called Virote to find out if he'd tracked down their identities yet.

"Nothing at this point," Virote said.

"Nothing? At all? That sounds to me like you haven't started checking yet."

"That's not what I mean, *khun* Mee Noi," the man said quickly. "I have several people working on it. We've been able to figure out what names they arrived under when they came from the States, but just like the ones they used when flying to Samui, they're dead ends."

"I want to know who these people are, and I want to know *today*. Tell me you understand."

"Yes, sir. We'll do what we can."

"I didn't say do what you can. I said *find out*."

He slammed the phone down. Virote had been one of Chayan's brother's hires. Clearly he was not of the caliber they would want to retain going forward.

Mee Noi was beginning to wonder if the organizational housecleaning was ever going to end.

He allowed himself a moment to calm down, and then called Pravat, who had, for lack of a better choice, been temporarily promoted with his partner Narong to Chayan's special assistants.

"Hello?" Pravat answered.

"Were you asleep?" Mee Noi said. Pravat's voice had sounded that way.

"No, I just...you're the first person I've talked to."

Mee Noi was pretty sure that was a lie, but he decided to ignore it. "And Chayan?"

"He is sleeping. I mean, as far as I know. We only got in

here a few hours ago."

"And the children?"

"Sound asleep when I checked a few minutes ago. Chayan had me put something in their drinks before we landed. Looks to me like they won't be moving around for hours."

"Where are you keeping them?"

"The guest room at the near end of the second-floor hall. Chayan had us block the window so the boy won't be able to signal one of the nearby buildings.

Mee Noi closed his eyes and recalled the layout of Hasam's Jakarta apartment. The room was a good choice.

"What about door locks? It has one, doesn't it?"

"No lock, but I don't think—"

"Exactly. Don't think. Get a lock on that door right away."

"Yes, sir. When Narong gets up, I'll send him out to get a padlock and a latch."

"Get him up *now*."

"Yes, sir."

"Do you have food for the prisoners?"

"Uh, I saw some stuff in the...hold on."

Before Mee Noi could tell him he would *not* hold on, he heard movement and then Chayan's voice over the line. "Report."

Mee Noi brought his boss up to speed.

"They arrived sooner than I would have expected," Chayan said.

They knew the monk would use his Bangkok resources to trace the jet there and follow the van, but they had assumed he would fly in on the first commercial flight that morning. The fact he was able to arrange other transportation was unanticipated but not surprising.

"Do you want to stay on the current timeline?" Mee Noi asked. "Or would you like to move things up?"

"We were only waiting for him, so I see no reason to delay. Let's accelerate."

"I'll get right on it."

Once the call was finished, Mee Noi opened the bag containing a disposable phone. He consulted his computer for the phone number he needed, and punched it into the mobile.

IN THE BEDROOM of the guesthouse on Koh Samui, Daeng's phone rang and rang and rang.

"EACH ONE OF these is a place we think he could have taken your children," Christina said, a hand on the pile of paper in front of her—some single sheets, some multiple pages stapled together.

It was just after nine a.m. and they were sitting around her dining room table. While Quinn, Orlando, and Daeng had tried to get a few hours' sleep—a mostly wasted effort—Christina and her people had continued working on locating Garrett and Claire.

"How many are there?" Quinn asked.

"Thirty-seven."

"Thirty-seven? No way of narrowing that down?"

"That's up to you." She looked through the papers until she came to a yellow Post-it, and then moved all those that had been above the marker into a separate stack. "These are all located here in Bangkok. Given that we're assuming the kids didn't get off the plane, and we're sure that the aircraft hasn't landed anywhere near the city since it took off again, we can probably ignore these. But like I said, the decision is yours."

Her logic was sound, but Quinn was uncomfortable ignoring even the remote possibility Garrett and Claire were there in the city. "Can you devote most of your resources toward the other places, but still have someone checking on the Bangkok locations?"

"Is that what you want?"

Quinn looked at Orlando.

"Yes," she said. "That makes sense."

Christina picked up the Bangkok pile and slid the second stack into the center of the table. "These are the other places. I was thinking it would help if you all took a look at what we have on them and see if anything jumped out at you." She stood up. "I'll be back soon."

As Christina started toward the door, Orlando said, "Why don't you leave those with us, too." She pointed at the papers for the Bangkok locations Christina was carrying away.

"Of course." Christina set the papers next to the others and left.

Quinn, Orlando, and Daeng each pulled a sheet off the stack. It took over an hour to finish the non-Bangkok group. With the exception of a few minor points, they spotted nothing of real interest. They started in on the Bangkok set.

It was almost eleven a.m. when Quinn set the last paper down. "If there's something here, I don't see it."

Orlando was taking longer to go through each set, and still had several left to check. "I'm not ready to give up yet."

"I'm not saying I'm giving up. I'm just saying what we're doing right now is busy work and not helping."

"I'm not so sure," Daeng said.

Quinn and Orlando turned to him.

"This might be nothing, but..." Daeng set a few sheets side by side, turning them so Quinn and Orlando could see them. "Here, here, and here." He tapped at the same spot on each of the sheets. "The acquisition date. These all came into Chayan's possession in the last month."

"According to Christina, he's shoring up his organization," Quinn said, not sure what Daeng's point was. "So it makes sense he's taking back what he can."

"You're right, but it got me thinking. Christina's ability to obtain information may be good, but it seems to me, in the current fluid situation, that there are some places her people have not yet found out about. If I were Chayan, I would take the children somewhere I controlled but was unlikely to be known by anyone else."

Orlando frowned. "So what you're saying is basically what Quinn said. We're wasting our time with this stuff."

"That's not exactly what I'm saying."

"Then what?"

Daeng put a hand on one of the papers he'd singled out. "He took possession of these places from someone else. I was thinking these same people would have likely controlled other locations Christina's people might know about. Maybe Chayan has taken those back, but they haven't been moved to his column yet."

Orlando nodded. "Yeah. That's not a bad thought at all."

"Let's tell Christina," Quinn said.

NARONG RETURNED FROM his errand and showed Pravat what he'd purchased.

"I told you to get a latch and a padlock," Pravat said. "Not another doorknob."

"This will be easier. We don't have to drill anything."

That was actually a good point.

"Fine," Pravat said, still acting displeased. "If something goes wrong, you will be the one to explain it to Chayan and Mee Noi.

"You worry too much."

Pravat glowered at him. "Just put the damn thing on the door.

GARRETT WOKE TO the rattle of metal.

He tried to turn toward the noise, but his body didn't cooperate right away.

His head felt weird. Like it was full of cotton, and every command he sent to his muscles had to fight through the fibers to arrive at its destination. Even his eyelids refused to part at first, and when they finally did, he found the room he was in to be dim, the only light coming from somewhere off to the side.

Beside him was a second bed, and on it lay Claire, sound asleep. At least someone had been smart enough to surround her with pillows to keep her from rolling off.

Garrett could now see the source of the light. It was coming through an open door past the foot of Claire's bed. But it took him a moment to figure out the two shadows squatting beside it were men, and another few seconds to realize he'd seen them before. One was Creep, and the other was the guy who'd been driving the van.

They were doing something to the doorknob. As Garrett watched, they pulled the whole thing apart and set it on the ground. They then picked up what looked like an identical knob and mounted it in the hole. They seemed to struggle with it at first, but soon Driver Guy was screwing it into place. When they were through, they played with it for a moment, and then stood up.

Garrett closed his eyes again, not wanting them to know he was awake. He was sure they would come over and check on him, but they seemed to have no interest in him or Claire. As they closed the door, one of the hinges let out a squeak. This was followed by the scratch of the key going into the lock on the other side of the door, and a click.

Worried that one of the men might have stayed in the room, he let the silence sit for several seconds before he reopened his eyes. With the door closed, the room was almost black, but his vision soon adjusted enough for him to tell he and his sister were alone.

He made the mistake of sitting up too quickly, as everything tilted one way and then the other. Grabbing on to the mattress, he squeezed his eyes shut until the world stabilized again. He then carefully pushed himself to his feet, stepped over to his sister's bed, and leaned in close.

Her breathing sounded like it always did when she slept, and her forehead was cool to the touch. That was a relief.

Moving slowly, he walked over to the door. He felt around until he found a light switch and gave it a try. The burst of light that filled the room forced him to jam his eyes closed, and he blindly tried to shut it off again but couldn't find the switch. Cracking his eyelids open, he saw Claire hadn't moved at all, so he left the light on.

He could now see why the room had been so dark. A large sheet of wood had been nailed to the wall, right where a window would be. Even from across the room, he could tell he wouldn't be able to pry it loose with just his hands.

He turned his attention to the doorknob, wondering why

they changed it. The fog in his head kept him from realizing the answer for several seconds. But then he saw the slot.

A keyhole.

He grabbed the knob and gave it a tentative turn. Sure enough, it was locked.

Panic rose in his chest again.

Don't, his mother's voice said. *Keep calm or you and your sister will never get free.*

Right, he thought. *Calm.*

Easier said than done, but after a few deep breaths, he was at least able to keep his panic from escalating.

Learn your surroundings. Assess the situation. Know your options.

He stood up and made a slow scan of the room. Besides the beds, there was a dresser, a closet, and another doorway. He walked over to the latter and peeked inside. A bathroom, the only thing on the sink a bar of soap. He checked the drawers, but all were empty.

Back in the room he did the same with the dresser, and then made a quick search of the closet, but also found nothing in them.

No situation is ever hopeless.

He wasn't sure if that was true or not, but knew his mother was really saying never give up. As he took another look around the room, his gaze stopped on the new doorknob.

Obviously the kidnappers wanted to keep him and Claire locked inside. Which meant...the previous knob *didn't* lock.

The gears spun in his mind.

If they hadn't changed the knobs, then...

Someone would have needed to keep an eye on the door once we woke up.

So putting on a lock meant there's no need for a constant guard.

He stepped back over to the knob and leaned down for a closer look. He had never seen this brand before, but a lock was a lock, right? He wasn't as good on door locks as he was on padlocks yet, but he could try to master it now.

Except—

His shoulders drooped. He couldn't undo the lock with only his fingers, and he had seen nothing in the room he could use for picks. He searched again to be sure, and came up empty.

You can't give up. You'll find a way. You have to.

QUINN AND ORLANDO followed the woman sent to escort them down to Christina's ground-floor office. Daeng was already there, as were two of Christina's advisors they'd met earlier.

Quinn was thinking maybe this had something to do with Daeng's idea concerning the properties, but as they entered, he saw that everyone's attention was on two video monitors on a table in front of the desk.

"What's going on?" Orlando asked.

Daeng waved them over.

At first glance, Quinn thought the camera feeds were of different buildings, but then he realized they were of the same place, just from different sides. It was a six-story structure that looked very well kept.

"We may have located Mee Noi," Daeng whispered.

"Where?" Quinn asked.

"A hotel near National Stadium."

"That's a hotel?" Orlando asked, motioning at the monitor.

"A discreet temporary residence," Christina said. "That's how they describe themselves, anyway. It's not a place you'd find on any website. You have to know about it. The rooms are like upscale apartments and run five grand US or more a night." She paused. "Earlier this morning, I put the word out to...people my group is associated with to keep an eye out for Mee Noi. A shop owner we've helped on occasion told us he'd seen Mee Noi going in and out of the building over the last few weeks."

"Did he see him today?" Orlando asked.

"No, but the sedan Mee Noi took from the airport is parked a few blocks away."

Quinn looked at the screens again. Nothing seemed to be

happening. "So what's the play here?"

"I have a team on the way there right now. At the moment we're just observing."

"What happens when they get there?"

"Until we know for sure he's there, nothing."

"So we're just going to stand around?" Orlando said. "Uh-uh. No way. Garrett and Claire might be in there."

"I think the likelihood of that is very low."

"But it's not zero," Orlando argued.

Christina nodded in tepid agreement.

After she returned her attention to the monitor, Orlando slipped her hand into Quinn's and squeezed. He didn't need to look at her to know what she was thinking, because it was exactly what he'd been thinking, too.

"We'll go back upstairs and continue working our contacts," Quinn said to Christina. "Let us know if something changes."

"Of course," she said.

"Daeng, if you're not too tied up here, we could probably use your help."

Daeng looked at Quinn, confused, but Quinn signaled him to say yes and not question anything.

"Sure," Daeng said. "I'm just standing around here."

The three of them left the office and went up to the guest room Quinn and Orlando had been using. When the door was closed, Daeng said, "What's going on?"

Quinn retrieved the guns they'd taken from the villa intruders. "We could use some more ammunition. Do you know where she keeps it?"

Daeng stared at him. "You're going after him."

"Damn right, we are," Orlando said, taking one of the guns from Quinn.

Quinn held another out to Daeng. "Like I said, we could use your help."

Daeng hesitated before taking the gun. "There's a storeroom in the basement. I can get us some spare mags."

"What else does Christina keep down there?" Orlando asked.

"The usual, I assume."

"Perhaps we should go with you," Quinn said.

CHAPTER
TWENTY FOUR

A MESSAGE HAD been waiting in Doha when the jet touched down to refuel. It was not meant for Nate or even Magnus, but for the manager of the facility.

The alert was from Helen Cho's organization, and had been sent to dozens of private airfields, telling them to be on the lookout for a missing and presumed hijacked plane. The instructions stated that if those aboard requested to refuel, they should be cleared for landing but then held until Helen's people arrived.

The problem was that the Doha facility manager felt no loyalty to Helen or her organization, and once he realized Magnus was not being held against his will, he allowed them to land and refuel unmolested. He thought the message funny, though, and gave them a copy before they left.

Nate knew it would take some fancy talking to make things right with Helen again after this. Though she might be sympathetic to Quinn, those feelings would not excuse Nate's appropriation of one of her planes and his kidnapping of the asset he was supposed to deliver. But dealing with her would have to wait.

"You wanted a two-hour warning until landing," Magnus said. "Here it is."

"Thanks. How are you feeling?"

With his copilot still unconscious, Magnus had had to do

all the flying. "Like I could sleep for a whole day."

"If you can hold off until we get there, that would be great."

"Do what I can. But I have a feeling even then I'm not going to be able to lie down for a while, thank you very much."

Nate's plan was for Magnus to call Helen thirty minutes after Nate and Liz left, using the story that Helen herself was already spreading—that Nate had hijacked the flight. Undoubtedly she'd send one of her local contacts there in a hurry, and Magnus would be stuck answering questions for the next several hours. Nate had thought it best for the pilot to plead ignorance of the reason for the change of destination. To do otherwise might make him look sympathetic to what Nate had done. Placing all the blame elsewhere should keep Magnus employed.

As for Dima, Nate still wasn't sure what to do about her. Initially, he had thought about leaving her with Magnus, but that's where the pilot drew the line.

"I'm responsible for transporting her, not protecting her," he had said.

He was right, of course. Protection was Nate's job, but taking her with him could expose her to more danger. Maybe Quinn could arrange for someone to watch her until she could be handed off to Helen's people.

One way or the other, he would have to figure it out before they arrived at their destination.

"I appreciate all you've done," he told Magnus.

"Just find those kids."

DOHA, QATAR

HELEN'S WASN'T THE only message received at the Doha airfield about the rogue jet. A mechanic whose job it was to service the planes had also received a directive concerning the aircraft.

If the plane were to land at the field, he was instructed to report back on the occupants and the plane's next destination.

If luck would have it that he was needed for some work on the aircraft, he was to do whatever necessary to make sure the plane couldn't leave.

Unfortunately, the jet stayed only long enough to refuel, and the closest the mechanic came to it was driving by in an airfield vehicle. He had seen two men outside and taken photos of them, albeit from a distance. As for their next destination, no flight plan had been filed, but a chat with his friend in the control center revealed the plane had headed east-southeast.

The mechanic passed the information on to his contact, who passed it on to the house in Pakistan, who passed it on to the fixer.

She'd arrived in Tel Aviv, Israel, about thirty minutes earlier. After discovering the others were on a jet heading east out of Spain, Israel was as far as she'd dared go until she had more information. Now that she did, she used it to create a list of the plane's next potential destinations, and then boarded a flight to Singapore, hoping it would at least put her in the vicinity of where the girl would be.

CHAPTER
TWENTY FIVE

BANGKOK

MEE NOI CALLED Chayan, knowing he could put it off no longer.

"Has the meeting been arranged?" his boss asked.

Mee Noi shifted in his chair. "Not yet."

"Explain."

"He's not answering."

"Did you leave a message?"

"Of course. More than one."

"But he hasn't called back?"

"No."

"I assume your messages made him aware of the time factor."

"They did indeed." The midnight deadline they had set for "freeing" the children was less than twelve hours away.

After a few silent seconds, Chayan said, "You know I want him here to watch."

"And he will be. I will find him. And I will get him there."

BANGKOK'S NOTORIOUS DAYTIME traffic was in full swing, so Quinn, Orlando, and Daeng grabbed separate motorcycle taxis. These were the fastest way to get across the city to where Mee Noi might be.

Concerned that if Christina caught on to what they were

doing she would try to stop them, they set about first locating the team she'd sent to be on standby. The men turned out to be a block away from the target building, sitting in a sedan and watching on their phones what Quinn assumed were the camera feeds. Leaving them undisturbed, the trio went to deal with the cameras themselves.

Among the things they'd taken from Christina's armory were two signal disrupters. Quinn and Orlando placed one within twenty feet of the camera covering the back of the building, while Daeng did the same with the camera in front. Now all they had to do was press the activate button on the two remotes and the cameras would go dark.

After Daeng rejoined Quinn and Orlando, they went up to the roof of a building down the alley from the rear of the hotel. Quinn studied the target building through the binoculars they'd procured. It had a walled-in area in the back that boasted a well-appointed swimming pool and deck area with lounges spread around, most empty.

He studied each person in the area. "Looks like just civilians, no security." He handed the glasses to Daeng. "Correct me if I'm wrong, but from what you and Christina have said, Mee Noi strikes me as someone who would have people guarding him."

Daeng studied the building. "He would, but he would also want to keep a low profile." He lowered the glasses. "I suspect that at the very least he has men in the lobby."

Orlando grabbed the binoculars and took a look. "We can hop that wall at the near corner. There's a lot of foliage on the other side. I don't think anyone will see us. The people at the pool all look like guests to me. There's a hotel employee near the building...no, wait, two staff members. A waitress and someone in charge of, I don't know, towels probably." She lowered the glasses. "We should be able to get almost all the way to the building without drawing attention."

"Yeah, but when those staff members see us, they'll raise an alarm," Quinn said.

"Leave them to me," she said.

"It might be safer if we found a way in through the roof."

"And in the amount of time it would take us to do that, we would already have Mee Noi and be out of there if we do it my way."

Quinn studied the building for a moment longer, but knew hers was the best option they had. He nodded and they headed down. Once they were back in the alley, he led them as close as possible to the wall surrounding the back of the hotel without stepping into view of Christina's camera.

"Everyone ready?" he asked, a remote in each hand.

"Just kill the cameras already," Orlando said.

Quinn pressed the buttons. "Go."

They ran to the corner of the hotel's white plaster wall, pulled themselves over, and dropped into the back. Keeping between the brush and the wall, they moved past the pool deck and stopped where the landscaping began to thin out near the building. Along the back wall, a set of double glass doors served as the hotel's entrance.

The guy at the towel station was halfway between the door and the deck. The waitress, however, was nowhere in sight.

"You two wait here," Orlando whispered. "When I distract him, sneak inside and I'll be there a few seconds later."

"How exactly are you planning on doing that?" Quinn asked.

"Don't worry about it. I'll figure it out."

"You can't just—"

"Wait," Daeng said. "Look." He pointed down the side of the building ahead of them, where the waitress had exited a door. "How about we use that?"

If they timed their movement with when the waitress was busy with one of the guests and the towel guy was looking the other way, they could scoot down the wall and get to the door unseen.

"Yeah, that'll work," Quinn said.

Ninety seconds later, they were inside a service hallway. They passed several closed doors and another corridor that smelled like it led to the kitchen, before Daeng nodded at a doorway near the end of the hall that had a stairs symbol above it.

Though they didn't know which floor Mee Noi was on, by unspoken agreement they went all the way to the top. With guys like Mee Noi, it was the logical move.

At the uppermost landing, they listened at the door.

A noise, muffled and distant. A radio, Quinn guessed. Or a TV.

A miniature snake camera they could slip under the door would have been very helpful right then. But that hadn't been one of the things they'd snagged from Christina, so they would have to do this the old-fashioned way.

Quinn knelt low beside the door and activated the front-facing camera on his phone. On his signal, Daeng opened the door just enough for Quinn to slip the top half inch of his phone out.

A low-angle view of the hallway appeared on the screen. The space was tastefully decorated with blue carpet and cream-colored walls. Sconces holding fresh flowers hung at various points along the hall, and in the very middle was the gold-framed entrance to an elevator. The only things he could see that weren't likely hotel issue were the two men standing in front of a door far down on the left.

Quinn pulled the phone back and whispered, "Suggestions?"

"The elevator's closer to them," Orlando said. "We go down one floor then take it up."

"And then what? We can't just take them out. They may not even work for Mee Noi."

"Of course we can. Who else would they be with?"

"I'm guessing a lot of people who stay here would be the type to employ private security."

She fell silent. Quinn could see she didn't want to admit he might be right.

"We should check the other floors first," Daeng suggested. "If there are no other guards around, then it'll be a lot likelier these guys are working for Mee Noi."

"True, but it still won't be proof," Quinn said.

"We could just ask them," Orlando said.

Quinn frowned at her. "The right move is to do what Daeng suggests and then reassess."

Orlando squeezed her lips together, but when they headed down, she followed.

The corridor of the floor below was empty, as was the one after that.

When Quinn reached the landing for the next one, he glanced back at the others but saw only Daeng. "Where's Orlando?"

Daeng looked around. "She was right behind me."

"Son of a bitch," Quinn said, heading back up.

ORLANDO UNDERSTOOD QUINN'S caution, but every second they weren't questioning Mee Noi was another second the kids remained in danger.

It became clear after finding no one standing guard on the next two floors down that Mee Noi was indeed ensconced at the very top. Unfortunately, she knew it would be impossible to talk Quinn and Daeng out of checking the rest of the building.

As the other two descended toward the next floor, Orlando slipped into the hallway they'd just checked, moved down to the elevator, and pushed the call button.

Since the building wasn't that tall, the car arrived quickly. She pushed the button for the top floor. The short ride ended with a *bong* and the parting of the doors. After securing her gun at the small of her back and putting on a disarming smile, she stepped into the hallway and turned toward the guarded room.

Though she knew a bit of Thai, she couldn't pass herself off as a native. She could, however, mimic a pretty killer Hong Kong accent.

"You can't come down here," one of the men said in Thai.

She kept walking and smiling as if she didn't understand him.

While his partner remained at the door, the first guard

208

started toward her. "Don't come any farther!"

"I'm sorry. I don't understand," she said, all sweet and innocent. "Do either of you speak English?"

Proving he spoke at least one word, the guard said, "Stop."

"Oh, I'm sorry." She took another step before doing as he asked, leaving less than five feet between them. "I must be in the wrong place. I'm looking for—"

"There," he ordered as he pulled a gun from under his jacket and motioned at the wall. "Hands on wall."

"Now, hold on," she said. "Who the hell do you think you are? I'm here to see Mee Noi. Is this the right place or not?"

The flash of surprise that crossed the man's face confirmed her suspicion.

He nodded at the wall. "I tell you already. Now do."

Putting her hands on her hips—her gun hand a little farther around back than the other—she said, "Absolutely not! No one touches me unless I want them to." She made as if preparing to turn away. "Tell your boss the next time he wants me to fly four hours to see him, I expect better treatment. I'm going back to my hotel. If he wants me, he can try me there, and if I'm in a good mood, I might answer."

In a deft sleight of hand, she plucked her gun from its hiding place and slipped it around front as she turned away.

"Wait," the man said. "Mee Noi want you here?"

Twisting around only enough to look at the guard, she said, "Of course he did. Do you think I came because I had nothing better to do?"

"Please. A moment."

The guard retreated to the door. As he talked in a low voice to his partner, Orlando turned to face them again, once more keeping her weapon out of sight. She was thinking things were going pretty well when the second man pulled a radio out of his pocket and started raising it to his mouth.

Crap.

She whipped her gun around and pointed it at the guards. "Don't move," she said, still in English but dropping the accent. "I will shoot if you do."

Both men froze.

"Guns and radio on the ground," she said.

The one who'd been talking to her let his weapon fall on the carpet. The other one did the same, but instead of dropping the radio, he pressed the mic button and shouted a word in Thai she didn't know.

With a pull of her trigger, a bullet flew down the hall and smashed through both the radio and the man's hand. The impact spun the guard into the wall as he yelled out in pain. He then doubled over, cradling his injured palm in his other hand.

"Kick the guns over here," she said to the other one.

He shuffled both pistols across the floor. Before she had a chance to pick them up, she heard a door behind her burst open.

QUINN RACED UP the stairs with Daeng on his heels. When they reached the top landing, it took all of his will not to rush through the door. Though the chances were slim, it was possible Orlando hadn't revealed herself to the guards yet. And if she was out there, his and Daeng's sudden appearance could get her hurt or killed.

He listened at the door. A man speaking in halting English, and Orlando using her Hong Kong accent. He couldn't make out all the words, but the conversation didn't sound overly friendly. Still, it wasn't until he heard the spit of a suppressor that he yanked the door open and he and Daeng rushed into the hall.

Orlando swung around, gun aimed at them. As soon as she realized it was them, she whipped back to the two guards. One was hunched over, clutching a blood-soaked hand.

"What the hell?" Quinn said. "What were you thinking?"

"Mee Noi's in there." She waved at the door the two men had been guarding. "I told you all we had to do was ask."

Quinn looked at the injured guard. "I'd say you did more than asking."

"He tried to send a message over the radio."

"Tried or did?"

She started toward the door. "What does it matter? I'm going in. Are you with me?"

"We can't just rush in. He might not be alone."

"You're right." She shoved the muzzle of her gun under the chin of the uninjured guard. "Is your boss alone?"

The man looked scared and confused.

"Daeng?" Orlando said.

Daeng translated her question and then the man's answer. "There's a maid. That's it."

"A maid maid? Or a bodyguard in disguise?"

Daeng talked to the man again. "Just a maid."

"And the children?"

Daeng asked.

The man looked confused again as he answered.

"They're not here," Daeng said. "He doesn't know anything about them."

Orlando closed her eyes and rubbed her forehead for a second, and then took a deep breath and looked at Quinn. "Mee Noi's in there, okay? And he's basically alone. So can we get him now?"

Quinn tried the door but it was locked. "Key card?"

When Daeng asked, the injured one nodded toward his waist. Daeng said something to the other guy, who retrieved a card from his colleague's pocket and passed it to Quinn.

To Daeng, Quinn said, "Tell our new friends that if they even *breathe* louder than normal, it's the last sound they will ever make."

When he was sure the guards understood the threat, he unlocked the door and quietly opened it. Off to the right in what appeared to be a kitchen area, he heard someone moving around.

He motioned for the others to stay where they were, and then inched over and peeked around the counter. A woman who appeared to be no more than twenty was looking for something in the refrigerator. She didn't notice Quinn until she shut the door. The finger he was holding against his lips and the gun he was flashing in his other hand were enough to keep her from yelling in surprise.

He motioned her over and pointed at the wall near the front door, indicating she was to sit. He had the others bring the guards in and have them take a seat with the girl.

Daeng knelt down next to the maid and had a quick conversation. Upon rejoining Quinn and Orlando, he whispered, "He's in the office. Last room on the right."

"Not sure if this guy speaks English or not, so Daeng has to go," Quinn said to Orlando, and then nodded toward the guards and the maid. "That means one of us needs to stay and watch them." He pulled out a ten-baht coin. "Heads or tails?"

"Just…go, dammit. I'll stay. But you had better bring him back here before talking to him."

MEE NOI COULDN'T understand what was keeping the monk from answering his calls. Could it be that the man actually didn't care about the children? It seemed implausible, but here it was, hours after Mee Noi had started leaving messages and not a peep in response.

Since his last message a few hours earlier, he had spent the time querying sources for any information on the monk's whereabouts.

He was in the middle of a phone call with another contact when he heard a voice over the radio. Whatever was said was short, and since it wasn't repeated, he assumed it wasn't important and continued with his conversation. In the end, though, the source proved as useless as all the others he'd talked to.

After hanging up, he checked his list and punched in the next number. Before he hit SEND, however, the door swung open and none other than the object of his search strode in.

CHAPTER
TWENTY SIX

JAKARTA

THE NEXT TIME the key slipped into the doorknob, Garrett was at Claire's bed, changing her diaper, using one from the package that had been brought aboard when the plane made its first stop.

The door opened with the same short squeak of the hinge he'd heard before, and then Creep stepped into the threshold. "Good, you up. Come now. Time for eating."

Garrett felt a tingle across the back of his neck. He would be leaving the room. Maybe there'd be an opportunity to get away. A plan started to formulate. He'd eat a little and then ask to use a bathroom. He'd have to come up with a reason to bring Claire with him, but he'd think of something. Once they were alone, they could escape out a window like they had at the villa. Not wanting to tip off Creep about his plans, he kept his expression neutral and took his time putting the new diaper on his sister.

Claire whined as he picked her up. She'd been fussy since she woke, but he was convinced it had nothing to do with any of the normal things that would upset a baby.

Though he hadn't realized it at first, he now believed he and his sister had been drugged, and her discomfort was due to the lingering effects. His own foggy head had taken nearly an hour to clear. Even now, he felt sluggish.

"Okay," he said to Creep. "I'm ready."

Creep wasn't alone. Driver Guy was waiting in the hall.

Garrett's dream of a quick escape vanished seconds later as they descended a staircase into a living room lined with floor-to-ceiling windows that looked out over a vast city. He had no idea what floor this apartment was on, but it was high. Really, really high. There would be no window escape. The only way out would be through a door.

Creep led them to a dining table and motioned for Garrett to sit. Since there was no high chair, Garrett held his sister in his lap. In front of him was some sliced fruit and a bowl of noodle soup that looked kind of like *pho* but turned out to be not as good.

"Where's the baby food? My sister can't eat this."

"Huh?" Creep said.

"Baby food." Garrett mimed feeding Claire.

Creep said something to Driver Guy, who walked into the kitchen area and grabbed something out of a sack. When he returned, he set it in front of Garrett. It was a plastic cup with a pull-off top. It reminded Garrett of yogurt cups back home, but he couldn't read any of the writing, and when he opened it, it was definitely not yogurt inside. He sniffed it before dipping his finger into the brown goop. He really didn't want to taste it but he wasn't about to let his sister try it first.

He brushed his tongue against it. It wasn't great, but not the worst thing in the world, either.

He looked at Creep. "Spoon?" Garrett did his miming thing again.

Before Creep could react, a voice behind them said something in Thai.

Immediately both Creep and Driver Guy rushed into the kitchen. Garrett looked back over his shoulder and saw the boss crossing the living room toward him. The man pulled out a chair at the end of the table and sat down.

"Good afternoon," he said.

Garrett didn't return the man's greeting.

"Garrett, yes?" the man said. "Is your name or not?"

Garrett tried very hard to not react.

"And she Claire, yes?"

Garrett picked up a piece of what looked like green melon and put it in his mouth.

"Names not fake?"

Creep and Driver Guy returned, the former carrying a spoon. Why it had taken both of them to get it, Garrett had no idea. But as Creep started to hand it to him, the boss said something and Creep pulled it back.

"You not respect me," the boss said to Garrett. "You answer, then you get spoon. No answer, girl can be hungry."

Garrett grudgingly said, "They're our real names."

"Girl. She sister you?"

"Yes."

Again the boss said something in Thai. Creep pulled a phone out of his pocket, fumbled with the buttons, and passed the device to the boss. The boss looked at the screen before turning it so Garrett could see.

Displayed was a picture that must have been taken the day before. It showed Quinn holding Claire and walking with Garrett's mom along the street in Chaweng Beach. Though Garrett wasn't in the shot, he and Daeng had been nearby when it was taken.

"Mama and Papa?" the boss asked.

It was a bit more complicated than that but Garrett knew the man wouldn't care so he just nodded.

"Who they?"

The question confused Garrett. "You just said it. They're our parents."

"No. Who they? What they do?"

Oh. Garrett realized what the man meant.

The boss probably hadn't expected his people to have any trouble when they went into the villa. Judging from the commotion Garrett had heard in the hall while hiding in the bathroom, though, he knew trouble was exactly what his mother and Quinn had delivered. So it was easy to understand why the guy would be interested.

But how was Garrett supposed to answer his question?

"What they do?" the boss repeated.

Garrett stammered as he tried to think of something that might help his situation. "They, um, work for the government. I-I-I don't know what they do. They don't talk about it. But they work for the government."

He cringed inside as he said the last sentence, thinking he might be overselling it. But the boss didn't seem to notice.

He asked, "American government?"

"Yes," Garrett said. He knew his mom and Quinn did do some work for the government, but they also worked for others and were not government employees. His thinking, though, was if the boss thought they *were* US government employees, he might be more reluctant to harm Garrett and Claire.

The strategy seemed to work. For several moments, the boss seemed dismayed and lost in thought. Then he pushed himself up, said something in Thai, and stormed out of the room.

A moment later, Creep tossed the spoon on the table.

CHAYAN SLAMMED CLOSED the door to the master suite and called Mee Noi. When the line rang and rang, he felt like his head was going to explode from anger.

US government employees? How did the monk know anyone like that? And *why* would they be vacationing together?

The people in Chayan's world tended to go out of their way to avoid getting entangled with the US government. The Americans had a way of gumming things up. The stupid pricks were even immune to generous bribes, for the most part. With his business in its current rebuilding status, the last thing he needed was to have US Homeland Security nosing around and asking questions about a family of dead American *government employees*.

Staring out the window at Jakarta didn't make him feel any better. He wished more than anything that it was Bangkok spread out below him. That was home. This most decidedly was not.

After a few minutes, the rage that had filled his mind

receded enough for him to think clearly again. The boy could be wrong. Or maybe even lying.

He raised the phone again, this time selecting the number for Virote.

"Who are the Americans?" he asked. "I need to know right now!"

"*Khun* Chayan," Virote said nervously. "We have been working very, very hard to find that out. But they have done an excellent job hiding their true identities."

"So you know nothing?"

"Uh…well…"

"What are the chances they work for the US government?"

A pause. "Is that true? Have you found something out?"

"I'm asking *you*."

"Oh, okay, um, along with searching through American driver databases, my people have also searched military, tax, and governmental records in both the United States and Canada with no matches. It's possible some records have been missed, but—"

"Did you check the CIA? NSA? Other US intelligence organizations?"

"Those are considerably harder to crack. I don't even know if we can. We've never needed to in the past."

"But you said it yourself. They are hiding their identity. What does that tell you?"

Another pause. "You think they're intelligence agents?"

"I don't want to *think* anything. I want to know. So find out!"

"Yes, sir. I'll, uh, get back to you."

"You have until eight p.m." That would give Chayan plenty of time before the midnight deadline to figure out an alternative plan if he needed to.

"I don't know if that'll be enough—"

"If you have nothing for me by then, consider yourself terminated."

BANGKOK

VIROTE HAD NO illusion about what *khun* Chayan had meant when he said *terminated*. If Virote couldn't find the information his boss wanted by the deadline, this would be Virote's last day on Earth.

He wasn't ready for it to be his last day. He had children in costly schools, and a wife who'd become addicted to shopping, and two mistresses he hadn't lost interest in yet.

There was much to live for, so he pulled out all the stops, sending inquiries that included Pravat's photos of the Americans to even the most unlikely contacts.

After the last message went out, he sat back and stared at his computer screen, waiting desperately for the *ding* of a reply.

JAKARTA

"I NEED TO use the bathroom," Garrett said when he finished eating.

Creep stared at him.

"Uh, toilet?" Garrett said.

The man's eyes widened a fraction of an inch. "*Hong nam.* Okay, you go."

He pointed at a door off the foyer.

Garrett readjusted Claire in his arms as the stood. When he turned to leave, Creep said, "No, no. She stay."

He held out his hands, but Claire buried her face in Garrett's shoulder.

"We'll be right there," Garrett argued, nodding toward the bathroom. "It's not like we can climb out the window."

"You go *hong nam*, she stay. You not go, okay, no problem."

With reluctance, Garrett handed her to the man. She cried and stretched her arms back toward him, while Creep looked like he was thinking he might have made a mistake.

"I'll be right back," Garrett said, but his words only made her cry harder.

Driver Guy followed him to the bathroom. Garrett was worried his escort would come inside, but the man stopped short of the threshold.

After Garrett closed the door, he sat on the unopened toilet and stared at the floor. He felt like he was about to drown in despair. How would he ever get Claire out of there? His breaths started coming in short bursts, and he could feel water gathering in his eyes.

It's impossible. I can't do this.

When a tear broke down his cheek, he heard his mother again. *Don't let the big picture overwhelm you. Focus on one thing at a time.*

"One thing at a time," he whispered.

He wiped his face, forced his lungs to relax, and repeated his mother's words until he regained some of his focus. With a clearer head, he realized that though he and Claire couldn't use the bathroom to escape, the room might hold something that could help them.

The sink was built into a counter that ran half the length of one wall. At the far end was a stack of four drawers, and in the middle, close to Garrett, was a large cabinet.

He moved over to the latter and quietly pulled open the top drawer. Inside he found soaps, little bottles of liquid, and a tube of toothpaste that looked barely used. The items were organized in neat rows. He picked up one of the bottles and saw it was shampoo. Another was labeled LOTION.

He closed the drawer and moved to the next. Brushes with hair still in them, and a handheld mirror. Next, Q-tips, small square sponges, and a palm-sized leather container with a metal snap enclosure. Inside the container he found nail clippers, a file, and a small set of scissors. He set the container on the counter and closed the drawer.

A knock on the door. "Okay, finish," Driver Guy said.

"I'm almost done. I just need a minute."

He stuffed the container into his underwear and searched the four drawers at the end of the room, but they held only towels and cleaning items.

He sighed, frustrated. The stuff in the grooming kit

would be helpful, but he was still missing a vital item that would help him execute his new plan.

After flushing the toilet to disguise his actions, he moved to the sink. As he ran water over his hands, he looked at himself in the mirror, but his focus soon shifted to the mirror itself. It was actually three separate mirror pieces that matched the length of the counter. The center mirror was narrowest and stuck out from the others maybe half the width of a pencil.

Garrett pushed on it. With a barely audible *thunk*, the mirror swung open. Ointments and bottles of pills and other types of medicine filled the shelves. He wondered if one of the bottles contained sleeping pills he could somehow slip to his captors, but he didn't even know what names he should look for.

The jackpot—or near jackpot—was on the bottom shelf. Sitting next to another hairbrush was a plastic container partially filled with safety pins. His only experience in picking locks had been with Quinn's or Daeng's set of tools, but he'd been told certain types of bobby pins would work, or even pieces of wire. He wasn't sure about the safety pin, but it would have to do.

He transferred several of the largest ones into the leather container, which he then slipped back into his pants. He closed the mirror, turned off the water, and headed for the door, but then stopped. There was one other thing he could use.

He pulled open the top drawer of the first cabinet and grabbed a small bottle of lotion. He was about to slip it in his pants next to the leather case when the door opened.

Driver Guy entered and pointed at the bottle. "What that?"

Garrett froze for a moment before holding it up. "Lotion. It's...it's for my sister. Helps keep rash away." The last part didn't get through, so he said, "My sister," and pretended to rub some of the substance on his butt.

The man chuffed and rolled his eyes. "Go now."

What Driver Guy didn't do was take the bottle away.

CHAPTER
TWENTY SEVEN

BANGKOK

WHILE MEE NOI was annoyed that the monk and his friends had somehow found him, he knew whatever advantage the men thought they had was an illusion. Chayan, after all, still had the children. And then there was the fact Mee Noi was always prepared for emergencies.

"Daeng, so good to see you. It's been far too long."

"Not nearly long enough," the monk said.

"And yet you're here." He glanced at the weapons in the hands of the monk and his friend, and said in English, "Better if you put guns down."

"I don't think so," the monk's friend said.

"Up to you. But soon you be outnumbered."

"I think what *you* need to do is set the phone down and put your hands in the air," the monk said.

Mee Noi smiled. "Of course."

As he set the phone on the desk, he pressed the three-fingered combination that would send a text to one of the organization's coordinators, signaling his need for help. The message would include his current GPS location. The coordinator would dispatch the closest men available. A delay of five minutes should be more than enough for backup to arrive.

"Hey!" a woman called from somewhere down the hallway. "You said you weren't going to talk to him until you brought him back here!"

Well, isn't that interesting, Mee Noi thought. They'd brought the mother along.

THE COORDINATOR RECEIVED the text four and a half seconds after it was sent.

Given the restructuring of the organization, she was hoping the more she shined in her job, the higher the position she'd obtain by the time all the dust settled.

With Mee Noi being Chayan's right hand, she had kept enforcers close to him whenever he was in Bangkok. At the moment, two teams were within three minutes of his hotel, and another only five away.

She activated all three groups.

SOMEONE WAS JAMMING the camera signals. Kiet's men had been unable to locate the devices causing the disruption, so he'd been forced to station a man on each side of the building to keep an eye on things.

Not happy that he had to divide his forces, he'd requested Christina send more men. But it would be fifteen minutes at least before anyone else arrived.

Until then, they would have to sit tight and pray Mee Noi didn't leave.

"YOU FIRST," QUINN said, motioning Mee Noi into the hallway. "And don't try to run. There's nowhere for you to go."

"I never run," the kidnapper said.

Quinn and Daeng followed him to the living room.

The moment Mee Noi entered the room, Orlando walked over, face blank. She stopped two feet in front of him and looked him over. "So this is Mee Noi?"

"In the flesh," Daeng said.

Without moving her gaze from their prisoner's face, she whacked the barrel of her gun against the man's ear.

Mee Noi fell sideways onto the ground.

"Where are my kids?" she asked, standing over him.

Mee Noi touched the side of his head, and looked at the blood that stained the tips of his fingers. "Not very friendly, are you?"

"Good to know you're not a complete idiot," Quinn said.

Mee Noi slowly pushed himself back to his feet. With a half smile, he said, "You know my name. If we have talk, better I know yours, too."

"Screw you. Were they still on the plane when it left Bangkok? Or are they somewhere here in the city?"

Mee Noi wiped away a drop of blood moving down the side of his head. "You make big problem for my men on Samui. I think maybe you military." He looked at Orlando. "Maybe you, too, yes?"

"Where did you take the kids?" Quinn demanded.

Mee Noi smiled. "Somewhere they are running out of time."

"What the hell does that mean?"

Mee Noi nodded toward Daeng. "Ask monk. I tell him, but still waiting answer."

Quinn looked over at his friend. "What's he talking about?"

"I have no idea," Daeng said.

Quinn shoved his gun against the man's shoulder. "This will hurt like a son of a bitch, but it won't kill you. Not right away, anyway. Now tell me what the hell you mean."

The asshole smiled. "I'm talking about deadline."

"What deadline?" Orlando said.

"The one at midnight," Mee Noi looked from Quinn to Daeng and back. "When sacrifice children unless conditions are met." Again he turned to Daeng. "But I not heard back from your friend yet."

"What con—"

That was all Quinn could get out before the sound of gunfire rose from the street.

KIET WATCHED THE hotel entrance from the steps of a 7-Eleven across the street and down half a block. With him was the fourth member of his team. The other two were still at their positions, one on the roof of a building behind Mee Noi's hiding place, and the other on the roof of the building directly in front.

He turned on his comm mic. "Anything?"

"All quiet," the man watching the back reported.

When the other man didn't reply right away, Kiet said, "Position one?"

"Sorry. The hotel roof is clear, and I don't see anything happening on the ground from here. I've got a partial angle into one penthouse suite, though. I thought I saw movement. Give me a moment. I think I can get a better view." The radio was quiet for several seconds before the man came back on. "Yeah, there's a woman standing in the room. Her back's to me. It's weird. It's like she's looking at the wall."

"Let me know if anything changes," Kiet said.

He returned his attention to the street. The area wasn't as busy as some parts of Bangkok, but there were still plenty of people working their way up and down the sidewalks on either side. Vehicular traffic came in bursts, followed by lulls of fifteen seconds or more.

"Kiet?" It was his man at position one.

"I'm here."

"I see Mee Noi."

Kiet couldn't help but tense. "Are you sure?"

"Absolutely. He's in that same suite."

"With the woman?"

A hesitation. "Yes. She turned when he came in and walked right up to him and put a gun to his head."

"What?"

"I recognize her," the man said. "She was at the garage. The American woman. Wait…there are two others." A pause. "It's the other American and *khun* Daeng."

Before Kiet could say anything, two vans came racing down the street and screeched to a halt in front of the hotel. As soon as the doors flew open, several men piled out. Kiet recognized a few of them as belonging to Chayan's organization.

Somehow Mee Noi must have been able to call for help.

Khun Daeng and his friends might be well trained, but Kiet didn't know if they'd be able to handle so many men at once.

Making a split-second decision, he took cover behind a parked car and opened fire on the vans.

QUINN RAN TO the windows.

The suite was too high up to get a direct view straight down, but he could see the roofs of two vans that had stopped in the middle of the street. A muzzle flash drew his eyes to the right. A gunman—no, two—were firing at someone in front of the hotel. Along the street pedestrians were racing away.

Whoever the target was returned fire. From the number of shots, there had to be at least four or five shooters.

As Quinn took a step back, movement on the roof across the street caught his eye. Thinking it was another shooter, he started to duck, but then saw the man was signaling to him. Quinn realized he must be one of Christina's. When the guy was sure he had Quinn's attention, he pointed at the base of the hotel, mimed a gun, and indicated they would be coming up to the top floor.

Exaggerating his motions, Quinn held up one finger, then two, three, and then shrugged.

Christina's man held up six fingers, changed it to ten, and then back to six. He didn't know how many people were down there, but the answer was somewhere between the two numbers.

Quinn ran back to the others. "We've got to get out of here now!"

"You should have left already," Mee Noi said. "Now, it's too late."

Quinn grabbed the man's arm. "You don't know me. It's never too late." To Daeng, he said, "Take care of them," and motioned at the two guards and the maid.

Raising his gun, Daeng barked at them in Thai. They got to their feet and he hurried them into the hallway.

Quinn yanked Mee Noi toward the front door and shoved him against the wall. "Can you watch him for a moment?" he asked Orlando.

She nodded, her gaze fixed on Mee Noi.

Quinn checked the central corridor. It was quiet but wouldn't remain that way for long.

He yelled back toward the bedrooms. "Daeng! We have to go!"

"There's nowhere for you to go," Mee Noi said. "In a few minutes you all be dead."

Orlando slapped his jaw with her gun. He staggered but remained on his feet this time.

Five seconds later, Daeng reappeared.

"I go first," Quinn said. "Daeng, you take our guest. Orlando, you've got the rear."

BETWEEN KIET, THE man with him, and his watcher at position one, they were able to disable two men and pin down three others. There were four, however, Kiet couldn't account for.

QUINN PAUSED AS he entered the hallway. The stairwell they'd taken up was at the other end, but a scan revealed a much closer one to the right.

Down they went, alert for the sounds of anyone coming from below, but they made it all the way to the ground floor without any problems.

As Quinn cracked open the stairwell door, he heard voices and the rattling of metal. Across the narrow hallway was the hotel kitchen.

Through a long window that filled the top half of the corridor wall, he could see a dozen staff members moving around the stovetops and prep tables. Apparently word of the chaos on the street had yet to make its way to them.

Quinn spotted two exits. The first was at the end of the hall along what would be the front of the building, and would put them right in the middle of the mess. The other was an open doorway on the far wall of the kitchen. If Quinn was right, it would get them to the same hallway he and the others had used upon entering the hotel.

He briefed Orlando and Daeng on what he'd seen and

what he wanted to do, and then got right in Mee Noi's face. "You will walk quietly and make no attempt to communicate with anyone or you *will* get that bullet in your shoulder. Do you understand?"

"I understand what you say."

"That was not the question."

With a wry smile, Mee Noi said, "Okay. I understand. But make no difference for you. You never make it outside."

"I guess we'll soon see, won't we?"

Quinn opened the door again and they filed out.

It took a moment before members of the kitchen staff started looking their way. Some immediately returned to what they were doing, while others gave them a who-are-you look.

When an older woman near the center of the room saw them, she stepped away from the table and yelled something in Thai. Daeng replied, but when she spoke again, her tone was even harsher.

Quinn kept going. The target doorway led into a short hall that did indeed intersect with the service corridor. They hurried through it and exited via the outside door to the walled-in pool area.

There was no missing the gunfire now as it bounced around the building into the back area. It had clearly driven those who'd been outside into the building in a rush, as towels and books and bags and sandals lay scattered on the deck.

Quinn didn't bother hiding as he ran to the back wall. He boosted Orlando up so she could take a look around. When she gave the all clear, he helped her over and then pulled himself up to straddle the top of the wall.

"Now you," he said to Mee Noi, holding a hand down to help him.

Daeng had to give the man a shove before he finally grabbed Quinn's hand. As Quinn began pulling him up, the hotel's main back doors flew open and two of Chayan's men ran out. They didn't at first see Quinn and the others at the back corner, but while the bushes hid most of the area, they didn't completely cover Quinn sitting where he was.

"Push him up!" Quinn said to Daeng as he pulled.

Despite Mee Noi's attempts to make it more difficult, Quinn soon had him bent over the top, with only his legs still on the wrong side.

A shout from Chayan's men rang out. They raced onto the deck and raised their guns.

Quinn ducked, leaning over on top of Mee Noi, a second before the men at the pool opened fire. Bullets flew over him while a few hit the wall near his leg.

He yanked out his gun and returned fire, sending Chayan's men scattering for cover. Quinn then grabbed Mee Noi by the waist of the man's pants and pulled.

Mee Noi fought back, twisting in an attempt to fall back on the hotel side. He snatched at Quinn as if intending to use him as an anchor. Quinn jerked out of the way, unwittingly pulling back enough for Mee Noi to get free.

Gunshots rang out again as the kidnapper wrenched himself up to sitting position on the wall. He didn't last long, though, as he lost his balance and fell into the alley.

"Daeng, get over!" Quinn said. "I'll cover."

He fired toward the two men, forcing them to temporarily break off their attack, while Daeng flung himself over the wall. When his friend was on the ground, Quinn sent off four more shots before dropping into the alley.

Orlando and Daeng were crouching next to Mee Noi, staring at the man.

"Come on. We can't waste time," Quinn said. "Get him up and let's get out of here."

Daeng rolled Mee Noi onto his back and looked at Quinn.

A bullet had hit Mee Noi just above his nose and had removed a large chunk of his forehead.

"How are we going to find them now?" Orlando asked as they escaped down the alley. "Quinn, how will we find them?"

Quinn wished he knew the answer.

CHAPTER
TWENTY EIGHT

JAKARTA

CHAYAN HAD KEPT as much as possible to the apartment's master suite, having no desire to "socialize" with Pravat and Narong. This day was already stressful enough without having to deal with them. Then again, a mind-numbing conversation with the two men might have taken his mind off the fact that Mee Noi had suddenly stopped returning his calls.

When his phone rang a few minutes after 4:30, he thought, *Finally*. But the name on his screen was VIROTE.

"You damn well better be calling with information."

"Yes, sir." Virote sounded surprisingly downcast. "I-I am."

"Who are they?"

"*Khun* Chayan, there's something else first."

"Nothing is more important than—"

"Mee Noi has been killed."

Chayan was not one to tolerate being cut off midsentence, but Virote's words stopped him cold.

Mee Noi was dead?

"How?" he asked, once his shock began to recede.

"The monk and his friends. They were attempting to take him hostage, and some of our men tried to stop them. He was killed in the process and left behind."

"*They* killed him?"

A slight pause. "Yes, sir. The security team thinks that he fought with them and was hindering their escape so they got rid of him."

"And did they escape?"

Another pause. "Yes, sir."

"Please tell me at least that some of them were hurt."

"I have no information on that."

"*Goddammit!*" Chayan yelled into the phone.

He stared across the room. Mee Noi's death was a colossal blow and would set everything back. He was Chayan's organizer, his sounding board, his weapon when he needed it. Now Chayan would have to do everything himself.

"I do, however, have information on the Americans," Virote said.

Chayan had almost forgotten the man was on the phone. "Tell me."

"The man's name is Jonathan Quinn. The woman goes by Orlando. They're operatives."

Chayan closed his eyes. As if this day could get any worse. "So they are CIA."

"Actually, no, sir. They're freelance cleaners, apparently."

Freelancers? That would mean they weren't official US government employees. So there would unlikely be any heavy-handed American response, and the kids *could* pay for the monk's sins. Nor would there be any issues taking revenge on the children's parents for killing Mee Noi.

The day might have been disastrous so far, but it wouldn't be a complete loss.

BANGKOK

CHRISTINA MARCHED INTO her living room, her face taut and her eyes ablaze. "What in God's name were you thinking?"

"What were we *thinking*? What do you think?" Orlando shot back. "He knew where our kids are."

They had returned only a few minutes earlier and hadn't had time to figure out what their next step should be.

"Did he tell you where?" Christina asked. "Because from what I understand, he's dead now. And it's also my understanding you would all be dead if my people hadn't bailed you out."

"And we're grateful for that," Quinn said.

"If you had just had patience, we might have been able to grab him."

"Even if you had been able to get him, it wouldn't have been in time," Orlando said.

Christina held on to her anger for a few more seconds before letting it go. In a calmer voice, she said, "Kiet mentioned something about a deadline."

Still seething, Orlando said, "Something we wouldn't have known if we hadn't grabbed him."

Quinn put a hand on her back. "Orlando's right," he said, but in a tone matching Christina's. He told the woman what little info they'd learned from Mee Noi. "We're not completely stuck, though. We did take his phone. The only problem is that it's locked, and we don't have the equipment to break the encryption."

"We can help with that." Christina sent her assistant to fetch someone from elsewhere in the house. She looked at Orlando. "I'm sorry for jumping on you like that."

Though Orlando's expression didn't change, she nodded and said, "It's all right."

Christina turned to Quinn. "I hope you don't mind, but I had your things sent here from Samui."

"Thank you," Quinn said. "We appreciate that."

"They're in your rooms."

"Did you have mine brought back, too?" Daeng asked.

"Yes."

"I'll be right back." Daeng hurried out of the room.

Before he returned, Christina's assistant came back with another woman—a girl, really. She was rail thin and couldn't have been more than nineteen or twenty. Her hair was cut short, boyish, and had been bleached blonde.

"This is Jar," Christina said. "If anyone can get into Mee Noi's phone, she can. Give it to her and she'll go check it out."

"I'll go with her," Orlando said, holding her hand out to Quinn.

He gave her Mee Noi's phone and she left with Jar.

Less than thirty seconds later, Daeng rushed back into the room. "Listen to this."

He hit a button on his phone.

Daeng translated as a voice message played. "Good morning, Daeng. It's Mee Noi. I think, especially after last night, that you probably remember me. I'm sure you're not having a very good day. If you don't want it to get worse, you should call me back right away. Unless your friends' children aren't that important to you."

A click.

"There are three more," Daeng said. "I haven't listened to them yet, but—"

"Play them," Quinn said.

Mee Noi again. "Perhaps you aren't taking me as seriously as you should. What you need to know is that there's a hard deadline, after which returning the children will no longer be an option. Midnight. So if you're interested in hearing the terms for their release, you'll call back well before then."

Message number three was a near repeat of number two. Number four, however—

"What is your problem?" Mee Noi began, not hiding his irritation. "Do you not care about the children? In case it wasn't clear before, no one will ever see them again unless you call. A simple trade is all it will take for them to go home again. You for them. I can't imagine the famous monk is heartless enough to let two children die in his place."

"I'm sorry," Daeng said. "If I'd only grabbed my phone while we were still on the island..."

"And what?" Christina ask. "You would have agreed to the trade and the children would be freed? Chayan's using them to lure you in, but I can't imagine him ever letting them go. He's never been a fan of loose ends."

"I could have worn a tracker, and by now you would

232

know where Garrett and Claire are."

"He would have searched you and found it long before you got anywhere near the kids," she said. "He's not an idiot. He would know that you'd try something to save them."

"But there would have been a chance," Daeng said. "That's better than anything we've got now."

"Stop it," Quinn said. "You didn't grab your phone because you were helping us look for Garrett and Claire. So there's nothing for you to feel guilty about."

"That's nice of you to say, but we both know that's not true."

ORLANDO SAT NEXT to Jar in a basement room filled with well-equipped computer stations. Jar's setup was particularly impressive, and rivaled Orlando's own back in San Francisco.

The girl rifled through a box filled with wires, pulled one out, and plugged it into a junction box next to the monitor.

She held her hand out to Orlando and spoke the first word she'd said since they'd met. "Phone."

Orlando gave it to her and Jar connected it to the other end of the wire. Orlando kept a close eye on the girl as Jar began working her computer, itching to be the one in the driver's seat. But Jar seemed to know what she was doing.

The encryption on Mee Noi's phone was first-rate. Jar tried all the standard methods that Orlando would have attempted, and each failed. Orlando was about to suggest another tactic when Jar tried something Orlando had never seen before. Much to her surprise, the phone suddenly unlocked.

She went to grab it but Jar blocked her hand. "Wait."

A few more keystrokes and the girl was looking at the source code of the phone's operating system. She scrolled through it fast and suddenly stopped. The corner of the girl's mouth ticked up in the first expression of emotion Orlando had seen.

Orlando skimmed the code on the screen and saw the problem just as Jar moved the curser to it. The trap was only three lines long. But if Orlando had tried to use the phone, those three lines would have erased all the data.

Instead of deleting the trap, Jar replaced it with a new string of code that would nullify any other bits of malicious garbage hidden in the software.

The girl disconnected the phone from the cord and handed it to Orlando. "Okay now."

"Good work," Orlando said.

Jar pressed her palms together and bowed her head in a *wai*.

Orlando went straight to the phone's call list. The names were all in Thai characters.

She showed the screen to Jar. "Can you read this?"

"It's Thai. Why wouldn't I be able to read it?"

Now that she'd said more than a word or two, Orlando realized the girl's English was very good. Her accent was also better than most Thais'. Not as good as Daeng's, but close.

"Could you read them to me?"

Jar shrugged. "I guess." She scanned the list. "There's a lot of names here. Mostly people but a few places, too, I think. What are you looking for?"

"Anything that might be Chayan."

Jar raised an eyebrow. "Whose phone is this?"

Orlando wasn't sure she should answer that, but she liked the girl and thought, what would it hurt? "Mee Noi's."

"No shit?"

"No shit."

Jar scanned the list again. "Nothing labeled Chayan. But he might be one of these nicknames."

"Does Chayan have a nickname?"

The girl grimaced. "Why are you asking me? I don't know him."

"I mean, do any of the names stick out to you as perhaps being his?"

"No way to know."

"Okay. How about this? What are the names associated with the numbers that have been called the most?"

"Why didn't you ask that first?" Jar studied the phone again. "Here's one he called several times. It's listed as Toy."

"Is that a girl's name or a boy's?"

"Could be either. Here's another. Name is Pravat. That's a guy's name." She cocked her head.

"What is it?"

"There are several calls here to something labeled Mo Chit."

"Mo Chit? Isn't that somewhere here in Bangkok?"

Jar nodded.

"Is there anything else?"

Jar scrolled through the screen, and shook her head. "These are the three most common."

"Tell me something, do you have a way of tracking down where the phones belonging to those numbers are now?"

"Of course I do," the girl said as if the answer should have been obvious.

"And how about their recent location history?"

"WE'VE GOT HIM!" Orlando said as she ran back into the living area, Jar right behind her.

"Chayan?" Quinn said.

"Yes. Well, at least we think so."

She and Jar moved over to the table Quinn, Daeng, and Christina were sitting around.

"I take it you got into Mee Noi's phone," Christina said.

"Oh, yeah, we did. Your girl Jar here is pretty good."

The girl looked uncomfortable with the compliment.

"There are three numbers he called the most. Jar was able to get a location on two of them. The third is obviously running some kind of masking software that's hiding its whereabouts. If you ask me, that's the one that belongs to Chayan."

"So you *don't* know where he is," Daeng said.

"Hold on. Jar was able to run a GPS history on the two she could locate. *Both* were in Samui yesterday. And both were in the air heading to Bangkok at the same time Mee Noi and Chayan were on that jet. One of them stayed in Bangkok and was in Mee Noi's hotel when we got there. I think he might have been one of the guards outside the door."

"And the other guy?" Quinn asked.

Orlando smiled. "*He* stayed on the plane. So I'm thinking he must be with Chayan. The signal from his phone cut out for a while mid-flight, but it doesn't matter. It's on now. And we know exactly where he is."

"Where?"

"Jakarta."

OVER THE GULF OF THAILAND

"SHOULD BE WHEELS down in about forty minutes," Magnus said over the intercom. "This is the last chance to use the facilities."

While the girls did as Magnus suggested, Nate checked on the copilot. When he was satisfied Barbier was still resting peacefully, he called Quinn.

The line rang four times before his partner answered.

"Wanted to let you know we should be at Suvarnabhumi in about a half hour," Nate said.

"You're almost here?" Quinn said.

"I could have sworn I just said that."

"What's your fuel situation?"

"Um, I'm not sure, but I would guess fine. We haven't come close to hitting the range on this thing since we refueled."

"Give me a second." Half a minute later Quinn came back on. "You need to abort Bangkok. I have a new destination for you."

CHAPTER
TWENTY NINE

JAKARTA

THE FIRST THING Garrett did upon returning to the bedroom after lunch was find a hiding place for the things he'd taken from the downstairs bathroom. The easy locations were in the bathroom connected to his room—behind a drawer or wedged in next to the sink pipe—but if they were obvious to him, they'd be obvious to the kidnappers, too. Under his bed would also be a lousy location, but just thinking about it made him realize what *would* work.

Using the scissors from the grooming kit, he cut through the seams along one side of his mattress and buried the kit inside. Since Driver Guy already knew about the lotion, there was no need to hide it. When Garrett pulled the sheet back down, his bed looked the same as before.

The rest of the afternoon was spent trying to keep his sister entertained between naps. Not an easy job. The good thing was that, with the exception of hourly checks, Garrett and Claire were left alone until dinnertime.

Once more they were brought to the dining room. This time a glass of milk sat waiting for him. Perhaps it was nothing more than Creep and Driver Guy trying to be efficient, but Garrett couldn't help thinking about the drink he'd been given on the plane. That, too, had been milk, and within thirty minutes he'd been sound asleep.

Not wanting to be drugged again, he periodically lifted

his glass to his mouth as he ate, but without actually taking any sips. He knew this wouldn't fool them for long because the level of liquid didn't change. Thinking quickly, he realized a partial solution was sitting on the table, next to his plate.

He wiped his mouth with his cloth napkin and put it on his lap so that it hung off his right thigh. The next time he took another faux drink, before setting the glass back on the table, he nonchalantly lowered it to his side and maneuvered the end of the napkin into the cup, letting it soak up some of the milk. He did it again a few minutes later, turning the cloth and using the dry side. His captors never noticed, their attention on the movie playing in the living room.

As he was finishing his meal, any doubt he'd had about the drinks being spiked disappeared when Claire's head began to slump forward.

To sell that he was feeling it, too, he yawned and blinked like he was having a hard time keeping his eyes open. There was still a chance his ploy might be wrecked as he'd been unable to completely drain the glass. If his captors saw how much milk was left, they might force him to drink it all down.

Realizing his only option was to be proactive, he put his glass and utensils on the plate, and then, keeping the wet napkin under the dish, stood up holding them.

"What you do?" Creep asked.

"I'm taking my dish into the kitchen."

"No, no, no. We take."

Garrett headed toward the kitchen area, saying, "I can do my own," and threw in another yawn for good measure.

Apparently neither man felt motivated to stop him. He put his plate in the sink, moved the napkin on top, and turned on the water, thoroughly soaking the cloth. While the water ran, he dumped the remaining milk down the drain.

That done, he picked up his half-asleep sister and said, "I'm tired. Can we go back to our room now?"

"You want to watch TV?" Creep said.

Garrett knew it was a test. "I'd rather sleep."

Back in the room, Creep watched Garrett put Claire on

the bed, and then said, "Have good night, huh?" He laughed as he pulled the door closed and locked it.

Garrett returned to the door and put his ear against it. He listened as Creep moved down the hall and descended the stairs. Before the man reached the bottom, he said something in Thai that provoked a laugh from Driver Guy. After that there was a moment of distant conversation, and then the rumble of the television as the volume was turned up.

With the kidnappers preoccupied, Garrett grabbed the lotion and applied a generous coat to each of the door's hinges. The squeak wasn't that loud but he didn't want to take any chances.

Next, he retrieved the grooming kit from the mattress. After removing the long metal file, he unhinged one of the safety pins and straightened the needle end so that it resembled a long pointer. Using the file as his tension wrench, he started working on the lock with the safety pin. As Quinn had taught him, he closed his eyes and visualized the space inside. When he could sense the tumblers, he gently pushed and wiggled the pins.

It wasn't the fastest he'd ever picked a lock, but when he finally turned the file, the latch retracted.

He opened the door and let out a breath when neither of the hinges squeaked. He crawled out of the room on his hands and knees. On the off chance that his sister cried, he closed the door again, checking first to make sure it was still unlocked.

Staying on all fours, he crept down the hall to the shadows at the top of the stairs. The living room area was directly below and to the right of the open stairway. An L-shaped couch faced the out-of-sight TV. The back of the sofa created a half wall at the bottom of the stairs. That would be very useful.

The big problem was that Driver Guy was sitting at the near end of the couch, his back to the steps. Creep wasn't in view, but was probably on one of the swivel chairs Garrett had seen earlier.

Garrett had never thought this would be easy, but it

seemed almost impossible now.

You can do this, he told himself.

He took a moment to build what courage he had, and returned to the room to get his sister.

PRAVAT AND NARONG were forced to watch English-language television since neither spoke a word of Indonesian and they had been unable to find anything in Thai.

It could have been worse. At least they were able to find an action movie where it wasn't important to understand the dialogue. Watching all the actors run around was making Pravat thirsty, though, so after about half an hour, he said, "How about a beer?"

"Sure," Narong said.

"I was thinking you could get them."

"It was your idea. You get them."

Pravat really didn't want to get out of his chair. He was too comfortable. But after another ten minutes, he finally rocked to his feet and headed toward the kitchen. On his way, he decided he might as well take advantage of being up and headed first to the toilet off the foyer.

GARRETT HAD BEEN sitting at the top of the stairs with Claire across his lap for over twenty minutes. The only thing that helped pass the time was listening to the movie. It was one of the *Mission Impossible* films he'd seen, and he could remember most of what happened just from the audio.

At the end of a motorcycle chase, Creep and Driver Guy started talking again, but it was a short conversation so Garrett refrained from peeking down. When he heard the creak of furniture, however, he decided it was time for a look.

At first, everything seemed as it was—Driver Guy still sitting on the sofa, the TV still lighting up the wall. Then suddenly Creep walked into view at the other end of the couch, seemingly headed for the bathroom. This was confirmed when Garrett heard the bathroom door shut.

Thinking it might be the best chance he was ever going to get, he picked up his sister and moved onto the first step, and paused. When Driver Guy didn't move, he continued down. The hardest part was when he came level with the man, but the action on the screen provided the distraction Garrett needed to reach the bottom and duck behind the couch.

For a terrifying second, Claire shifted in his arms. He was sure she'd cry out, but instead she settled back down. He slunk to the end of the couch. Now all he had to do was cross a small open space, go around the corner, past the bathroom door, and across the foyer to the apartment's entrance.

He made it across the open space fine, but as he was about to round the corner, he heard the bathroom doorknob turn. He was caught. There was absolutely nowhere he could go that Creep wouldn't see him on his way back to the living room.

Maybe if he sprinted for the exit, he could get out and find a way off the floor before they could grab him. He just needed Creep to come out and move toward the living room so he wasn't between Garrett and the front door. He knew he'd still be seen before Creep made it two steps past the corner, but it would have to be enough.

Garrett shifted his weight so he could push off with maximum speed when the time came. But instead of heading back into the living room, Creep went on a diagonal into the kitchen and never looked in Garrett's direction.

Garrett eased around the corner and tiptoed to the front door. He looked back in time to see Creep walk into the living room with two bottles of beer and disappear behind the wall.

Garrett unlocked the deadbolt, turned the doorknob, and ever so carefully opened the door.

SINGAPORE

THE FIXER'S LOCAL contact was waiting for her after she passed through Customs and Immigration at Changi Airport.

"So where did they land?" she asked, anxious to pick up the girl's trail.

"They haven't yet."

She looked at him, surprised. She was sure the other

plane would be on the ground by now. If they were still in the air, that meant they could be heading for Shanghai or Manila or maybe even Tokyo, in which case she was even farther behind than she'd feared.

"What's their destination?" she asked.

"Jakarta."

"What?" She looked at him as if he were speaking gibberish. "That can't be right. If they were going to Jakarta, they should have been there at least two hours ago."

"They were on approach to Bangkok but then rerouted in flight."

"Are you serious?"

"Completely. When I checked a few minutes ago, they had just begun their descent."

She started for stairs that would take her to the departure level. "How long will it take me to get there?"

"Flight time is just a little over an hour and a half."

If she left right this moment, she'd still be over an hour behind the target, but the situation was a lot better than it could have been. "Do you have anyone in Jakarta who can follow them after they arrive?"

"I thought you might ask that. I already have someone on standby."

"Activate them."

"Yes, ma'am."

"What airline will have the first flight out?"

"Singapore Airlines has a plane leaving in forty minutes." He pulled a ticket jacket out of his pocket. "I hope you don't mind, but I've already secured you a seat on the flight."

Grinning, she took the ticket. "I don't mind at all."

JAKARTA

NATE HAD HOPED to enlist Quinn's help in arranging for someone to watch Dima, but that had been when they were headed to Bangkok. Here in Jakarta, Nate was on his own. Maybe if it was someplace he knew well, he could have put her in a safe house until he could get her out of the country, but he had no in-country contacts. For the time being, he had no choice but to bring her with him and Liz.

A taxi took them into the city, and then on what seemed like a very roundabout way to the location Quinn had sent Nate. The building the tracked phone was supposedly in was a good thirty to forty floors high. The skyscraper was one of dozens in the area, half of them in various states of construction.

On the ground floor of the building across the street was a café. Nate situated Liz and Dima at a table far from the window, and instructed his girlfriend to text him if she got even a hint of trouble. He didn't like leaving them alone, but Quinn had asked him to do recon before the others arrived, and that would be impossible if they were with him.

The entrance to the main part of the target building was tucked between a ground-floor dress shop and a convenience store. Given that it was going on eight p.m., he thought the door might be locked, but it opened automatically as he approached.

The lobby took up the center of the building. Behind a counter to his right sat two well-dressed women wearing head scarves, looking at computers. A concierge service perhaps, or building management. The wall to his right hosted three elevator doors, but neither these nor the women were the most interesting sight. That honor was reserved for the three hard men in a lounge area directly across from the entrance. Their attention had immediately focused on Nate as he walked in. He had seen their type countless times in his work.

Acting the innocent foreigner, Nate wandered over to a directory mounted on the wall near the elevators. Most of the names seemed to be businesses, none of which located on a floor higher than nine, meaning ten and above were likely residential only.

Nate pulled out his phone and pretended to consult a message on the screen as he turned away from the directory and gave the room a more thorough examination. He was sure Garrett and Claire weren't somewhere here on the ground floor. So how would Nate and the others go up without drawing the attention of the three steroid users?

His examination revealed that even if the men could be lured out of the building and neutralized, there was another problem. Cameras were mounted high on the walls in all four corners. Boxy things that probably hadn't been replaced in years, but that didn't mean they didn't work. Nate had no idea how this building was set up, but plenty of places like it allowed residents to access certain security feeds. If the people who had taken Garrett and Claire happened to be watching, there would go any element of surprise.

The curious thing was that he saw no alternate ways up other than the three public elevators. Where were the stairwells? Though he was unfamiliar with Indonesian building codes, a tower this high must have at least two emergency stairways for God's sake. And what about a service elevator? There should be one of those somewhere, too.

Acting confused, he walked over to the counter. Both women looked up, each wearing a businesslike smile.

"May I help you?" the one on the left said in English. It was probably standard protocol when dealing with non-Indonesians.

"I hope so," Nate said. "I think I'm a little lost. This isn't the Palace View Apartments, is it?"

"Palace View?" the woman said. "No, sir. This is The Mills."

"The Mills? Oh. Wow. I guess I am lost. You wouldn't happen to know where the Palace View is, would you?"

The woman frowned. "I am sorry. I do not recognize the name."

Nate pointed at one of the computers. "Is it possible for you to look it up for me? I don't have data on my phone over here." He put on his best helpless smile.

"Of course. One moment."

As the woman began fiddling with her computer, Nate leaned over the counter like he was trying to watch the screen with her. What he was doing instead was take in everything else hidden behind the façade. In addition to the computers, tucked under the counter was a row of smaller monitors showing what appeared to be security footage. He could see the feeds from the lobby, but there were also some showing the doorways outside. Like the cameras, all the equipment looked a bit dated.

"I am sorry," the woman said, turning from her screen. "I cannot find anything with that name. Are you sure you have it correct?"

"I thought I did." Nate made a show of checking his phone. "It's what my friend wrote." He shrugged. "I'll just call him. Hopefully he can talk me there. I appreciate your help."

"You're welcome."

As he walked back across the lobby, all but one of the guards had lost interest in him, and Nate was sure even that one would forget about him the moment he left.

Outside, he did a walk around the building. Not counting the door he'd already used, and those to the ground-floor shops, he found five more entrances. One was a set of tall and wide double doors that opened off a loading dock located directly behind the concierge station. If the building had a service elevator, that's where it must be.

The other four doors were near the corners of the structure. These had to be the emergency stairwells. Mounted about five feet above each was a camera, the same make, style, and age of those in the lobby. As far as he could tell, they were the only cameras covering the outside of the building.

He stopped when he came around the front again and took a final look at the tower. An aging security system. Muscle hanging out in the lobby. Exterior entrances to the stairs. A loading dock.

Child's play.

He headed back to the café to wait.

GARRETT WOULD HAVE run the moment he closed the apartment door if he weren't worried that Creep and Driver

Guy might hear him. So as nervous as it made him, he walked quietly down the hall, looking for an elevator.

He was at first surprised by how few doors there were, but then he realized if all the other apartments on the floor were as big as the one he'd been in, there could be only a handful of residences.

The floor had three hallways, set up like a giant H. The place Garrett and Claire had escaped from was down one of the arms. The elevators, however, were in the middle of the cross section. He hurried over and jabbed at the down button over and over and over.

Every sound he heard made him think Creep and Driver Guy were coming down the hall after him and Claire.

"Come on, come on," he whispered.

A creak.

He shot a glance back the way they'd come.

Was that a door?

He didn't hear any footsteps, but maybe they were walking quietly.

Ding.

He whirled back toward the elevators just as the one on the left arrived. He rushed inside and pressed the button for the ground floor.

As soon as the doors shut, he thought, *We did it. We're getting out.* He leaned heavily against the wall and closed his eyes, exhausted.

THE FIXER RECEIVED two texts moments after her plane touched down in Jakarta, both from the watcher that her Singaporean contact had hired. The first had been sent over an hour ago.

TARGETS UNDER SURVEILLANCE

The second had come in later and contained directions to a meeting point.

By the time the Fixer was in a cab headed into the city, it was 9:07 p.m.

QUINN, ORLANDO, AND Daeng took the same plane from Bangkok that had brought them from Samui. Joining them were Kiet and three of his men. Christina had also sent Jar along to help pinpoint the location of the phone, and to be in charge of the bag of equipment they were bringing. The girl took a seat in the back and had her nose in her laptop before they'd even started taxiing toward the runway.

At 9:06, when they were about forty minutes from Jakarta, Jar said, "Got it."

She fumbled with her seat belt and hurried forward with her computer to where Quinn and the others were sitting on either side of the built-in table. Jar set her laptop down so they could all see. On the screen was the picture of an Asian man, though he didn't look Thai to Quinn.

"Who is it?" Orlando asked.

"Hasam Kazi," Jar said.

Quinn frowned. "Never heard of him."

"I have," Daeng said. "He's one of Chayan's lieutenants."

"*Former* lieutenants," Jar corrected him. "When Chayan went to prison, Hasam was one of the people who took a piece of the business for himself. He'd been doing pretty well by it, too, apparently. Well enough to buy an expensive apartment in Jakarta."

Orlando looked at her. "In the same building where the phone pinged?"

"Same building."

"Hold on," Quinn said. "If he struck out on his own, why would he help Chayan?"

"If he were still alive, I'm sure he wouldn't have."

They all stared at her, waiting.

She brought up another picture, this one of a water-damaged corpse. "Early this morning his body was pulled out of a canal near the airport."

GARRETT STARED AT the panel, watching the numbers change—15, 14, 12a, 12, 11, and on.

When it hit 4, he moved in front of the exit, marking off

the final floors by the muted *ding* the panel made as it passed each one. He could hardly believe it when the car slowed.

Clutching Claire tight to his chest, he inched as close as he could get to the door.

The moment between when the elevator stopped and the doors slid apart felt like an eternity. When they finally opened, he started to step through, but froze when he saw the three men sitting directly across the room. At least one of them had been on the plane with them, he was sure of it.

Garrett glanced right and left, looking for a nearby exit, but didn't see any.

The elevator buzzed a warning, wanting him to move so the doors could close again. Garrett wasn't the only one to hear it. One of the men was turning toward him.

Garrett jumped back into the car and let the doors shut. Before they closed all the way, he saw the man shoot out of his chair, having recognized Garrett.

Garrett blindly slapped at the control panel. The number 11 lit up and the elevator started to move. Hyperventilating, he reached for the wall to keep from losing his balance.

"Focus," he told himself.

He and Claire were still free, and if he wanted to stay that way, he couldn't give in to his fear. By the time the elevator stopped on eleven, the sense that the world was spinning out from under him had faded a bit. He leaned through the opening and took a look around.

The hallway looked exactly like the one outside the apartment on the sixteenth floor. He hadn't seen any places to hide there, so he thought it unlikely he'd find something here.

He pushed the button for twelve, and then realized something. The men downstairs would only have to wait until his elevator stopped. The display would tell them where the car had been. They might already be heading up to eleven. If he got off on twelve, it would be too close.

He stared at the panel for a second and then began pushing buttons, skipping the sixteenth floor. Every time the elevator stopped, Garrett stuck his head out and checked around. But hallway after hallway turned out to be a repeat of what he'd already seen.

When the doors opened on twenty-two he was expecting the same, but even though the hallway was laid out like the others, only a few lights were on, and against the wall was a cart with construction equipment on it.

Garrett put his foot between the doors to keep them open, and then pushed all the rest of the buttons, forcing the elevator to go all the way to the top. Just as the car began to buzz in warning again, he stepped into the corridor, hoping he'd made the right choice.

THE ALARM WENT off on Pravat's phone.

"It's your turn," he said.

"What are you talking about?" Narong said. "I was the last one to check them this morning."

"I got the beers."

"Doesn't count. It's your turn."

Pravat glared at his colleague, but Narong acted like he didn't even notice.

Pushing out of his chair, Pravat said, "You owe me," and headed upstairs.

He was nearing the top when Sunan, one of Chayan's men on watch in the building lobby, called.

"Yeah?" Pravat answered as he continued toward the bedroom.

"We just saw the boy trying to get off the elevator."

"What boy?"

"The one you're supposed to be watching."

Pravat chuffed. "You're seeing things. He's asleep. It was probably some kid who looks like him."

"Then why was he carrying a baby? And why did he look scared when he saw us and head back up before we could get to him?"

As troubling as that sounded, the boy couldn't have gone anywhere. A) he was drugged, b) he was locked in his room, and c) Pravat and Narong had been between him and the only exit all night. He started to say as much to Sunan as he slipped the key into the bedroom lock and opened the door, but the words never left his lips.

"Are you still there?" Sunan asked.

The door wasn't locked, and when Pravat pushed the door open, he saw the beds were empty.

"It's him. Find him!"

He hung up and hurried back downstairs.

After a glance toward the downstairs hallway that led to Chayan's master suite, he moved over to Narong and whispered, "They're gone."

"Who's gone?"

Pravat slapped a hand over Narong's mouth. "Not so loud." He glanced up the stairs. "The kids aren't in the room."

"Are you serious?"

Pravat nodded and told him what Sunan had said. "It would be better for *us* if we find them before Chayan knows anything is wrong, don't you think?"

"If he finds out..." Narong said.

"Yeah, which is why we need to get them back here fast."

Narong stole a look toward the master suite. "If he comes out and finds us both gone, he'll check the room himself and think that *we* took them."

It was a good point. If Chayan did leave his room, someone would need to convince him nothing was wrong. "Okay, you go help Sunan. But keep me updated."

"Why me?"

"Because I'm the better actor."

THE FIXER MET her contact two blocks from the café where the target had apparently been for an hour or so. He showed pictures that confirmed it was her, and that her escort from the Barcelona-bound train was still with her. They had been joined by a woman. The fixer assumed she was another operative.

Why they had flown all the way to Indonesia was a mystery. The fixer would have thought they'd take the girl somewhere like the US or the UK, put her someplace the fixer could never reach.

Indonesia was another matter altogether. There were resources she could pull together here, and officials she could pay to look the other way if necessary.

"Show me," she said, handing the photos back to the man.

He led her to a position across the street from the café and handed her a pair of compact binoculars. The girl was still seated at the same table as in the pictures. Her back was to the window, but her shape and clothing were the same. Across from her were the other woman and the target's original escort.

It was obvious they were waiting for something. The next handoff perhaps? Another exchange in another country to further confuse the girl's trail?

If so, it hadn't worked because the fixer was here, her eyes on her prize.

She lowered the glasses. "My requests?" She had asked her Singapore contact to arrange for weapons and a team to back her up.

"Thirty minutes to an hour."

She didn't hide her displeasure.

"If we had had more time…" he said, letting her fill in the rest.

As far as she was concerned, the man had had plenty of time already, but arguing about it wasn't worth it.

"They serve coffee, I assume," she said, her gaze back on the café.

"I'm sure they do."

"I could use a cup."

It took him a moment to realize what she meant. "Oh, um, I'll get that for you. Milk or sugar?"

"Black."

THE TWENTY-SECOND floor turned out to be an even better choice than Garrett had hoped.

The low light continued in each corridor. And from the condition of the floors and some of the hallway walls, he was pretty sure the level was unoccupied.

He started trying some knobs, looking for an unlocked one. The fifth door swung open. He flicked the light switch but nothing came on, so he was left to rely on moonlight drifting in through the windows.

Unlike the apartment he'd been held in, this place was a single story. There was no tile or carpet on the floor, and many of the walls were down to their studs. He searched for a nook he and Claire could hide in.

The last room at the end of the hall was a master. Its size wasn't much different from that of the other bedrooms, but it had an en suite bathroom. Like the rest of the place, the bathroom had been gutted and was in the process of being rebuilt. The shower stall looked like it was going to take up the whole back wall. To the side, there was a spot that might be a place for a tub. It was really hard to tell in the dark. That was why Garrett almost missed the hole. The only reason he took a second look was that it was slightly less black than the rest of the wall.

With a hand cradling Claire's head, he leaned down next to the tub space. Sure enough, there was a hole in the wall. It appeared wide enough to crawl through, but not with Claire in his arms. He patted the floor next to the hole to make sure there was nothing sharp, and then set his sister down.

He poked his head through the opening and scanned the new space. Another bathroom, but this one looked further along in its construction. Thankfully, the tub had not been put in place yet. He crawled through and reached back for Claire.

A search of the apartment revealed it contained no good hiding places, either. He'd have to hope his kidnappers would never check the twenty-second floor or, if they did, only search the corridors.

He checked the lock on the front door to make sure it was engaged. Leaving Claire in the bathroom, he reentered the other apartment and locked that door, too. When he returned, he leaned some loose boards against the hole and jammed them in place with a toolbox. Maybe if the others somehow got into the neighboring apartment, they wouldn't notice the unofficial exit.

Then again, maybe they would simply bust down the door to this place and it would be all over.

He carried Claire into the living room, sat down in the middle, and stared out into the night, wondering if he'd done enough yet to keep his sister safe.

CHAPTER
THIRTY

A VAN WAS waiting for Quinn and the others when they arrived at Soekarno-Hatta airport in Jakarta, and by the time they reached the rendezvous point, it was nearing 10:30 p.m.

Quinn texted Nate, telling him where they were parked, and two minutes later his partner arrived at the van.

"I thought you had a package with you," Quinn said.

Nate nodded at a building down the block. "She's in the café with Liz."

Quinn's jaw tensed involuntarily. He should have realized Nate would bring Liz along. Quinn hated it when his sister got drawn into their world, but he could do little about it right now.

Nate climbed into the van and gave them a briefing of what he'd seen in and around the target building. From Jar, they knew Hasam Kazi's apartment was on the sixteenth floor. Quinn felt sure they could swiftly deal with the guards in the lobby, but it would be much better to get in unnoticed and avoid the possibility of anyone calling the police.

"My thought is, the service elevator would be the best bet," Nate said. "Since this guy's got people in the lobby, he might have more waiting outside the elevators on sixteen. To avoid running into a concierge, we should take one of the stairways up one floor, and then get on the service elevator there."

Quinn nodded, liking the plan.

"You bring jammers?" Nate asked.

Jar zipped open the duffel bag on the seat beside her. "What brand are the cameras?"

"No visible markings, but they're old." He pulled his phone out. "I took a picture of one."

"Let's see it," she said impatiently.

Nate shot a is-she-for-real glance at Quinn before opening up his photos and turning his phone toward her. She grabbed it and magnified the picture.

"June-Jeong Electrosystems," she said. "Korean. Out of business seven years ago. Their gear is crap."

She dug a palm-sized device out of her bag, tinkered with an embedded dial for a moment, and then held it out.

Orlando grabbed it and looked it over.

"Point that end at the camera," Jar said, indicating the side covered in smoky glass, "and then press the yellow button. It will fire the circuit board."

"We don't need to destroy it," Quinn said. "We just need to knock it out for a while."

Jar looked unmoved. "Maybe this will motivate them to get better equipment."

While weapons were handed out, Quinn said to Nate, "You've been using that café for a while. Might be a good idea to get Liz and your package—"

"Dima."

"All right, Dima. Might be a good idea to get them out of there. They can wait here with Jar."

"No offense to you," Nate said to Jar before turning back to Quinn, "but I can't leave Dima here unprotected. At least in the café there are other people around."

"Why would I be offended? Protection's not my job," she said.

Quinn looked at Kiet. "Pick one of your men to stay. Once things are underway, if we're not back in thirty minutes, he's to take them to the plane and immediately fly back to Christina." He moved his gaze to Nate. "That work?"

Nate nodded. "I'll be right back."

LIZ DID HER best to keep Dima's spirits up—talking about her art history studies, about trips she'd taken with Nate, and even about what it was like growing up in northern Minnesota— but she wasn't sure if it was working or not. Though there were moments when Dima seemed somewhat interested, she spent most of the time staring off into nothing, looking worried and tired.

The café staff had glanced at them with curiosity when Liz and the others had been there for over an hour and a half, but soon lost interest and only paid enough attention to occasionally ask if they wanted anything else. Even though the place had never filled up, Liz couldn't help but feel self-conscious about staying so long. So she was more than a little relieved when Nate returned and said they were going.

When she saw Quinn and Orlando outside the van, she ran over and hugged them. Searching for the right words to say, she could only come up with a lame, "They're going to be fine."

Orlando and Quinn seemed to appreciate it nonetheless.

"You and...Dima, is it?" Quinn said, turning to the girl.

Dima nodded.

"You'll be staying here in the van. Jar and Lamon will be with you." He motioned to a sullen-looking young Thai woman in the back and the man in the driver's seat.

"Are the kids really here?" Liz asked.

"We think so."

"How long will you be gone?"

"Just long enough to bring them back."

THE FIXER WAS seldom surprised.

When the escort returned after a brief disappearance and led the target and the other woman out, she was annoyed that they were on the move before her help arrived, but accepted it as inevitable.

Keeping to the shadows, she followed them to the next intersection and around the corner. That's when her jaw dropped. Standing outside a van that turned out to be the target's destination were six people, with at least two others inside. There was no mistaking the look of those she could see—pros, every one of them.

Goddammit.

This must be the handoff, and not to another solo escort but a whole team.

She had requested only three men herself, which now seemed insufficient if it came to a firefight. As long her Jakarta contact came through on the gear she asked for, though, then the men wouldn't be necessary.

Her second surprise came when all except the target, the woman who had been with her, and the two people already in the van headed down the street in the fixer's direction.

I've been made.

She scurried backward into some bushes that paralleled the road, looking for an escape passage, but on the other side she ran into a wrought-iron fence. She looked both ways for a break but found none. The footsteps nearing, she crouched low, hoping they hadn't seen where she slipped away.

When the operatives passed, though, they made no indication of knowing she'd been in the area, and continued on down the road. She was able to get a good look at them and saw at least a few were armed. That was probably the first thing that hadn't surprised her in the last few minutes.

Quietly, she crawled back out. She glanced at the van and saw that the four who'd remained were all inside. The engine was off, and it looked like they weren't going anywhere soon.

Since she was still waiting for her equipment and her curiosity was piqued, she headed after the larger group.

PRAVAT WAS GOING stir crazy.

It had been over an hour since the brats were seen in the lobby, and yet they were still free. How was that possible?

He'd called Sunan back right after Narong left, and Sunan had told him the elevator seemed to be stopping on every floor.

Hoping he'd get lucky and recapture the children on his own, Pravat had chanced a short trip to the elevators. But after several minutes passed without the *ding* of an arriving car, he realized the boy must have been smart enough to skip the sixteenth floor altogether. Disappointed, he returned to the apartment.

Every noise he heard made him look nervously toward the hallway to the master bedroom, sure that Chayan was on his way. If he did appear, Pravat was so wound up now, he'd have a hard time convincing his boss everything was fine.

He went into the kitchen area, thinking another beer might help calm his nerves. Naturally, this was the moment Chayan's voice rang out.

"Where is Narong?"

Pravat whirled around to find his boss standing near the bottom of the stairs, outside the first-floor hallway. Chayan looked tired and stressed. Not a combination that made Pravat feel any less anxious.

"He, um, went to, uh…pick up some food."

Chayan's eyes narrowed. "You didn't think to ask if I was hungry, too?"

"We d-d-didn't want to disturb you."

Even as Pravat was replying, Chayan seemed to lose interest in the topic. The man glanced up the stairs, and for a few horrible seconds, Pravat thought he was going to go up. Instead, Chayan said, "I want them ready to go in fifteen minutes."

"It's not midnight yet."

Chayan twisted back around and locked his eyes on Pravat. "I don't care what time it is! The monk has not contacted us yet. That's all I need to know. He's going to pay for his inaction. You will prepare things, and we will do what we came here to do. And then we will get out of this cesspool. Is that *clear*?"

"Yes, *khun* Chayan. Very clear. I-I-It will be done."

"Fifteen minutes." With that, he retreated to the study.

I'm a dead man, Pravat thought.

If the children hadn't been found in the last hour, what were the chances they'd be located in the next fifteen minutes? Ten, really. They'd need to be brought here and prepared.

Pravat had no choice. He needed to go help with the search. If Chayan came back out while he was gone, so be it. And if the fifteen minutes passed without the kids being located, maybe that would be the sign for Pravat to search for new employment.

He grabbed his gun and headed for the door.

ORLANDO ACTIVATED THE jammer and waited ten seconds before saying, "That should do it."

Taking the cue, Quinn sprinted to the stairwell door, picked the lock, and signaled the others to join him.

Per Nate's plan, they went up one floor. While everyone else stayed in the stairwell, Quinn and Nate exited for a look around.

The scuffed walls and well-worn carpet were proof enough that they had entered a non-public area.

The hall took a ninety-degree turn twenty feet down.

After coming around the corner, Nate whispered, "There it is."

Along the wall on the left were the wide doors of a service elevator. When they reached it, they found that a key was needed to call the car.

Once more Quinn set to work with the picks.

THE SURPRISES JUST kept coming.

The group the fixer had followed had broken into a nearby high-rise and disappeared inside. It appeared to be an assault team about to make a raid. Which was bizarre. What did an assault team have to do with her target?

For a moment she wondered if the girl had led them to this building. Maybe the fixer's employer had an interest in something or someone inside.

Maybe her employer *was* inside.

That thought made her pause. She had no idea where he was located, just like she had no idea why the target was a problem for him. Would the fixer's payment be affected if her client met an untimely death?

That would be…unfortunate.

But she couldn't do anything about it. She would have to hope her client had the appropriate security measures in place if he was indeed about to be attacked.

Her job was the target, and one way to guarantee not getting her fee would be by botching the mission.

She pulled out her phone and texted the local watcher.

Where the hell is my stuff?

The reply came in seconds.

The men are pulling up now

She smiled and texted:

On my way

THE DING WAS so soft, Garrett wasn't sure he'd actually heard it.

Gently, he laid Claire on the floor, tiptoed over to the front door, and listened. The only thing he could hear, however, was the ever-present hum of the building's air system.

False alarm, he thought as he returned to his sister.

As he picked her up, she squirmed a little, so he rocked her while saying, "Shhh." All this activity was dulling the effects of the drug she'd been given.

With a soft whimper, her mouth contorted in discomfort.

"Oh, great," he muttered when the odor of a newly soiled diaper enveloped him.

There had been extra diapers in their prison room, but he hadn't thought of grabbing any when they left.

Way to go, idiot. You really thought things through, didn't you?

He couldn't do anything at the moment but live with the smell. Claire, however, was not content with the situation. She started to whimper again, louder this time.

"Quiet. It's going to be all right."

His words were like gas on a fire, turning the whimper into a cry.

"Hey, hey, hey. It's okay. I'll change you as soon as I can, I promise."

When that didn't work, he tried sticking his finger in her mouth again. She didn't look completely at ease but at least stopped crying.

"It's going to be all right," he said, over and over again.

NARONG'S LAST TEXT said he and Sunan were on the eleventh floor.

Pravat knew they'd been working their way up from the lobby, and that the two other security men had been left below in case the kid tried to sneak back out. Pravat decided his best move would be to work his way up from sixteen.

With Chayan's deadline looming, he rushed through each floor, focusing on nonresidential areas where the kids might hide, specifically the maintenance storage and service-elevator space.

There was always the chance the boy had been able to convince a resident to let him and the girl into one of the apartments. If that had happened then Chayan's men would never find them. But Pravat didn't think it likely, as the building would surely have been crawling with police by now.

The service area on seventeen was deserted.

As was the one on eighteen.

And nineteen.

And twenty.

And twenty-one.

As he rode the elevator to twenty-two, he checked his watch. At the speed he was going, he could check maybe three more floors before he'd have to admit defeat and get the hell out of there. And if it came to that?

He thought for a moment. Going straight to the airport would be tempting. But it was late and his choices of flights would probably be limited by both destination and departure time, turning the airport into a place where he could easily be trapped.

No, a more under-the-radar approach was called for.

A long-distance bus across Java would do the trick. Not the tourist kind. One favored by locals, where they took your money and didn't care who you were. His looks were ethnically mixed enough that he felt he could blend in well with the local Indonesians, as long as no one tried talking to him.

Maybe he could pretend he was a deaf mute. That would deflect some of the—

Ding.

The doors opened onto the twenty-second floor.

His brow furrowed as he moved into the corridor. Unlike the floors he'd checked already, only about half of the hallway's lights were lit and the carpet was missing, leaving the cement floor exposed.

Floor twenty-two was apparently being renovated.

If I were looking for somewhere to hide, this would be the place.

Still believing the maintenance area would be the kids' most likely destination, he headed there first. But as he reached for the knob, he heard a baby's cry.

He cocked his head.

There it was again, prolonged this time. It wasn't coming from behind the maintenance door, but from the other way. Swiftly and silently, he followed the cry back to the central corridor and into the connecting hallway on the other side before the noise finally stopped.

He had no doubt which door they were behind.

He sent Narong a text.

22. They're here.

CHAYAN PACED THE master suite, his confidence that Pravat would get the children ready in the allotted time eroding by the second. When he could take it no longer, he marched back into the living room so he could supervise them, but neither

Pravat nor the kids were there.

He headed up to the second level, ready to ream the incompetent asshole for taking too much time. Only the children's room was empty. He checked the attached bathroom and the other two guest rooms, but those, too, were empty.

Furious, he pulled out his phone. He almost pressed Pravat's number but knew he'd just hear more lies, so he called Narong.

"*Khun* Chayan?" the man answered.

Chayan instantly picked up on the nervous tension in the man's voice.

"What the fuck is going on? Where are the children? And where is Pravat? He left with them, didn't he?"

"Left? Uh, n-no, sir. He's, um, looking for them."

"He's *what*?"

Narong hesitated before spilling the story. "He may have found them, though."

"Where?"

"Floor twenty-two."

Chayan retrieved his pistol and stormed out of the apartment.

QUINN LED THE team off the service elevator and onto the sixteenth floor.

Like on the floor where they'd boarded, the elevator was in a self-contained area at the end of one of the halls. Quinn cracked the door open for a peek, and was just in time to see the leg of a man moving into the central corridor.

Quinn eased into the hall. As he approached the corner the person had disappeared behind, he heard the *ding* of one of the public elevators arriving. Before he was able to look around the edge, the man had entered the car and the doors were closing.

There was no way to know if the guy was a civilian or someone they needed to keep tabs on, but Quinn noted the elevator's directional indicator was pointing up, not down. He continued on to Hasam Kazi's apartment.

The team fell in line behind him as he knelt in front of the door. As he always did, he tried the knob first.

The door was unlocked.

He tensed.

He signaled Nate to move right behind him, and then gently pushed the door open, both men pointing their weapons into the room.

The sound of racing cars and high-energy music blared from a television deeper in the apartment, but no one was within view.

Quinn stepped into the foyer and the others followed.

The entrance area opened into a grand room consisting of a kitchen and dining area to the left and a large living room ahead to the right. The blaring TV was in the living room, playing some kind of action film, but no one was watching it. There were, however, two cans of beer sitting on a coffee table.

As Quinn cleared the end of the foyer, he saw a stairway to the right, and behind it a hallway.

Quinn motioned for one of Kiet's men to watch the front door, and assigned Daeng, Kiet, and Kiet's other man to search the rest of this level. He then led Orlando and Nate up to the second floor.

They split up, each taking a room. Quinn's was a bedroom that looked like it hadn't been used in a while. He barely stepped inside for a closer look when Orlando shouted his name.

As he rushed back into the hall, Nate popped out of the room he was checking.

"What's going on?" Nate asked.

"I don't know. I'll deal with it. You finish checking."

Passing the stairs, Quinn saw Daeng racing up toward him. Since Kiet and his men were covering below, Quinn waved for his friend to follow.

They found Orlando standing in the middle of the front bedroom, holding a stack of unused diapers. "Look," she said, pointing at the beds.

There were indents on each, small on one bed, teen-sized

on the other. On the former, pillows had been set up between the depressions and the bed's edges.

"They were here," Orlando said, and hurried into the attached bathroom.

He followed just in time to see her grab two used diapers out of the trash can.

"This one's still warm," she said. "They haven't been gone long."

When they returned to the bedroom, Quinn said to Daeng, "I assume there's no one downstairs."

"No one," Daeng said. "But I spotted a laptop and some papers. They could be Chayan's."

"Get them."

Daeng nodded and ran out of the room.

"Check this out," Nate said. He was looking at the doorknob.

Quinn stepped over and saw there was a keyhole on both sides. Anyone inside the room could be locked in.

With a start, he said, "The elevator! The middle car. We need to know where it just went!"

When they reached the elevator area, Quinn and Nate pulled the doors open as far as they could, and Orlando leaned inside.

"Is it still up there?" Quinn asked.

"Yeah," she said, and pulled back out.

"Which floor?"

"Twenty-two."

THE FIXER WAS not impressed with the men her contact had brought in. As promised, there were three of them. Bruiser types without an above-average IQ among them. Good thing she probably wouldn't need them.

What she *would* need were the weapons they had brought with them. The first was a 9mm pistol with suppressor. They had also brought the shoulder holster rig she had requested. She donned the holster under her windbreaker, slipped the gun into it, and picked up the other weapon. Like the pistol, the sniper rifle was a Chinese knockoff. She would have preferred Tango 51, but since distance wasn't going to be much of an issue—she could probably get as close as a hundred feet if she was very cautious—the weapon should do the trick. The suppressor for it was first-rate, so that was a bonus.

After donning a pair of shooter's gloves, she pulled back the bolt, checked the chamber, and inserted one of the 7.62 NATO cartridges. As she slid the bolt back into place, she looked at the watcher. "Stay here. All of you."

Keeping to the shadows, she went in search of the perfect vantage point to finish her assignment.

"HOW LONG DO you think they'll be gone?" Dima asked.

"Not too long, I'm sure," Liz said.

"What if they don't come back?"

"Trust me, they always come back."

CHAPTER
THIRTY ONE

GARRETT WAS STARING out the window when he heard a squeak from the door behind him. He looked over his shoulder. Though it was dim, he was sure the knob was moving back and forth.

Someone was trying to get in.

This was it. They were going to break through the door and catch him and Claire. He could move to the back bedroom, but they would find him eventually.

He had chosen the wrong apartment. He had come through the hole in the wall only to put his sister and himself in—

The hole in the wall.

He was on his feet in a flash. He wanted to sprint across the room but forced himself to tread lightly. Claire twisted in his arms, and he feared she would cry out again, but she kept quiet.

In the bathroom, he removed the toolbox and boards from in front of the hole and climbed back into the other apartment. He set Claire down and pulled the boards through so he could block the opening from this side. When he reached in to get the toolbox, he heard a scuff and realized whoever had been at the door was inside the apartment now.

He pulled his arm back and propped the boards over the hole, hoping they'd stay in place without the box. He then picked up his sister, crept out of the bathroom, and headed for the front door.

His only chance was to get off this floor while the apartment next door was being searched.

PRAVAT FOUND SOME loose wire and a nail in the construction cart in the hallway, and used them to pick the lock on the apartment door.

After stepping inside. he noted that though the apartment didn't have two stories like Hasam's place, it did have the same basic layout for the living room and kitchen. He shut the door so the boy couldn't sneak by him, and then hurried through the entryway to the main room. It was unoccupied but he knew the kids were here somewhere. There was no hiding the distinct odor of a dirty diaper.

The cry had come from this apartment, all right.

Some of the tension that had been gripping his chest eased. If he could quickly round up the brats, he should be able to get them down to sixteen with just enough time to save his own skin.

As he headed toward the bedrooms, he had to admit the boy deserved points for not simply giving up when Pravat had entered. But it was over. Pravat knew it, and the kid would know it, too.

The first bedroom was empty.

Not surprising. They'd be in the farthest corner of the last room. Kids were predictable that way. Still, the boy had proved resourceful to this point, so Pravat needed to check everywhere just in case.

Hall bathroom, empty.

Second bedroom, empty.

And now for the master.

The bedroom portion was empty. As was the walk-in closet.

"Finished now," he said as he approached the master bathroom. "Time to come out."

No sounds from inside, but he'd expected the boy to be defiant to the end.

Stepping through the doorway, he said, "That's enough. I've got you. Now let's—"

They weren't there.

He walked all the way to the other side and back, but they *still weren't there.*

He hurried back to the living room.

The cry *must* have come from this apartment. He could still smell the diaper. There was no other exit, and no way they could have gotten around him.

A vent maybe? No. The vents in the living area were not large enough for the boy to fit in, never mind the fact they were all in the ceiling and the boy couldn't have reached them.

A secret storage area, perhaps? But he hadn't noticed anything like that. Of course, in the dim moonlight he could have missed it.

He turned on his phone's flashlight function and swung it around the room. Nothing.

He was about to head back to the bedrooms for another look when he heard Chayan shout in the corridor.

CHAYAN WAS AS angry as he'd been on the day he was sent to prison. So when the doors to the elevator opened on twenty-two, he stormed off, ready to tear Pravat to pieces.

He strode down the central hallway to the corridor left of the elevators and turned down it, listening for signs of his soon-to-be-terminated employee. He hadn't gone far when he heard someone back in the central hall. He whipped back around in a rage.

But as he rounded the corner, he saw it was not Pravat at all.

GARRETT OPENED THE front door quietly and peeked both ways down the hall.

If he could get to the elevators, he could find another floor to hide on. He stepped into the hallway and crept over to the intersection with the central corridor. As he turned the corner, he accidently kicked a loose piece of carpet, sending it skidding a few inches across the bare concrete. He paused, sure his pursuer had heard the noise. The footsteps he heard, though, weren't coming from the hall he'd just left. They were approaching from the one at the other end.

Before Garrett could even move, the big boss came around the corner.

For a second, they both stared at each other, and then Garrett twisted and ran the other way.

"Stop right there!" the boss yelled.

Garrett had spotted the entrance to the stairs when he was searching for an open door, but being so high in the building, he hadn't even thought about using it. Now he raced toward it, blasting past the two apartments he'd been hiding in.

Another yell, only this time in Thai.

IT TOOK PRAVAT a second to realize Chayan had yelled in English, and another second for it to dawn on him that it could mean only one thing.

He yanked the door open and raced into the hall. Chayan was to his right, running toward him fast.

"Don't stand there! Get them!" his boss yelled, pointing past Pravat.

Pravat spun around and saw the boy nearing the end of the hall, angling toward the door with the emergency stairway sign above it.

Oh, no, you don't, he thought, and sprinted after him.

GARRETT HIT THE door handle to the sound of footsteps racing up behind him. As he shoved the door open, Claire started to cry again.

He flew across the stairwell landing and took the first step down.

Before he could take a second, a hand grabbed him by the arm and jerked him back, causing him to almost lose his grip on his sister.

"No more run!" Not the boss's voice. Creep's.

Garrett tried to struggle free but Creep wasn't letting go. The man hauled Garrett out of the stairwell and back onto floor twenty-two.

CHAPTER
THIRTY TWO

"THERE'S PLENTY OF room if you'd like to lie down for a bit," Liz said to Dima.

"I want to get out of here," Dima said. "I want this to be over."

Liz smiled sympathetically, "How about something to drink?"

Dima said nothing, so Liz took that for a yes.

She looked back at Jar. "Is there any water?"

Jar looked up. "I don't have any."

"Anywhere in the van?"

The girl frowned. "How should I—"

A crunch of glass, and an instant later something wet hit the side of Liz's face.

Turning around, she saw the man in the driver's seat had slumped forward, with a large hole in the back of his head.

"Get down!" she said, pushing Dima to the floor.

A second later, another bullet punctured the windshield.

THE FIXER FOUND an excellent spot on an elevated walkway surrounding an office building about a hundred yards from where the van was parked. The walkway was deserted and only partially lit, the corner she found completely in shadows.

She checked to make sure the sound suppressor was properly attached, and then extended the barrel-mounted tripod, placed it on the cement wall that surrounded the walkway, and took aim.

The target was in the first row of seats behind the driver, sitting next to the woman operative. The fixer centered the crosshairs on the woman's chest, took a breath, let a little out, and squeezed the trigger.

A moment later, she muttered, "Goddammit."

The scope was off. Her shot had gone a good two feet to the left, taking out the driver.

She cranked back the bolt and loaded a new cartridge. Taking the deviation into account, she aimed and fired again, but the target moved as the fixer was depressing the trigger.

"What the hell?"

She played the scope through the van's interior. The target and the other two still-breathing occupants had all dropped out of sight.

Annoyed, she picked up the gun and hurried to find a spot from where she could finish the job.

LIZ KNEW THEY were dead if they remained where they were. Driving the van out of there would be the quickest way to safety, but if any of them tried to get behind the wheel, they'd likely wind up in the same condition as the man still occupying that seat.

The only other choice was to get out of the van and find someplace to hide.

Dima trembled below her, saying something under her breath over and over. A prayer, probably.

Liz reached for the side door handle and pulled it down. "Come on. We're getting out of here."

"What? No!"

"Dima, I'm trying to keep you alive." Liz crawled outside, grabbed Dima by the armpit, and pulled. "Move it."

Dima hesitated a moment before allowing herself to be helped out. As she stepped from the van, Liz shot a glance toward where Jar had been sitting, but the girl had also moved out of sight. "We're going. Are you coming with us?"

When Jar didn't immediately respond, Liz took hold of Dima's hand, said "Keep up with me," and ran past the back of the van and down the road.

FOR A COUPLE moments the van was out of sight as the fixer weaved her way to a spot that would give her a better angle. When she could see the vehicle again, the side door was open.

"Shit!"

She looked past the van and saw two shadowy forms running away.

"Shit, shit, shit!"

So much for her original plan. She dumped the rifle in some bushes, pulled out the 9mm pistol, and took off in pursuit.

JAR HAD DROPPED to the floor even before Liz had forced Dima down. She hadn't panicked. She'd experienced plenty of violence growing up and was good at keeping her head in dangerous situations.

Her immediate thought once she was out of the shooter's sight was of the duffel bag. She pulled it onto the floor at the same time Liz opened the door. When Liz asked her if she was coming with them, Jar was too focused on going through the duffel to answer.

She found the Taser at the bottom, under the other items Christina had sent along. It wasn't as good as a gun, but those had all been doled out to the others.

She checked to make sure it was charged and zipped up the bag. With the dead man in the front seat, she knew she had to take it with her as there was no way they'd be using this vehicle again.

She was about to head out when she heard footsteps, light but fast, move past the van in the direction Liz and Dima had gone.

She hurried out. There, running down the sidewalk, quiet but not hiding, was the person who had killed Jar's colleague.

Jar shoved the duffel under a parked car four places behind the van, and sprinted down the block.

LIZ SCANNED AHEAD, looking for someplace they could hide. But they'd run into what appeared to be an upper-class residential neighborhood, where all the homes were behind ten-foot walls that butted up against the cracked concrete walkway.

If they could find an open car, maybe they could hide inside, she thought. Or would that just expose them more because they'd need to slow and check doors? Then again, perhaps they'd already run far enough, and all they had to do was wait for Nate and Quinn to come get them.

She had no idea what the right answer was. She didn't have the same training her boyfriend and her brother had.

Ahead she spotted a break in the walls along the sidewalk. It was the best option she'd seen, so she pointed it out to Dima and led the girl across the street.

The break turned out to be an undeveloped lot. Walls ran down either side of it, and it looked like another was at the back, but it was hard to see because several trees were between there and where she was. It was troubling that she could see no other exit, but the lot would get them out of view. Liz headed deep into the darkness, until they reached a clump of trees they could move behind.

There had been no time to do anything but focus on staying alive since the bullet killed the man in the van. Now that she had a moment, Liz pulled out her phone. She desperately wanted to call Nate but worried that her voice would be heard, so she sent him a text.

> Someone shot at van. Killed guy
> you left w/us. Dima and I got out
> and are hiding. Don't know where
> Jar is. Or the shooter. Come quick.

She stared at the phone, hoping he would text her right back, but her screen remained blank.

THE FIXER KNEW they were in the empty lot somewhere. She'd seen them scurry across the road and disappear into the darkness.

Though she had yet to be impressed by the skill level of the operative shepherding the target, she approached with care and entered the lot in a low crouch.

There were a few piles of garbage to the left, and farther back some trees, and then another wall. As she scanned for movement, a small, faint glow of light spilled from around one of the trees. It lasted less than fifteen seconds.

Thank you for that, she thought with a smile.

JAR HAD LOOKED away for only a moment, and nearly missed seeing the shooter cross the street. She then lost the shooter completely a few seconds later when the person melted into a dark void between homes.

Jar had to pause for two cars speeding by before she, too, could make her way to the other side.

The void turned out to be an empty lot.

Jar hunkered near the opening, searching for signs of the shooter or Liz and Dima. The moon was out but the forest of skyscrapers two blocks away blocked it, turning the lot into an inky pit of black.

A barely audible crunch of dirt.

Jar heard it, though. Listening for quiet footsteps was a survival skill she had developed in childhood that had saved her from beatings—and worse—many times.

The sound had come from down the wall nearest her.

Tightening her grip on the Taser, she advanced.

LIZ SENT ANOTHER message.

Pls hurry!!

THE GLOW AGAIN, brighter now that the fixer was close.

She eased forward until she could see behind the tree.

The target and the escort were crouched side by side.

She crept as close as she could, and then stood up and said, "Hello, ladies."

WHEN THE SHOOTER raised the gun, Jar knew she wasn't as close as she needed to be, but it would have to be enough. She

275

pointed the Taser and fired.

AT THE SAME moment the fixer pulled the trigger, her world all but disappeared in an electric blaze.

She fell backward onto the ground, the gun flying from her hand. As she hit the dirt, she saw what looked like a string running from her arm to the third woman who had been in the van. Her mind recognized the weapon in the woman's hand, but it took a moment for the message to get through.

A Taser.

Another string was loosely attached to the fixer's jacket, while two more lay on the ground, having missed their target.

No wonder she hadn't been completely knocked out. She ripped the wire from her arm, and did the same with the one on her jacket.

Pushing unsteadily to her feet, she looked at the ground around her.

My gun.

It had to be there somewhere, but she couldn't see the damn thing.

The third woman had tossed the Taser to the side and was picking something up off the ground.

The gun?

Not wanting to stick around to find out, the fixer stumbled toward the street, her speed increasing as her strength returned.

A part of her wanted to keep running until she could find a ride out of the neighborhood. But the professional in her would not let her do that. She didn't know if her shot had taken out the target, and until she did, the mission was still on.

She made her way down the road toward where she'd left the rifle.

CHAPTER
THIRTY THREE

IT FELT TO Quinn like whole lifetimes could be shoved between the *ding*s that announced each floor they passed on their way up to twenty-two.

When the car finally slowed, he said, "Everyone hold here for a moment," and then looked at Nate. "Out and left. I'll go right."

Nate nodded.

As the doors slid open, Quinn heard another *ding*, this time from the hall outside the elevator. As he stepped into the corridor, he saw that the car to his right had just arrived.

Two armed men rushed out.

"Hands in the air, guns on the ground," Quinn ordered, aiming at the closest one's head.

The men twisted toward him in surprise. Quinn sensed Nate and the others move in behind him and add their gun to the mix.

Though the two men hadn't raised their weapons, they hadn't dropped them, either.

"Daeng," Quinn whispered. "Please help our friends here understand the situation."

As Daeng translated Quinn's order, the shadows of at least two more men came around the corner at the dim far end of the hall.

Before they could slip away again, Quinn switched his aim to them. "Stay where you are!"

The closest shadow stopped at the edge of a pool of light,

revealing itself to be Chayan. He said something in Thai, and instead of lowering their weapons, the two men from the other elevator car raised them.

"I see you bring me monk. And ahead of deadline, too."

"If you think we're here to make a deal, you'll be disappointed," Quinn said.

"Quinn?" Garrett called from behind Chayan.

"Garrett?" Orlando said. "Sweetie, are you all right?"

"Yeah. I'm okay."

"Where's Claire?"

"I have her. She's fine, too." He paused. "She needs a new diaper, though."

"The boy cares very much for the little girl," Chayan said. "You should be proud of him."

Ignoring him, Quinn said to Garrett, "Bring your sister over here."

"You not tell them this," Chayan said. "I tell them what to do, or my colleague will shoot them."

Quinn could see the man who was still in the shadows shift his weight.

"This is what will happen," Chayan said. "You give monk to me, I take him and your children with me. If you not follow, maybe I let kids go."

"Let me tell *you* what's going to happen," Quinn said. "You have ten seconds to send them over or we'll drop you all where you stand."

Daeng repeated the deal in Thai for the others.

While Chayan sneered, the two men from the elevator looked uncertain, and after a moment they lowered their weapons. Chayan shouted an order at them. Though Quinn was sure the man hadn't told his guards to drop their weapons on the floor, that's exactly what they did.

"You're down to six seconds," Quinn said.

His face red with anger, Chayan glared at Quinn until the time was almost up before motioning for Garrett to move around him.

Garrett stepped to the side to get around his kidnapper, and then inched forward. As he came level with Chayan, the man suddenly twisted toward him and snatched Claire out of his arms.

Claire wailed as Garrett shouted, "Hey!" and tried to get her back.

Chayan took a step back, holding Claire in front of him, her head partially obscuring his, and pointed his gun at Garrett.

"No!" Orlando yelled.

Garrett dove to the side as the gun went off, landing hard on the hallway floor, the bullet missing him by inches at most.

Chayan backed away, now pointing his pistol at Claire. "You shoot me, I shoot her."

Quinn advanced toward him, Orlando at his side.

"Get back, or I kill her!"

Quinn had multiple shots—the man's gut, his legs, groin, even the part of his head he wasn't hiding behind Claire. Any would drop the son of bitch, but Claire would fall, perhaps even with Chayan landing on top of her.

Still, they couldn't let him get around the corner.

"I got shoulder, you get waist," Quinn whispered without moving his lips. If they hit their spots, it should send him backward so that Claire would land on top of him. "One...two..."

Before he could say three, Garrett pushed off the floor, bellowing, "Let her go!" and charged Chayan.

The move caught everyone off guard, including the kidnapper, who took an extra second before swinging his gun back toward Orlando's son.

Quinn and Orlando, in sync as they almost always were, pulled their triggers at the exact same moment.

WHEN THE BOSS had taken Claire from Garrett, Garrett noticed the man's gun move just in time to jump out of the way.

All he could think of as he lay on the ground, trying to get his wind back, was that it didn't matter what he'd done. In the end, he'd failed to keep his sister safe. He could have lain there in a pool of self-pity, but what he felt instead was anger.

An anger that boiled over when the boss threatened to shoot Claire.

Shoving himself off the ground, he yelled, "Let her go!"

In his mind, he was going to tackle the boss and grab Claire back. But there were still five feet between them when the man pointed his gun at him again.

Thup. Thup.

The boss twisted sideways, blood flying from his shoulder and hip. Garrett raced forward and ripped Claire from his arm as the boss bounced against the wall.

Holding his sister with one arm, Garrett channeled one more lesson his mother had taught him. He slammed a fist into the man's face, knocking him to the ground.

ORLANDO RACED OVER to the kids and hugged them tight while Quinn made sure Chayan's gun was out of the man's reach.

After only a few seconds, she pulled away and ran her hands over Garrett's face and shoulders and arms. "Are you okay?"

"Mom, I'm fine," he protested.

"No cuts? No bruises? Nothing broken? How about your hand?" As Quinn joined them, she was inspecting the hand Garrett used to punch Chayan, which had blood on the knuckles. "Does this hurt?"

Garrett pulled his hand back. "I said I'm fine."

She checked him for a moment longer, and then said, "And Claire?"

He handed his sister over. "She's okay, too. I made sure she got enough to eat, and I-I-I keep telling her everything was going to be all right." He looked worried, as if thinking he hadn't done enough. "But I should have remembered to take some diapers when we escaped."

Orlando's eyes widened. "When you *what*?"

"Perhaps we should discuss that later," Quinn said. "We don't want to stay here any longer than we have to."

Orlando nodded, and then hugged Garrett and Claire again. "You did great. I'm so proud of you."

Quinn put his hand on the boy's shoulder, relieved beyond measure at having both his kids back in one piece. "Even better than great. You did amazing."

NATE HELPED KIET and one of the men move Chayan's soldiers into an apartment and zip-tie them to an exposed pipe.

As he was coming back into the hall, he remembered his phone had vibrated in the middle of all the action. He pulled it out and stopped in his tracks.

"Something's wrong!" he said, heading straight for the elevator.

"What?" Quinn asked.

Nate punched the down button. "Liz says there's a shooter." The center car was still there so the door opened right away. Holding it open, he looked at Kiet. "The man you left in the van is dead."

"We're coming with you," Kiet said, and motioned his men to follow him.

Nate could see that Quinn was torn between dealing with Chayan and helping his sister, so he said, "I'll call you if we need you," and let the doors close.

As they rode down, Nate texted Liz, asking where she was, and then said to Kiet, "There were three men in the lobby when I checked earlier. Only one of them was up here, so I'm thinking it must be the other two. Maybe they were searching around and came across the van. Is it possible they recognized your guy?"

"Possible, yes."

"Then that's got to be it."

The problem was, when the doors opened on the ground floor, Chayan's men were still in the lobby, sitting on the same couch Nate had seen them on before, looking very much like they had gone nowhere since then.

When they saw Nate and Christina's men exit the elevator, they jumped up, hands going for their guns. But Kiet said something to them in Thai, his volume normal but his tone hard, and he and his men flashed their guns. Chayan's men froze.

Creating a human wall to block the view from the concierge desk, they confiscated the men's weapons.

"Neither of these have been fired," Kiet said.

"Then who was shooting?" Nate asked.

He checked his phone. No answer from Liz.

"Tell these two that their boss is done, and if they're smart, they'll get the hell out of here right now. Make sure they know if they have any ideas about coming back, we'll kill them on sight."

Kiet delivered the message, and the men didn't even hesitate to accept the terms.

They all left the building as a group. As soon as they were outside, Kiet spoke a few words. The moment he finished, Chayan's men ran up the road in the opposite direction of where the van was parked.

Nate spotted the two holes in the van's windshield from half a block away. They hurried over.

Kiet and his men tensed when they saw what had happened to their colleague. If there was any consolation, Nate thought, it was that the shot had killed the man instantaneously.

Nate glanced inside. A lot of blood splatter, but all of it consistent with the dead man's wound, and there were no signs anyone else had been injured.

But where the hell had they gone?

PRAVAT FLEW DOWN the stairs from twenty-two all the way to the ground floor. His speed only increased as he raced out the door into the night.

In a way, it was a blessing that the monk and his friends had found them. If they hadn't, once the kids had been dealt with, Chayan would have turned his anger to Pravat.

He circled the building and headed toward the main road before he realized he was still carrying a gun.

Right. Must get rid of it.

Then again, maybe not, he thought. Perhaps it would be a good idea to keep it until he was sure he wouldn't need it.

When he reached the road, he veered to the right toward the heart of the city. There he could get lost and then start a new life. Maybe take that bus he'd been thinking about out of the city. That really was a good idea. He had no doubt Chayan would find a way to extract himself from the situation he was in, and after things settled down, Pravat's former boss would come looking for him. So the more Pravat could cover his tracks, the better.

There was someone to the side of the walkway ahead, kneeling next to several bins. A scrounger, probably, who made a living from others' trash. He didn't give the person a second thought as he focused on how to create a new identity.

THE FIXER RETURNED to the area where she'd discarded the sniper rifle, and had to feel around for a few seconds before her hand hit the stock.

As she pulled it out, she heard footsteps running in her direction. She turned and saw the silhouette of a man running down the walkway. As he briefly passed through the halo of one of the streetlamps, she spotted a gun with an attached suppressor in his hand.

Though she couldn't see his face, she was certain he was one of the men who had gone with the male operative into the building. The operative who'd been with the target must have sent out a warning, and now her friends were coming back to help. The running man didn't seem to have noticed her, though.

She waited until he was abreast of her to thrust the stock end of the rifle into his knee. He crumpled to the ground in a groan of pain, and she easily wrenched the gun out of his hand before he even realized what was happening.

"Looking for me?" she said, pointing his own gun at his head.

He looked confused, and was able to get out a "Wha—" before she pulled the trigger.

This job had gone from pain in the ass to seriously messy in less than fifteen minutes. She looked down the street toward the distant empty lot, wondering if she should try again or let it go.

The universe apparently decided to provide her with an answer, because only a few moments later, she spotted the male operative and a few more members of his team exit the building they'd been in. She adjusted her grip on the pistol, but instead of heading in her direction, the men turned the other way, toward the empty lot.

Nope, she thought. This assignment was over.

There were too many variables. Perhaps she could hang back and hope for an opening later, but enough was enough.

Her client could keep the fee.

She was done.

She disassembled the rifle, sent her contact a message to release everyone, and then walked out of the neighborhood, dropping pieces of the gun here and there along the way.

KIET PULLED HIS phone out of his pocket and answered a call. As the conversation continued, he glanced at Nate.

"What?" Nate asked.

When Kiet finished the call, he said, "This way," and hurried into the street.

"Who was that?"

"Jar. She is with your friends."

"TAKE CLAIRE AND Garrett down," Quinn told Orlando. "Find a place to wait nearby and we'll join you soon."

Orlando shot a glance at Chayan, but Claire cooing in her arms seemed to steady her. She nodded and ushered Garrett onto the elevator.

Quinn and Daeng set about wiping down every surface Garrett had said he'd touched. They would do the same on sixteen. The boy was barely a teenager. No sense in his young life being potentially hamstrung by a set of prints stored away in a criminal database.

When they finished with the floor, they returned to Chayan.

While Quinn and Daeng had been otherwise occupied, the man had apparently tried to slither away, but the damage to his hip and shoulder and all the blood he'd lost prevented him from going more than a dozen feet.

Fire still simmered in his eyes, though, when he looked up at them. "My men will find you, and they will kill you."

Daeng looked down at him with pity. "Your operation was already half gone when you broke out of prison. As we speak, Christina's people are in the process of dissolving the rest of your assets." Not entirely true, but it would be within the next twenty-four hours, the task greatly aided by the information on the laptop they'd found. "You should have stayed behind bars where you belonged. You have no men. You have no one who will avenge you. You have reached the end of this life. Maybe you will inch closer to enlightenment in the next."

"You will kill me, monk? I think that not help your own enlightenment."

"No," Quinn said. "That's my job."

He pressed his gun against the man's forehead and pulled the trigger.

NATE FOLLOWED KIET into an empty lot.

"Over here," Jar called from some trees near the back.

When they arrived, Nate sucked in a breath and dropped to ground next to where Liz lay. Her shirt was covered with blood.

He put a finger on her neck and could barely feel her pulse. He checked her wounds, and any thoughts of telling the others to call for an ambulance disappeared. Even if a team of doctors were already there, it would probably be too late for them to do anything.

"Nate?" Liz's voice was weak. She peeled open her eyelids a fraction of an inch. "I'm sorry."

He caressed her cheek and kissed her. "Shhh. It's okay. Nothing for you to be sorry about."

"I tried to...keep...her safe."

"You did fine, sweetheart."

"I didn't mean to...get hit."

"Don't worry about that. It's not your fault."

"I love you."

"I love you, too. More than anything."

She closed her eyes and for a moment he thought she was gone. But then she whispered, "Be careful, okay?"

She took her last breath before he could say, "Always am."

KIET CALLED AS Quinn and Daeng were riding the elevator down to sixteen. When the car stopped, instead of getting off, Quinn jabbed the button for the lobby.

One of Kiet's men was waiting for them outside the building, and led them at a run to an empty lot down the street. Orlando was already there, while Garrett stood a dozen feet away from everyone, holding Claire.

Nate was sitting in the dirt, Liz's head in his lap. Her eyes were closed, and if not for the blood, she would have looked asleep.

Quinn lost all sense of balance as the pull of gravity seemed to increase a hundred fold. Daeng grabbed his arms to keep him from falling, and then helped him to kneel.

Quinn took his sister's hand. It was already cold.

He opened his mouth to speak, but couldn't. He didn't know he was crying until he tasted the tears.

"Was it one of Chayan's men?"

"Chayan didn't have anything to do with this," Nate said, his tone as broken as Quinn's.

Quinn looked at him. "Then who?"

Nate glanced over at where Jar stood with Dima. "They saw her."

"Her?"

"Yes. Dima recognized the shooter as one of the people who were trying to stop us in Barcelona."

"*Your* job?"

"Yes."

Quinn had to fight hard not to lash out at his former apprentice. But in truth, the only reason the woman had been able to get to Liz was because Quinn had forced Nate to interrupt the job he was on. There was plenty of blame to smear on both of them.

Once Quinn had nominal control of his voice again, he said, "What's her name?"

"I don't know," Nate replied. "But I *will* find out."

CHAPTER
THIRTY FOUR

IT TOOK SOME bribing, but they were able to get Liz's body onto Christina's plane without the Indonesian authorities raising an alarm.

On the flight, Quinn contacted a very irate Helen Cho.

After a litany of very choice words, she all but yelled, "Where is my package?"

"I have her," Quinn said.

"*You* have her? Is she all right?"

"She's fine. But…we lost someone while helping her."

"Nate?" Helen managed to sound almost concerned.

Quinn looked out the window. "Not Nate."

"Who, then?"

Having no intention of ever answering that, he said, "You need to send someone to pick her up."

"Where?"

CHRISTINA'S PEOPLE WERE waiting for them when they arrived in Bangkok, and saw to it that Liz was put into a proper coffin that would be loaded onto the flight Quinn, Orlando, Garrett, and Claire were taking home.

Nate and Daeng would not be returning to the States.

"As soon as you know where she is, you tell me," Quinn said to them outside the security checkpoint on the departure level at Suvarnabhumi Airport. "Don't do anything until I get there."

"I promise," Nate said.

"Even if you have an opportunity."

"I said I promise."

Quinn glanced at Daeng, who nodded to indicate he'd make sure Nate complied. Quinn wanted to stay with them, but he had to go home first. He needed to tell his mother about Liz, needed to attend the funeral for the last of his siblings.

"Where will you start?" Quinn asked Nate.

"Not sure yet," Nate said. "Jar's doing some digging for us."

"I want daily updates."

"You know I can't promise that."

Quinn frowned. "As often as possible, then."

A hesitant nod.

Quinn gave Daeng a hug, and then, more tentatively, did the same with Nate.

"Find her," Quinn said.

"You can count on it."

Made in the USA
Lexington, KY
03 January 2017